RETURN TO PHANTOM CREEK

Howard,
I think we started it all, way back on Big creek. Best wishes, and hope you enjoy this novel!

Bud Ziller
Boise Id. 83704
July 25, 2017

Also by Bud Filler

Two-Man Stick, A Memoir of the Smokejumpers

RETURN TO PHANTOM CREEK

BUD FILLER

Burning Mountain Press
Boise, Idaho

Return to Phantom Creek
Copyright © 2017 Bud Filler

All rights reserved.

This story has been inspired in part by historical events and contains fictitious characters, places, and circumstances. Any similarities to actual persons, living or dead, or to actual events, is purely coincidental. Ownership of this story is protected by copyright and other applicable laws, and any unauthorized duplication, distribution, or exhibition of this story could result in prosecution, as well as civil liability.

Published by
Burning Mountain Press
P.O. Box 45534
Boise, Idaho 83704
budfiller@hotmail.com

Library of Congress Cataloging-in-Publication Data

Filler, Bud, 1934 –
    Return to Phantom Creek: A Novel / Bud Filler
1st ed.
      p. 242
      ISBN-13: 978-0-692-03407-1

Printed on acid-free paper

Cover art by Mike Flinn
Edited by Dennis Held
Cover and interior design by Gray Dog Press

This story is dedicated to those in our family who
fought for America in foreign wars:

Lt. Colonel Ted Filler, Army Special Forces, Middle East
Brigadier General Brad Richy, Idaho Air Guard, Iraq
Colonel Guy Claire, Army Infantry, France, North Africa, and Italy
Private Robert Ruggles, Army Infantry, KIA, Southeast Asia
Colonel John Bright, United States Air Force, Southeast Asia

For Ellie,
Always ~

Contents

Whiskey Bravo and the Smoke-Eaters 1
Trapped on the Yellowstone 9
The Road to Sun Valley 17
Between Seasons 27
Liz Hollis 32
Phantom Ranch 41
Take-off at Owyhee Crossing 45
Baker Brindell 51
Rustlers Noose 56
Otto Takes a Hit 67
North of the Slot 73
Death on the Switchback 85
From the Treeline 97
Fight Below Stoddard Peak 109
Jammer Swings a Pulaski 118
The 800-Foot Runway 126
Return to Phantom 134
Fightin' General Joe Hooker 140
The Man in the Forest 152
Parachutes Over Rush Creek 157
Dry Martinis 171
Kentucky Long Rifle 178
Three Fires 187
Hostage 197
South to the Desert 202
Destroy the Power Grid 208
I Owe Them One 218
In the Spring 225

"There is a Catskill eagle in some souls that can dive down into the deepest gorges, and soar out of them again and become invisible in the sunny spaces. And even if he forever flies within the gorge, that gorge is in the mountains, so that even in his lowest swoop the mountain eagle is still higher than other birds upon the plain, even though they soar."
—Herman Melville, *Moby Dick*

Whiskey Bravo and the Smoke-Eaters

At a thousand feet above the airfield in central Idaho, a red single-engine airplane banked left for landing. An orange windsock, mounted high on a post in the grass, fifty feet to the side of the runway, bounces from a northwester coming over and blowing down from the mountain. The wind is across the runway, strong, gusting, and tricky.

From the cockpit I was watching the swing and snap of the windsock sleeve. *Twenty to twenty-five knots.*

The plane rolled left again to line up to land on runway three-four. The wind blew the plane to the right of the runway and I dropped the left wing into the crosswind, straightened the plane with power and right rudder to come back in line. The left tire and tail wheel kissed the tarmac and chirp-chirped together. The nose of the plane lifted, the wings leveled, the right tire contacted the runway, and not to be outdone by the other two, came down hard with a solid squeal.

Whiskey Bravo had landed itself again. I smiled to myself, pushed left rudder and turned onto the first taxiway. *That* landing, challenged by the crosswind, was perfect.

The FAA registration number, bold on the fuselage of the Aviat Husky, was N09WB: November-Zero-Niner-Whiskey-Bravo. The FAA flight controllers at the Idaho airfields where we land—the airplane and I—shortened the radio call sign to Whiskey Bravo, the airplane with a painting on the tail of a fearless black and tan sled dog.

Indian summer had arrived in the Idaho high country. Out past the spinning prop, green mountains surrounded the valley and the airfield. To the north was the small village of McCall, and beyond the houses and the trees, a blue lake shining in the sun. A right turn here, a left turn there, and I swung the plane to the government buildings of the United States Forest Service Smokejumper Base.

I was coming home.

The morning wind stirred the aspens along the river, and the September morning air held a chill. The De Havilland Twin Otter jump plane assigned to the smokejumper base was missing. The firefighters must have received a fire call. I idled Whiskey Bravo to the largest brown shingled buildings, shut down the prop, set the brakes, and walked into the office. The forest fire season was coming to an end. Or so I thought.

James Tecumseh Deming, better known as Jammer, was the smokejumper base operating manager. Fifteen years ago Jammer, Link Barrett, Mike Romano and I strapped on parachutes and fought forest fires together. Link, Mike, and I went into the Rangers, then the Special Forces. Jammer stayed at the smokejumper unit and was now the boss of the outfit. After the Army days, Link became an FBI agent, and I went into the timber business. Mike fell in a firefight with the Taliban in the Hindu Kush. That battle, over a decade and half ago, was a son-of-a-bitch.

Dammit, Mike, we need you here, with the jumpers, you hardheaded sergeant. You were too damn brave.

"Morning, Casey," Lori said, when I walked into the office. She cupped the mouthpiece, pointed to the phone, and whispered, "Fire lookout on the Salmon. Wait one."

"Morning, Lori." Lori was office manager and secretary at the base, and had been handling the administrative work for ten years. She had her black hair pulled back in a bun. Nice. The color matched her slacks. She was single, very attractive, and all business. It crossed my mind that she paused a second or two longer when I came through the door.

I waited. Behind Lori on the paneled wall was a framed photograph of four jumpers, suited up in front of the Twin Otter—Jammer, Link, Mike, and me. That picture had been there for eighteen years.

Lori recorded something and then disconnected. "Jammer is talking to West Yellowstone. Phones are bouncing. Lots of smokes."

"I see the jump plane is gone."

"Eight jumpers went out this morning—three fires reported on the Salmon."

"We haven't had any lightning storms for two weeks. What's up?"

"Three more fires were reported in the Bitterroots. The Missoula base is covering those smokes. We're short-handed," Lori added. "Jammer just got off the line."

When I heard of multiple fires in a line, I thought of somebody setting fires as they traveled, from a plane, road, or trail. My mind worked that way. Lightning-caused fires in the backcountry ignited along jagged ridgetops, far from the roads.

Jammer came out of his office, his hand outstretched. I noticed he was getting more muscles at this job, or he was buying his T-shirts too small.

"Is your hunting gear ready?" I asked, smacking him on the shoulder, about the same as slapping a tree trunk.

"Can't go hunting with you next week, Casey. We're up to our asses in late summer fires."

In the fall of the year Jammer, Link and I got together for an early archery hunt for elk in the Idaho backcountry. We'd camp for two weeks, catch up on past adventures, and make a serious dent in the Idaho bourbon supply. I'd start by flying Whiskey Bravo solo into an airstrip along the river and set up a spike camp. Link and Jammer would charter a plane and bring in a cook tent, stove, cots, and boxes of food. Lots of food.

Jammer was calm, in command, doing what he loved. He had a voice like an infantry colonel.

Lori looked up from her computer screen.

"Sorry, Lori, excuse the French."

"Never heard the French speak that way. And I do speak French." She smiled and went back to typing on her keyboard. The office phones continued to ring. "Line two shows the FBI on caller ID. You better take it, Jammer."

"FBI? Casey, it must be Link. Talk to him. Tell him we're short-handed, and I'm suddenly up to my neck in fires."

Link was on the line when I picked up. He had an edge to his voice. I knew Link well enough to know he was busy. "I'm delayed for our hunt, Casey. I'll meet you later in the mountains. We've been tracking some questionable people moving up this way, suspect they are affiliated with a subversive group. The trail has gone cold. I can't tell you exactly what's going on and who we are watching, but when you and Jammer are out there on the river camp I'll keep in touch with the satellite phone."

"Terrorists?"

"I didn't say that."

"Call them badasses, then," I said. "I was cleared for Top Secret in the Army. Remember? I won't breathe a word. Most people don't even know these mountains out here exist."

"Your Top Secret clearance doesn't mean squat anymore." Link laughed. "But I will tell you our intelligence people say they have intercepted information regarding a possible strike on a large government building, hospital, or electrical facility. Location unknown."

"There isn't anything like that where we're going."

"The major electric transmission lines are in the desert of southern Idaho."

"The power grid would make a good target," I said.

"Yes, it would," Link said.

"Jammer has fires all over Idaho. Let's delay the hunt until mid-October. If he agrees on a date, I'll call you back."

"Okay. I'll see you when I see you." Link disconnected.

I relayed the message to Jammer, who'd hung up on the second line. "If anybody can do it, Link can," Jammer said.

"Do what?"

"Keep those fucking terrorists out of Idaho."

Lori looked up from her keyboard. "Terrorists?"

Jammer and I both glanced at her.

"That other call was from the park manager at Yellowstone," Jammer said. "He has a new smoke near the Idaho border. A big smoke were his words. The fire is burning in dead lodgepole pine inside the park boundary. The fire is moving fast. He sounded excited—and desperate. Those park supervisors are a different breed, you know, they don't like to see their tourist forests going up in smoke. The other Montana smokejumpers went out on a series of fires in the Bob Marshall this morning, and we're short of people here. Most of the crew are back in college or teaching school. We only have six on the jump list, plus me. The De Havilland will carry eight. We need to help the Yellowstone people, until they can bring in ground crews."

"The woods are still dry and suddenly there are fires everywhere—this late in the season. That's unusual," I said.

"Yes, it is. Go out to the Middle Fork solo. We'll meet you there in two weeks, three weeks max," Jammer suggested. "You love roaming the mountains alone. The bears won't eat you. You're tough enough to eat them."

"I don't eat bears. Link's chasing bad guys and you're throwing dirt on burning branches and cutting smoking snags. And you want me to drink whiskey in the mountains without you. I'd go crazy out there, thinking of all the fun you're having. You only have six jumpers here, plus yourself. I'll solve your problem and go with you. I'll make eight."

"Can't do that, Casey. Although I can see you're keeping yourself in good shape."

Jammer was standing at the wall looking at a map of the Yellowstone country. The light from the morning sun through the windows was bright in the Forest Service office. I glanced outside. The day was warming, the noon winds increasing and the branches of the firs next to the warehouse were swaying.

I turned again to Jammer. "The weather's dry. Your camp is empty. Missoula smokejumpers are working on our fires in the Bitterroots and their own fires in the Bob Marshall. Does it strike you some of these late season fires have been started in series? Intentionally?"

"Possible. This many fires late in the summer is unusual. Now, let's go. We're going to load up for the Yellowstone fire. Lori, hit the buzzer six times."

The loud rasp of the klaxon on the side of the parachute loft broke the silence. In an instant, jumpers working around the warehouse and loft were running to get their chutes and jump gear.

"I remember how to steer a parachute, Jammer. If I break a leg out there, you can shoot me."

"You're serious, aren't you? You haven't qualified for the season. You're not an official government employee." Jammer emphasized the "official" part.

"Qualified? I have fifty jumps with the Forest Service and another fifty in the Army, plus a couple of free-falls."

"You must have hit your head when you landed on those free falls," Jammer said.

"I can't miss a fire, Jammer. I'm only thirty-eight, for Christ sake, still under your jump age."

"I know how old you are. You and Link had to go out and join the Army and get your asses shot at. The Forest Service raised the maximum jump age to accommodate guys like you returning, but you had to be here at the beginning of the season, hired, qualified, and trained."

"I sure as hell know how to use a Pulaski and a chain saw," I said.

"Wish I could." Jammer's voice was softer now. "Go out to the mountains and hunt elk. You're a solo guy, Casey. I heard you were a one-man army in Afghanistan. Besides, you can't join up again. Forest Service regulations won't allow it. Somebody will have my butt for letting you go with us as a jumper."

As a jumper? An opening! I liked arguing with Jammer. Like old times. "You need firefighters. You're down to seven, including you."

"You can ride along with us in the Twin Otter as an observer. No parachute. Sometimes an ex Forest Service employee will do that—with my permission."

"Well, that's a start," I said.

"Lori." Jammer laughed. "What am I going to do with this guy?"

"Let him jump. Get him out of my hair," she said.

I nodded and smiled back at Lori. She was on my team now.

"I can't believe the two of you," Jammer said, shaking his head.

I turned to Jammer. "If I was in the plane with you as an observer, and you all went out the door, I'd follow you by reflex. There'd be no one in the plane to hold me back. And me without a parachute. My untimely death would be on your hands."

"You're crazy. What justification do I have for taking you along?"

"I'm a free-lance journalist. I'll write a story."

"A journalist. When did you think up that one? God damn," Jammer said, and shook his head. "Okay, I'll get you something to sign, so they don't hang me out."

"I'll sign anything to climb aboard that De Havilland."

"You can't stay away from the smoke-eaters, can you? Aren't you happy flying your red airplane around, and staying up in the sky?"

"Once a smoke-eater, always a smoke-eater," I said.

"You must be nuts," he said. "No, I must be nuts. Check out a chute and reserve from the loft. You know where the jump suits are, and if anybody asks, I don't know you. If they do, I'll say you're a writer working on a story. Ask Lori for a release."

"Thanks," I said, and gave Jammer my goofiest smile. *I knew Jammer would cave.*

"When you see this fire, you'll change your mind. When you worked here the forests weren't all dried out bug-killed pines. These forests burn like gasoline. Deadfall is everywhere."

"Won't happen. Hell, this is like old times."

"Old times, huh! We'll take extra rations. You'll eat everything in sight."

"Just a growing boy."

"If you break something, or get burned up out there, it's your body. You have insurance and medical?"

"Of course. Link will be envious."

"For God's sake, don't tell Link," Jammer said. "I couldn't handle the two of you."

"Just me," I said, and gave Jammer a half-assed salute. "Link's busy chasing terrorists."

"Take-off is in fifteen minutes. The Twin Otter just landed. They're refueling. By the size of this fire, with the camp empty, plan on a week in the mountains."

"Okay to tie down Whiskey Bravo outside the chain link?"

"The red airplane? The plane you fly to scare me on hunting trips?"

"Nothing scares you. That's why you're the boss. Yes, that's the one. Give me five minutes to call the plant. They think I'm on a hunting trip."

"If these winds keep up, you'll wish you were. Sure, tie down Whiskey Bravo next to the Otter. Lori, handle everything here. I have my phone and radio."

I followed Jammer into the locker room. Not much had changed, I found the tan jump suits and pulled one from the warehouse locker. Next, the helmet, two parachutes, a backpack and a reserve. Jammer slipped into his jump outfit. He was smiling, watching me trying to remember how to organize the parachute harness.

"I'm the one who's crazy," he said.

Trapped on the Yellowstone

We carried our chutes to the plane. I walked stiffly through the cabin, shaking hands with the other firefighters, until I came to the last one. The sixth jumper was sitting next to the pilot's cabin: a woman, tall, blonde, good looking, with a beautiful smile.

"I knew we'd get you back, Casey," she said. She was holding her jump helmet in her lap.

"Baker! My God. Baker Brindell." Baker was one of the first woman smokejumpers, over a decade ago. I had a crush on her for a couple of summers, as did all the other guys. I leaned over, stiff from the unaccustomed jump suit, and kissed her on the cheek.

"Baker Cameron for a while. That's another story. I'll tell you sometime."

Baker was an ash blonde, an athlete, a triathlon competitor, stood at five feet seven in her bare feet, weighed 118 pounds, and that was her problem, or the Forest Service's problem. The minimum weight was 125 pounds, and she was rejected the first season. The minimum was adjusted the next year to 120 pounds. Baker qualified easily then, shocking the old guard, who couldn't imagine a woman wanting to jump from an airplane to cut smoking trees and dig trenches next to a flaming forest fire.

Number one engine of the De Havilland revved, stopping our conversation. Number two followed. The pilot took a heading east to the Wyoming border. Two hours later we were over the fire and circling the smoke. Thick timber stands on the west edge of the park were dead and dying lodgepole pine and fir, bug-killed from decades of neglect. The fire was burning hot on the face of a long steep mountain. The flames had already consumed a thousand acres. This was more like a fifty-man fire. We'd try to knock it down with eight.

Jammer was the jump spotter and was kneeling in the open door of the Otter. "The big meadow below the burn near the creek is the jump spot," he shouted, turning away from the slipstream. "Stack your gear near the creek. We'll split up the crew, dig line around the bottom, and work up both flanks. The head of the fire at the top of the mountain is hot. Let's squeeze it off on the sides."

The pilot banked into the smoke, banked again for a one-eighty for the jump pass. The smoke from the fire came in through the door—the smell of heat and burning pine needles.

Jammer was the spotter and last jumper. After the first six firefighters disappeared over the mountains below, he gave me the signal to get in the door. I placed my gloved hands on the edges of the door, looked down, then concentrated on the horizon. Jammer was tight behind me. When he slapped my thigh we both went through the door and into the sky.

I didn't tell Jammer ten years had passed since I was under a parachute, pulling on the risers. Some things you never forget.

The afternoon winds had been buffeting the De Havilland but the meadow below looked soft. The green clearing was downwind and half a mile from the bottom of the fire. Jammer had picked the safest spot. The alternate was to make tree jumps and that wasn't always fun. Seven jumpers were in the meadow, next to the stream, gathering up their gear. All had landed in the grass except Carson Conley, who found a large ponderosa pine on the edge of the clearing and treed up, his jump boots swinging fifty feet off the ground.

"Wasn't the meadow big enough for you?" a jumper yelled up at Conley.

"Use your guidelines the next time," someone barked at the lofty firefighter, who was pulling out his let-down rope.

"We didn't know you were a tree-hugger," another shouted.

"That's Carson Conley," Baker said, organizing the chain saw and fuel containers. "The bull of the woods. He pushes the maximum weight limit. He likes tree landings, says his legs are fragile, but we don't believe him. He lifts and works out when he's not on a fire. The jumpers tell him he doesn't know how to use the guidelines, but they smile when they say that."

Conley was in the branches, untangling kinks in the coil of rope. The jumpers were gathering below, some looking up at Conley's white and orange parachute, taut and securely hung over the top of a large ponderosa. The jumping part of the attack on the fire was over. The firefighters had grips on their shovels and Pulaskis, eager to start work, waiting for Conley to join them.

Conley was slowly making the descent, applying friction on the rope with his gloved hands.

"Are you going after this fire, Conley, or waiting for the next one?" one of the smokejumpers yelled up.

"I'm going to break somebody's arm when I get on the ground," he barked through his face mask.

"If you ever get down," another jumper snickered. All the firefighters were gathered in a group, smiling at the descending Conley.

I looked at Baker. "Nothing changes. There are no thin-skinned smokejumpers."

"Definitely not," Baker said, looking up, watching Conley. "This is his tenth season. Nobody, but nobody, teases him on the ground. I got some flak from the guys my first summer, but not much, because I could swing a Pulaski, hit the same place twice on a log, and outrun most of the guys, even wearing jump boots."

Conley was down. "Like a feather," he mumbled, when his logging boots kissed the top of a clump of sagebrush. He moved faster on the ground, removing his helmet, parachute harness, and jump suit.

Jammer walked up, looked over the crew, rolling his eyes when he paused on Conley, who was untangling himself from his let-down rope. Jammer issued orders. "We'll split up the team—Conley, Baker, and Casey—with me. Donovan, you're the team leader on the right. We'll dig line on both flanks and work to the ridge. The winds are down. We should be at the top or near it by daybreak. Stay in contact with the radios."

I stuffed a candy bar in my shirt pocket, adjusted the canteen on my belt, took a strong grip on the shovel and Pulaski, and stepped out behind Jammer. Just like old times.

We did work through the night. At eight o'clock in the morning a red sun topped the mountain and showed through the smoke:

the weather was warming, and we stopped for a moment to catch our breaths.

Jammer sat on a sun-bleached log, opening a dented can of peaches with his jump knife, while keeping his eyes on the fire and the smoke at the top of the mountain.

The morning winds were beginning to stir. Smoke from the burn eddied through the trees. A Douglas fir widow-maker, burning at the base, fell and crashed into the ashes. The smoke rolled outward, and we checked the perimeter of our location for other burning snags.

Below us a park ranger came huffing and puffing up the fire line we had dug. He was tall, wide shouldered, with a big belly for a ranger. His cheeks were red from the exertion of the climb. I had him figured. *This will be interesting.*

Jammer was also watching the ranger. He turned to me and smiled. "Here we go." The four of us had ash-blackened hands, faces, and pants. The night's work was showing.

The ranger looked newly minted out of ranger school. He bent over and coughed.

I was rather proud that we had worked through the night digging fireline and securing one flank of the fire. Our other team had stopped the fire on their side. The ranger didn't comment about that. "You the fire boss here?" the ranger asked me. His voice was tentative. I pointed to Jammer.

"Get on your feet, people. Pick up your tools, take a chain saw, and build a fire line above those flames," he said, gesturing at the top of the mountain. He was out of breath. He coughed again.

"God damn." Jammer swung and embedded his Pulaski carefully into a black log. Jammer was by nature a friendly-looking dude but I knew that underneath that nice-guy macho image he could be meaner than a mountain lion. The ranger didn't stand a chance.

"What?" the ranger said.

Jammer said "God damn" again.

Smoke from the burn drifted past us. I could feel the heat from the flames on the slope above us a hundred yards away. Baker arrived with the chain saw. She set the saw and a fuel container of gasoline on the top of a flat rock, took off her yellow hard hat and placed it next to the saw. A strand of blond hair dropped over her face and she brushed it back with a gloved hand. She had been listening to the ranger and she shook her head.

"Not a good idea," Jammer said. "We're not going to send people in front of that fire—too dangerous. The winds are getting stronger and the fire will cross the ridge and burn into the next drainage, whether we like it or not. We'll continue to work the flanks today, knock it down there and the bottom, then squeeze the fire off at the front. We'll assign people to take out the spot fires. The weather will be cooler tonight and the temperature and winds will drop."

I smiled. I was a journalist signed up on this trip. It was good to see Jammer earning his pay as fire boss.

The park ranger didn't say another word, coughed again, turned and walked away.

"What a jerk," Conley snarled, "trying to get us roasted."

The ranger heard him. He stopped between the trees, raised his shoulders in a fierce move, got up his nerve, and stomped back through the ashes. The first person he came to was Conley.

"That's an order!" The ranger's arm was extended and he was pointing a finger at Jammer and Conley. Smokejumpers are independent types and don't like fingers pointed at them. I sure as hell didn't.

"You give us an order like that again and I'll knock you on your ass in these ashes," Conley snapped. Underneath the dirt and ash streaks on his face Conley was getting red. He had been up all night throwing dirt and cutting logs. The ranger best not want to rile up Carson Conley.

"Conley!" Jammer barked. "I'll do the talking!"

"He's trying to get our asses fried up there."

Jammer gave Conley a "be cool" motion with his hand.

The ranger settled on Jammer. "The other crew needs help."

"What other crew?' This time the ranger got Jammer's attention. "I'm in touch with our other team by radio. They're on the right flank of this fire."

"There is another crew. I dispatched a twelve-person ground crew to the top of the mountain this morning."

"You did *what?*"

"The crew is digging line on the ridge. I can't reach them with my radio."

"In front of this fire? For God's sake, man, that's dangerous. That *is suicide.*"

Jammer tried to contact the ranger's crew with the frequency the ranger gave him, but received no answer. "We've got to get up there," Jammer said. "Casey, you and I can go to the top. Baker, you and Conley stay here."

"I'm going," Baker shouted. "The saw is too heavy to run with uphill. Casey, give me your shovel."

"If the crew is in trouble, you're going to need all the help you can get," Conley said. "I'm with you."

The smoke clouds above were a sickly rolling yellow, with fire in them. We could see live embers blowing high, then dropping into the pines on the left flank. The fire was already burning across the ridge.

We moved faster as we approached the top of the mountain. This fire was creating its own wind, adding oxygen from below. The white smoke on the flanks was turning to billows of yellow and black. The fire was spreading to the sides on the ridge. Firefighters up there could not outrun a fire of this intensity. What in the hell was the ranger thinking?

I hoped we weren't too late. Jammer radioed Donovan on the right flank and told him what we were doing.

We ran up through the black of the burn, sometimes among the green trees on the edge, wherever the climbing was the easiest. Two hundred yards below the ridge, Jammer stopped and hooted—the smokejumpers' call. It echoed across the mountains. We listened, and the only response was the crackle of flames above us, and a thump when a burning tree fell. Our chests were heaving, but the adrenaline made it easy. There were no answers. Except for the fire noises and murmurings, the silence was creepy. *Where were the firefighters? On the ridge? Black bodies in the ashes? Hell, I came along as a journalist!*

The ranger was below us, making his way several hundred yards outside the burn, moving from green tree to green tree. We ignored him and kept running uphill.

"There they are!" Baker shouted. "Two yellow shirts on the other side of the rocks."

Two firefighters were under some burned-out trees. The lodgepole pines on the ridge above us were on fire. The four of us raced through the smoke and ashes to the firefighters. I smacked down pieces of smoking pine needles landing on my shoulders.

Two fire shelters had been deployed. Both firefighters were outside the shelters. One was standing and the other was pinned under a smoking log. The other was trying to lift the log.

"Over here," the standing one shouted.

"We'll get you out of here," Baker said. Jammer and Conley moved down the log, struggled for a hand hold, then lifted one end of the black log. Baker and I, one on each side, tugged and slid the injured worker from underneath the log to a level place in the ashes.

"I think my shoulder is broken," he said.

"We're going to move you. The winds can shift and this area can reburn," Baker said. She was cool and calm. I thought about all the "two manners" I had been on with Baker. What a woman.

"Where is the rest of your crew?" Jammer asked the men.

"They high-tailed it down the ridge," the other firefighter said. "My leg won't support me. I stayed with Tim and we deployed our fire tents."

"Shake and bake shelters, eh?" Conley said.

Jammer glanced at Conley, then toward the firefighters. "We can't wait for a stretcher, or a lift-off. Not here. Too much smoke and no clearing. Climb on my back. There's no time to splint your shoulder. Casey and I will change off until we get to a clearing below us," Jammer said, nodding at me. "Baker, take what tools you can carry."

We had the two injured firefighters on our backs, and as clumsy as it was moving through the ashes and around burned logs, we made it to a clearing below. Jammer radioed for a helicopter extraction, and within an hour a Lakota came clattering over the ridge. The yellow shirts were easy to spot from the air.

The small opening wasn't large enough for landing and a moment later a basket at the end of a cable dropped for the first firefighter, then descended again for the second. The helicopter took the two off to the emergency room at West Yellowstone.

The ranger went down the mountain and that was the last we saw of him.

Jammer was on the radio with the park managers. He turned to our full team, now assembling around him in the burned-over clearing. "A hundred-person ground crew is busing and then hiking in from West Yellowstone and expect to arrive on the fire line tomorrow. They will have their own boss. An incident commander will be appointed."

The fire boss wouldn't be Jammer. He had his hands full in the Idaho backcountry. The Yellowstone fire burned over the ridge and into the next drainage. A day later the hotshot ground crews arrived, dug more line and stopped the flames on the flanks and the front. In the morning eight of us boarded a charter bus to West Yellowstone. The Twin Otter picked us up, turned west and landed in McCall in the afternoon. The other jumpers went to sharpening their tools and preparing new fire packs, ready for the next fire call, which could come at any moment. I took a shower in the bunkhouse, checked out Whiskey Bravo, and walked into the office.

Lori and Jammer were at their desks, shuffling paperwork.

"If you need any more jumpers to put out fires in this country, let me know," I said, giving Lori a hug and moving toward the door.

Jammer came out his office. "You'll be the first we'll call," he said, and smiled. "I remember adventure follows you. And best get that red airplane out of here, or we'll use it for cargo drops."

"I'm the only one who knows how to fly that plane," I said. "See you at elk camp. Bring your hunting arrows and lots of food."

Then I remembered Link's comments about some badasses moving up this way.

Here in the backcountry? Hell, those days in the mountains of Afghanistan were behind Link and me. I must have been dreaming.

The Road to Sun Valley

I was untying Whiskey Bravo from the ground rings when Lori came to the door of the Forest Service parachute loft. She said to "wait one" as Jammer was on the radio again but *she* had something to give me. In a moment Lori and Jammer walked out to Whiskey Bravo. Lori handed me the framed picture of the four smokejumpers from his office wall.

"Casey, for you, the four amigos," she said.

Jammer nodded. "For helping pack those two firefighters off the mountain," he said.

I held the picture for a moment. "Thank you. Three amigos now. Mike's gone."

"He was a Green Beret, wasn't he?" Lori asked. "I heard a lot about him. Killed in Afghanistan. I wish I'd known him."

"One of a kind. A legend in his time."

I turned to Jammer. "Thanks for letting me swing a Pulaski. We did good work on the Yellowstone. Eight of us stopped the fire from taking out the big drainage."

"Yes, we did."

"I love the smell of burning pines in the morning."

"Saw that movie," Jammer said. He shook his head. "Journalist, eh? I can't believe you talked me into that jump. See you at elk camp. We will have some early fall rains soon and the fire season will slow. Call me when you and Link have the date set."

Whiskey Bravo was ready to fly. An hour later, when I returned to the office at our plant at Owyhee Crossing on the Snake, I expected a call to testify about the incident with Jammer, Carson Conley, the shave-tail ranger, and the injured firefighters on the Yellowstone. I didn't get the call. Neither did Jammer. Packing those guys off the ridge was all in a day's work.

The lumber operation was running well. My managers, Tony and Ellen, were good operators. Production was up without having to crack the whip. After spending a week behind a desk, my plan was to call on distributors in Utah and Colorado to discuss their timber requirements for the coming year. Driving the Porsche seemed like a good idea and I'd blow the carbon out of the engine on the mountain roads before winter set in. There was a speech to give at the lumber meeting in Sun Valley and the 911 looked at home there among the Mercedes and Maseratis.

The sales work in Utah and Colorado was completed. The turbo was in sixth gear and purring at eighty-five. Route 287 took me north and the sign for the Wyoming state line had just blurred behind me. My eyes were open for state troopers parked in the arroyos. This was high windy country, the land of junipers and sagebrush. A dusting of snow had settled on the barren peaks, and the occasional flurry followed me north. Beethoven's Ninth played on the CD, and when "Ode to Joy" came over, the car liked the music and started tracking nicely at ninety. Okay, so I liked classical.

Interstate 80 was to the north. There was a motel in Laramie to stop for the night, and then I'd arrive in Sun Valley the next day, make the technical presentation to the lumber audience, and drive west on the second morning to Owyhee Crossing. The distance was 750 miles. That was the plan. The plan was about to change.

There is a bar on a wide turn on the left, appropriately named Lefty's, a dive frequented in the past by cowboys and sheepherders. Now it was a stopover for bikers moving north and south, drinking and doing things bikers are wont to do. Lefty's was the only joint in this desolate land where a traveler could get a whiskey, a beer, a cup of coffee, or all three. I was opting for the coffee.

The tavern was weather-beaten, desolate, run-down, and dangerous looking. Instinct again. The stiffness started in the back of my neck. Like Afghanistan. This wasn't Afghanistan. The Taliban weren't here. I pulled into the parking lot, turned off the ignition, and swung open the door, leaving a small .25 caliber Beretta in the center compartment. There were places in foreign lands where I would have slipped it into my pocket.

The parking lot was empty except for three dust-streaked and roughed-up motorcycles. Two were crotch rockets, and the third, a well-used Harley. Harley owners didn't usually let them get that scruffy. The bar was deserted except for three assholes sitting at a table. Their eyes were red rimmed in the dim light, and those eyes were focusing on me when I walked in. From the looks of the wet table with the empty bottles, glasses, and cigarette butts, they had been sitting there most of the day. The tallest one with a shaved head displayed a black Swastika tattoo above his right eye. Stunning. The second biker had long greasy brown hair to his shoulders. A blue chain tattoo adorned his forehead. His decoration to the clan was a leather thong necklace, strung with black beads and a dozen claws of some large animal. The third was the youngest of the group, a newbie wearing a shiny leather vest, a size too large. Splotches of tattoos darkened his neck. Prison ink. He would be taking orders from the Swastika guy.

I took a seat at the bar. The view through the front windows of Lefty's was stunning. The first shades of darkness was settling on the sagebrush hills. In a moment the door to the kitchen swung open and a small white-haired old man appeared.

"What'll you have?" He appeared surprised to see anyone.

"Coffee. Black."

"That's it?"

"That'll do it."

The three bikers turned at their table and were now facing me. Their comment came sooner than I expected. There wasn't much to do at Lefty's. "Why are you drinking coffee?" the newbie asked. He was the youngest and the dumbest.

"Because I like coffee," I said, without turning around on the barstool. "You got a problem with that?"

"We'll buy you some whiskey," the Swastika guy said.

"Coffee is fine."

"You handling drugs?" the same biker asked.

There was no response to such a stupid question.

"He don't look like a druggie to me," the one with the chain head said.

I took a drink of the coffee. The black stuff was left over from the morning's brew. I would have been better off with whiskey. Time to find the men's restroom. I slid off the stool and spotted the sign, down a dark and smelly hallway.

I washed my hands, found the paper towels, and pushed open the door. The door stopped with a thud. Someone—a big guy—was blocking the door. I pushed harder. The door opened and I walked out.

"Hey, watch it, man," the biker said. He said the words slow, changing his manner, trying to be non-aggressive. He wanted to talk.

I nodded.

"You the runner?" he asked.

"Not me." I pushed past him, uncomfortably close, enough for knife action, if he had one. I walked down the hall, and slid onto the barstool.

The biker returned to his table and the three of them talked among themselves for several minutes. The big man tried again to get my attention. "Mister, you're driving a Porsche with Idaho plates. You a point man?"

"Nope. You're mistaking me for someone else."

"Which way you driving?"

"Doesn't matter."

"Are you connected, or a smart ass?" The Swastika guy again.

Connected?

"You a soldier? Driving back to Idaho?"

"Was."

"You tough?" The tall leader was getting bolder, showing off to his two followers.

"Can be."

"You got no drugs, and you don't drink whiskey. You soldiers think you're heroes. You're out there in the sand chasing them A-rabs, while we're here fucking your women."

Oh damn, here we go.

"He looks rich," the newbie said.

"Got any money?" Chainhead was getting bolder.

The newbie looked on. His cheeks were sunken, mouth open. He had bad teeth. I expected him to start drooling.

20

"Nope."

"We think you got some money."

"Hey guys, I want a cup of coffee to wake up, and then move on. Maybe some other time we can have a real party." I was evaluating each of them, instincts from the Army. Who was the fastest, the strongest, and who might have a weapon, and if he could use it.

"You fucking rich guys piss us off. You say you got no money or drugs, and you don't drink whiskey." Chainhead again.

The old man behind the bar was half asleep. He looked up from washing the bar glasses. His bifocals fell forward into the dirty dish water.

"You want to buy us a drink?" Chainhead tapped his glass on the table.

"Next time." Now they were getting my dander up.

The three of them turned toward each other. I heard the newbie say, "He's not the one."

I put a five on the bar for the lousy coffee, and headed for the door. The newbie stopped drooling for a moment and closed his mouth. I walked to the door and glanced back. The newbie gave me the finger. Another tough guy.

I slid behind the wheel of the Porsche, then lifted the Beretta out of the center compartment and laid it on the seat next to me. The black automatic fit in the palm of my hand. The magazine was loaded but the chamber was empty. I didn't want to use it. I put the car in gear, listened to the welcome rumble of the Bavarian engine, took one last look at Lefty's and headed north.

The road through Wyoming was lonely, gray, isolated, with the occasional cow silhouetted on the top of a windswept hill. A high, dark overcast was moving in from the west, and the September night settled in over the forlorn landscape.

The lighted digits of the speedometer on the panel showed ninety. I kept my eyes open for antelope or deer, knowing I could stop if I had to. A headlight would show to the front, then be past and gone. At one time a single headlight, like a motorcycle, appeared behind me, but I touched the accelerator and the light disappeared. If those three jerk-offs were behind me, they couldn't catch up. After twenty-five miles I needed a break and pulled off at a state rest stop.

The rumble of the car slowed. A few cottonwoods circled the brown grass and the standard yellow-brick government building with the restrooms.

Another car was parked at the far edge of parking space near the exit lane. When I came out of the restroom ten minutes later the same car was parked there with exhaust showing in the cool evening air. And now, the three motorcycles from Lefty's were parked past the restrooms at the edge of the grass with their front tires pointed out. They weren't as far behind me as I thought. Where were the bikers? They must be behind the restroom building.

The other car pulled away, and in answer to my question the three bikers came out from behind the building. I walked to the Porsche, keyed the unlock in my pocket, and slipped behind the wheel.

"Wait soldier, we want some money," the big Swastika guy barked. He was moving fast toward me, out in front of Chainhead. The newbie was moving toward his bike. He wanted to be out of this action, and away. This raised another alarm in my head.

I lowered the window on the driver's side. "Okay, Jack, move on, we've had enough fun. You can get in trouble here in more ways than you can count."

"Big talk, soldier boy." He was ranting now, his hand on the door handle. "You may not be the guy we're waiting for, but you'll do."

"That is, if you can count. And get your fucking hands off the door."

"Give me your wallet or I'll cut the canvas top to shreds." Chainhead reached behind his leathers and produced a Bowie knife.

That did it. I pushed the door open against him. I didn't want to use the Beretta.

He came in fast for the ignition key. His arm was inside the car and it was all the leverage I needed. With both hands I grabbed his arm, pushed him back from the door, rotating the arm up and back, trying to dislocate his shoulder. He was a muscular bastard. He wasn't fazed.

He side-stepped and reached for the keys again. The knife was in his left hand. "Nice car," he ranted. The ignition key was on the left side and he missed it. He tried to slice the canvas top, feinting with the knife. The big guy wanted the car intact and I wanted the car intact. Keeping my eyes on the other two I grabbed the hand inside the car, found his finger, bent it back and felt it break.

"You dirty mother—"

At the same time I looked for the second man. Chainhead pulled a pistol from his belt, behind his back, but he hesitated, tangled up in the fringed leather, or Lefty's whiskey, or both, and he lost the advantage. I wrapped my hand around the little Beretta, dove past the open door, past Swastika, who was holding his hand and cursing.

I got to my feet, snapped back the slide of the little automatic and in the night air the sound was sharp and metallic of a cartridge locked into the chamber. I pointed the short-barreled pistol at Chainhead's nose.

"Drop it now," I said, "or you're dead. And so is your friend." The little automatic was pointed at Chainhead, then I swung to the other biker, who was ready to jump me.

"Holy shit, take it easy, man," he said. "We just wanted a couple of bucks. Thought you were someone else." The biker dropped the pistol.

His weapon was a revolver, and keeping the automatic pointed at his face and not taking my eyes off his hands, I knelt down and picked it up, stepped back, opened the cylinder, and pocketed the cartridges. Then I slipped the revolver into my pants pocket.

The first guy had dropped the knife. He tried flexing his fingers. "You son-of-a-bitch. You broke my hand."

I swung the Beretta back to Swastika. "Stay where you are."

The bikers were ripping mad. The dark hills and the parking lot were silent. An owl, startled by the noise of the scuffle, flew out of the cottonwoods, and quietly disappeared into the night.

I had also been watching the newbie. If he had pulled a weapon the fight could have got nasty. He swung his leg across his motorcycle, wanting out of this game. He started the engine and a single light cut a broad swath out to the blacktop. Without looking back, he turned right on the highway, and headed south. I watched his headlight disappear in the distance. Miles beyond him the lights of another vehicle appeared, coming this way.

The big man moved toward me, ready to swing again with his good arm.

Now I was pissed. "Did you say, we fuck your women?"

"You've got the gun, soldier boy," he snarled, his good hand holding his other hand.

I walked over to the two motorcycles and fired one bullet each into their tires. The tires hissed as they went flat. The two bikers were going to say something or jump me, but their attention diverted to a large black SUV coming toward us on the other side of the restrooms. The SUV stopped and the headlights went out, but no one exited the vehicle. The two bikers were hypnotized, staring at the black car.

I threw the revolver and the Beretta on the front seat, and slid into the Porsche. The bikers knew these people and the situation looked like it was going to get deadly.

The Wyoming night was like the bottom of a black bucket. I was in a hurry to get the hell out of there. A movement at the other end of the parking lot got my attention. The lights of the big SUV came on and the vehicle made a slow turn on the gravel and the driver positioned the vehicle facing the two remaining motorcycles. The headlights lit up the bikes like a stage. The rear doors of the SUV opened and a man got out on each side and stood behind the bikes in the glare of the lights. The two men looked dark and dangerous and I wish I had my M4, with four full mags.

The two bikers moved toward the SUV, talking frantically. Swastika held one hand. The Chainhead guy waved his arms. This was a circus, a dangerous circus. The lights on my car were off, and it would be a matter of seconds before they saw me.

I let out the clutch for the first gear, drove by the feel of the road, went up four gears, drove on the blacktop for the next half mile, turned on the headlights, dropped to sixth gear, and the engine hummed. I relaxed and the speedometer moved to eighty-five. They couldn't catch me if they tried.

The bikers might report the scuffle, saying they were roughed up and someone damaged their motorcycles, but I doubted that. They were up to no good. The brass from the little automatic lay scattered on the ground, easy to find. The authorities couldn't trace the casings to the Beretta. The gun was unregistered, came from a dead Taliban chieftain in the Hindu Kush. I kept driving and in the darkest part of the night parked just off the bridge crossing the Snake River in Idaho, walked to the center of the bridge and threw the revolver, the cartridges and the little pistol fifty yards downstream into the fast current. No one would find those guns.

At seven in the morning the high beams were still on and the car was purring at a modest eighty on the Interstate. The light from the east touched the sagebrush and the grain fields. I punched the seek button on the panel and Salt Lake Radio came on. The morning news got my attention.

A female newscaster, guaranteed to wake everyone at this time of day with her happy strident voice, narrated a shootout in Wyoming:

"Early this morning two motorcyclists were found dead at a rest stop facility inside the Wyoming state line, south of Laramie. Their motorcycles were disabled, the tires shot out, and the riders died of multiple gunshot wounds. The sheriff said that a gunfight had taken place, sometime before midnight. Bullet holes were stitched across the outside walls of a public restroom, the sheriff said, leading him to suspect that automatic rifles were used, as well as pistols, in a violent gunfight. Pistol and rifle casings were scattered over the grass and the parking lot. FBI agents from Cheyenne and Salt Lake City were dispatched this morning to the crime scene. Authorities suspect gangs were involved. The victims identities have not been disclosed."

After a cup of black coffee and an egg with sausage biscuit I turned north off the Interstate to Ketchum and Sun Valley. The air was crisp with a tease of the snows that were coming. A decade ago I had tangled with the worst of hostiles in foreign lands. Who was in that black SUV? Those bikers had run up against people who were a hell of a lot better armed than I was.

Between Seasons

The Sun Valley lodge, tucked away in a high valley in the Sawtooth Mountains, was living up to its name. Two rows of spruces lined the driveway. Above the trees the sky was a brilliant blue. The winter ski crowd was two months away. I pulled the Porsche up to the *porte cochere* and caught the attention of the two uniformed doormen, standing rigid, on high alert. One jumped to take my bags, the other offering to park the car.

"Thanks, I'll take care of the car," I said, and pocketed the keys. Nothing in the car would tell of the action at the Wyoming rest stop. The two pistols and the cartridges were in the river. The two jerks didn't get the chance to slice the canvas top. Now they're dead.

"We're between seasons, summer and skiing," the lovely young woman behind the desk informed me when I registered. She was, I was certain, hired for her good looks and Swiss accent. "You can have a suite at the same rate as a single."

"Thank you." I had driven all night, needed a couple hours sleep, an easy workout, and a drink. Make it a double.

"I believe you have a gym here."

"Yes, second floor. Open twenty-four hours, with your room key."

Lumbermen were arriving for the meeting and moved around in the lobby. Several I recognized, nodding to them, shaking hands with others.

"Heard you were on the docket," one timber owner said. I'd see them tomorrow at the meeting.

A tall woman in an unbuttoned cashmere coat walked through the lobby toward the elevators. She had slim gorgeous legs and carried a large handbag over her shoulder. The light from the high windows caught her brown hair, and I stopped. She brushed her hair back with her hand, entered the elevator, turned and took a last look at the gathering crowd in the lobby. For an instant our eyes met and each of us, stunned, held for a long moment. The elevator doors closed.

Only one woman walked that way. Liz Hollis, a girl I once knew in Idaho. Before the wars. A woman I was once in love with.

If the beautiful woman getting onto the elevator was Liz, if she was staying here, I would find her.

"Sir, your credit card."

"Thank you. And could you tell me, is a Ms. Hollis registered here?"

"We have no one registered by that name."

Of course, she'll be married, with another name.

The pretty Swiss receptionist beckoned to a bellhop, who was standing at the side of the desk, spring loaded. He was on the two duffels in a flash. He had an accent, sounded French. The Sun Valley people were great marketers. They emulated the luxury hotels of Bavaria and did a fine job of it. The Lodge, surrounded by the spruces, had been there since the days of Ernest Hemingway and Gary Cooper, and had not changed a whit.

The suite had all the amenities I expected in Sun Valley. If it was good enough for Ernest, it was good enough for me. I opened the duffels, threw back the bed covers, slept until two, went to the workout room, moved some weights around, pounded away for a short stretch on the treadmill, then back to the room. The plan was for an early drink in the bar. I thought about the dead bikers. They weren't that tough, or well-armed, for whatever they'd had in mind. They were up against automatic rifles. Who were those guys in the black car? The two men who got out of the SUV were professional and deadly. That was certain.

When I stepped out of the shower the message light on the desk was blinking. I pushed the button. The recording was startling.

CASEY, MEET ME IN THE DUCHIN ROOM AT EIGHT TONIGHT. LIZ

Liz is here at the hotel! Five hours to meet her. An eternity. I opened the papers of the speech I had to present. The words were a blur. That wasn't a problem because the subject was memorized. I had promised myself that drink and with hours to go, I changed into jeans, a blue shirt and polished western dress boots.

The Duchin Room, the famous lounge off the lobby, at five o'clock was almost empty. On weekends a local band provided the music, taking requests far into the night. The atmosphere has not changed much since Hemingway held court here, telling stories of his years in the wars in Italy and France. He had his stories. He was a writer. I was a rifleman, and had my own stories. Hemingway was handsome. I touched the scar on my cheek. What the hell, some women said it was macho.

In the Duchin Room were the bartender, two serious business men, talking rapidly to each other about the price of something, and a single male patron, seated around the corner of the bar. The man eyed me when I walked in, maybe wanted to talk with someone other than the barkeep. He was about forty-five, curly black hair, six foot two or so, wore a button-down shirt and rep tie. I took him as Ivy League, played sports at Princeton, wealthy family background.

He swung his drink toward me in a gesture of greeting. He had soft hands. He had been talking to the bartender. Both were watching the elevated television screen behind them.

The commentator was talking about a shooting in Wyoming. Two motorcyclists had been found dead at a roadside park. The victims had been shot numerous times, with automatic weapons. Some drugs were found on one motorcycle. The sheriff said the killings looked like a drug deal gone bad. Both motorcycles had the rear tires shot out. Authorities said the killings were gang related, and they were concerned this lawlessness was coming up across the state line.

The bartender turned to me and smiled. "Maker's on the rocks," I ordered. He ignored the TV to work on the drink. Nice.

"Good choice," the man at the end of the bar said, turning away from the screen and giving me his full attention. He twirled his fingers at the barkeep. "Another vodka martini." His voice slurred. The evening was early.

"New in town?" the man asked, leaning closer to me.

"Passin' through," I said, giving him my best crooked smile. That sometimes slowed people down. It didn't. He moved another bar stool closer.

The TV commentator was winding down from the dead bikers and was switching to a story of a polygamist in Utah. The polygamist had four wives and was trying to make it legal. Good luck. The bartender said he usually turned off the screen at five. "Okay by me," I said.

"Every one of those drug-dealing bikers should be shot. But then where would I get my coke?" the rep-tie guy said, and laughed. "You? Going north or south?"

"North," I lied.

"The roads are open to the north. I come out now and again to warm up the Mercedes. Took it across Galena Summit yesterday."

"Good to know." *For God's sake, this is the first week of October.*

"Hanson Porter. Boston. And you are?"

"McConnell. Idaho. Near Boise."

What did he say? Handsome Porter?

He gave me his card. The gold embossed print read, "Hanson Porter III – Investing."

"I keep a car here when I check on the house. Parked it next to a black turbo 911 off the lobby. I'd like to talk to the guy driving that baby. What do you do?"

"Manufacturing." I left out the lumber part. Tree huggers were prolific here in the valley. I also didn't tell him the Porsche was mine. "And you?"

"Investments. I'm in investments," Hanson said. "I can work from a computer anywhere. If you need to diversify, let me know. Got some deals. Don't offer them to most people. Flew out here Tuesday to check if the caretakers are keeping the place fit."

"Are they?"

"Are they what?"

He leaned toward me again. The intimate type, his breath too close, as he worked on the vodka.

"Keeping it fit?"

"Fabulous, just fabulous. As soon as the skiing starts, I'll be here for a month."

A trust fund baby from Boston. Next he's going to tell me he skis the steep and the deep, off the face of Baldy.

"I get in twenty-five ski days a season. Keeps me in shape."

"This is the place to be."

"About those deals. I can get you a twenty percent return. Risk is low." He winked at me.

Winked? Wow. Hanson's breath was bad. This was Idaho sheep country. He should have tried sheep dip. I wished he had someone else to talk with. I was getting queasy.

Twenty percent return. I'd kill for twenty percent. "I'm good."

"Well, think it over. There are some high rollers out here who work the big numbers."

I'll bet.

The bartender turned to wipe down glasses, pretending he wasn't listening to the conversation. "Fact is," Hanson Porter continued, "this could be your lucky day. I'm meeting a gentleman tonight who is locked into a nice real estate project. Want in? Won't take much cash."

"Nah—I'm saving for a new pair of skis."

"This deal is not showing on the big board, if you get what I mean." He gave me the knowing wink again.

I took a sip of the Maker's.

"Excuse me," Hanson Porter the Third said, "I got to get some papers from my room, get ready for the meeting." He moved wobbly off the barstool.

"Would you like me to turn the TV back on?" the bartender asked. "You were interested in those dead bikers?" He must be Swiss. He had that cool European accent.

"No, I'll catch it later." After the black SUV arrived at the rest stop there was a one-sided shoot-out. One of those bikers was lacking a gun. I took it.

The Swiss bartender smiled and slid another Maker's my way. "On the house," he said. "We're between seasons."

My cell phone chimed. Ellen, the company's office manager, was on the line, working late on a Friday night. "Ready to take down some numbers? I think you'll like them."

"I'll call you from my room in five minutes." I gestured to the barkeep to keep my seat warm. "Be right back." Liz would be here in the Duchin room in an hour, and the butterflies were already starting.

Ellen and I spent twenty minutes going over the month's numbers. She had remarkable accounting skills and enough knowledge of the lumber business to alert me if something was changing. The bottom line, as they say, looked good. My mind was somewhere else.

Liz Hollis

When I walked back into the lounge Liz was sitting at the bar, wearing a red sleeveless dress with a high collar. Her legs were crossed, just so, long slim legs like no other woman had. Her eyes were large, brown, and laughing. She was more gorgeous than before.

"I'm early," she said. I leaned over and kissed her on the cheek. "I can't believe this."

"Of all the gin joints in the world," I said, trying my best Bogie.

"You're better looking than Bogie."

"And you are more beautiful than ever." I kissed her again, this time lightly on her lips. I was watching her reaction. It was positive.

"This is wonderful. You are looking fit. Haven't changed at all."

"Just got off a fire on the Yellowstone."

"You're back to jumping. I can't believe that."

"One jump, and I'll tell you about that, after we talk about everything else we've missed these last fifteen years. How did you know I was here?"

"Your name was on the speaker board in the lobby, Mr. Big Shot."

"The directors of the association who sponsor this meeting couldn't find anyone else," I said, feigning modesty.

Liz laughed then. "That's not true. Tell me everything. Start from the beginning."

I slipped onto the bar stool beside her. "First things first. What are you drinking?" I circled my hand and smiled at Swiss.

"Tanqueray and tonic."

The barkeep was watching her also. He set the drinks down, glanced at Liz again, and gave me a devilish smile.

"Friendly guy. Hope he isn't reading my mind."

"I don't think anybody can read your mind. I couldn't."

I wasn't sure where that comment might take us. We touched glasses, neither saying a word. Then we both laughed and gave each other a long hug, there in the Duchin Room.

Liz said she was in Sun Valley for an investment seminar. I had seen the hotel agenda in the lobby. This seminar wasn't for the low-end investors.

"How many companies are you going to buy this week?" I asked.

"Don't be facetious," she said, and laughed. "I like to stay in touch, do some financial management of my own."

"Great, I'll let you cover my expenses for our next meeting in Sun Valley." I gave her a mischievous grin and touched her hand.

"Are we going to have another meeting?" she asked, measuring me to see if I was the same guy she had once been in love with.

"I'm planning on it."

"I remember you talked me into spending some weekends here with you, back when."

"Yes, I did. They were great."

"You smokejumpers move fast." She smiled, changing to a lighter vein. "We all started at the bottom, remember? Summers at the lodge on the river. I was the chief cook and bottle washer, and you were throwing dirt on burning trees."

"Jumping out of airplanes and throwing dirt on forest fires is not the bottom, it's the top, the best job in the world." I was thinking of the fires in the pines on the Yellowstone last week. "But I can't go back now. To keep the record straight."

"Okay, you're a modern day Viking. Smokejumpers and Rangers. You were hard to keep track of."

"I remember the summers at Fall Creek. One special night. We were at the end of the runway, the moon was out, and I asked you to marry me."

Liz's eyes brightened. "It took you a whole year to ask me. Remember, we were at that same place the summer before."

"And you asked me to marry you," I said. "We were both in college."

"No, I asked you if you were going to ask me to marry you."

"Is there a difference?"

"Of course there is."

"We were asking each other some serious things backwards then, weren't we?"

Liz smiled and took a sip of her drink.

"I believe you would have turned me down," I said.

Those large brown eyes were looking at me now, serious.

"Always the blonde hair," Liz continued, like she was thinking of what might have been. "There were some Scandinavians in your background, weren't there?"

"Somewhere," I said and laughed.

"Our kids would have been cute."

"If they had taken after you." We had drifted apart. I had been in a hurry to conquer the world. "What happened?"

"Not sure."

"Those crazy days we thought would never end. You went to California and became an airline attendant."

"Yes, but I wrote."

"I was in the Rangers, then the Green Berets. The wars came, one after another."

"And you came back to Idaho?"

"I worked for a small sawmill, bought it from the owner who wanted to retire, got a bank loan, built it into a high-tech timber operation."

"I always knew you would be successful in whatever you did."

"Thanks for the kind words. And you?" I asked.

"While you were across the ocean chasing al Qaeda, I met and married a nice man, older than me by eighteen years. Alec Champlin. He's an investment banker, owns several companies, one of which is a ranch in Nevada, where we live most of the time. No children."

"Most of the time?"

Liz gave me a devilish smile. "Yes, two years ago we bought a lodge on the Middle Fork of the Salmon in the primitive area of Idaho. We call it a ranch. I plan to spend the summers and falls there, along the river."

"There aren't many private acreages on the river in the backcountry."

"The ranch is upstream from Phantom Creek," she said, and sipped her drink.

"I know it well, but never had the occasion to land a plane on that airstrip. Your place is about as far back in the mountains as you can get. You always did love the Idaho backcountry."

"Like you," Liz said. "Ever marry?"

"No," I said. "Being thirty-eight, there might still be time." Liz gave me a serious look, which I couldn't decipher, then she touched her glass. Her eyes seemed suddenly larger and brighter.

I ordered another round of Tanqueray.

"What happened to Mike Romano?" she asked. "You guys were close, jumped together, joined at the hip. The wild Italian you called him. We always had fun, in those summers, the three of us."

"Mike's gone. Fell in Afghanistan. He was a brave bastard. I was with him when he died. Hard to talk about it."

"I knew him almost as much as I knew you." Her eyes filled with tears. "Want to tell me?"

"Maybe someday." I had to change the moment. We each had a drink in our hand. "To you. More beautiful than ever."

"It's the gin." Liz laughed. "It's misleading. Now that we're telling each other how wonderful we are, you have the blue eyes. Dangerous blue eyes."

"I thought they were twinkling."

"Dangerous *and* twinkling."

"What a combination."

Liz slid her drink away, reached up and touched my cheek, below my left eye. "The scar makes you look even more handsome. Like a knight." She reached up and her finger traced the scar from under my left eye to almost my ear. "You must have scared the troops. Afghanistan?"

"A grenade fragment. The scar is fading. In ten years it should be gone."

"The important thing is you survived the Middle East."

"The second time we went in, everybody on the team made it. Three were wounded, not seriously."

"You loved the Army—yes."

"Yes I did, but moving on to us."

"We had a lot of fun, back then, didn't we," Liz said. "Before those days."

"A lot of fun." I smiled.

Liz gave me an inquisitive look. Maybe that was best. She was married.

"Let's have dinner downtown in Ketchum, and we can catch up."

The bartender reached up and turned off the TV again. Thank goodness. He slid a small plate of cashews between Liz and me. What manners he had. We both took some.

"Thanks again. Slow, isn't it?" Liz commented.

"We're between seasons," the bartender said.

A moment later Hanson Porter the Third returned, his vodka martini in his hand. He spotted Liz at the bar and kept his attention on her as he settled, clumsily, onto his familiar stool.

Hanson Porter wasn't shy and he made his move, oblivious to the fact that the good-looking woman and I were talking. He picked up his martini, came around the corner of the bar, crossed behind me, and sat next to Liz. I heard him introduce himself, said the action was quiet in the valley. He produced a pack of cigarettes and offered her one, which she declined.

Then I heard Hanson tell Liz—she of the brown eyes and red lips—of all the great restaurants he frequented in New York, Chicago, and Boston, and of all the elegant wines he had tasted from California and France, and some, God forbid, from Idaho and New York.

After a few minutes of hearing how wonderful Hanson was, I was getting bored, and Liz, who had not said a word, looked straight ahead and declined another cigarette. She winked at me, then excused herself for the powder room, leaving Hanson again sitting alone.

The golden boy, with no one to talk to, declared he was going to the lobby to buy more cigarettes. He also was going to meet some men, to tie up an important deal. Wants to buy Brazil.

The moment he left the lounge Liz returned from the powder room, glanced around the bar, and said, "I'll buy you dinner. Let's get out of here."

I gave the bartender my room number for the tab and tip. I escorted Liz out of the lounge and into the lobby, my hand on her waist.

Hanson Porter sat on the edge of a large brown sofa near the windows, facing us. He was talking to a tall, strikingly handsome man, who looked to be Middle Eastern. The man had black hair, a salt and pepper mustache, trimmed beard, and wore a black sports coat and white shirt, open at the neck. He had the look of a successful international businessman. He also had the body language of being physically strong, even athletic. Another man, also dark complexioned, sat in a leather chair with his back to the wall, facing the entrance. He had the stoic appearance of a bodyguard. These people looked big time, big money. Hanson and the tall foreigner were both leaning forward, talking in noisy, animated terms. The bodyguard was watching me.

Hanson passed the man a large envelope, stuffed, it appeared, with cash. The transaction was clandestine, an impression I got, the way my mind worked. There had been press lately about drug and illicit oil money from the Middle East, being laundered in the West, where high-end real estate was being purchased and figuring into the transactions. Some of this cash was being used by extremists.

The two of them hadn't seen us. The bodyguard had. They were both speaking in Farsi, a language I knew well and used in-country. Hanson Porter was also communicating in this language. I thought that surprising.

Only twenty feet from the lobby entrance Hanson spotted us, did a double take, and jumped up from the sofa. "Wait," he said. "I want to buy you both a drink." The tall business man was watching us. His bodyguard, unmoved, staring, had his eyes on only me.

"Fauod," Hanson said, "I'd like you to meet some new friends." Fauod stood up, I'm sure because of Liz's presence. I introduced myself and gestured to Liz.

"Liz," she said. "From Nevada."

"Fauod Saeed," the tall bearded one said, his countenance unchanged, nodding toward Liz. "I know Mrs. Champlin."

My head jerked. *Middle Eastern men speaking Farsi, and Fauod knows Liz.*

"Mr. Saeed flew into our airstrip and lodge on the river," Liz said.

That got my attention. I looked from Fauod to Liz and back to Fauod. What was going on here? Fauod spoke impeccable English. His manner was that of a leader. "I did visit Mrs. Champlin's lodge," he said.

"I offered to lease the property, perhaps even buy it. Unfortunately, she turned down my offer. There are, however, other opportunities to find a mountain retreat."

For what purpose? These two guys didn't look like elk hunters.

Fauod was unhappy talking about this, and appeared to want to put the matter to rest. He turned his attention to me. Was I a visitor, ski bum, or CIA? I had passed the age of a Sun Valley ski bum.

Hanson picked up the conversation. "Fauod is a pilot. He flew up here from Texas, wants to buy a condo up here."

A pilot from the Middle East. *We've been through this before.*

We talked about Sun Valley condos. Hanson said it is a good time to buy. The market was hot.

"Looks like you fellows have some business to discuss," I said, including the man whom I classified as a bodyguard, "so we'll be going."

Liz nodded in agreement. *We were not going to dinner with these guys.*

"Might see you in town later," Hanson Porter said. "Ciao."

"*Ciao.*" I echoed. *Ciao?* Mike, the crazy Italian, used that word.

I touched Liz's elbow and led her to the hotel entrance. The two hotel uniforms, flanking the door, bid us good evening. The bodyguard sat watching from the lobby.

We walked around the fishpond, past the spruces, onto the parking lot, and slid into the Porsche. I suggested the Frontier restaurant, she said yes, and we drove the mile into Ketchum. The maître d' found us a table behind a wood-slatted screen, and I ordered drinks, a Grey Goose and tonic for her, and a Maker's neat for me.

The drinks came immediately. She raised hers and we touched glasses. Liz was looking at me seriously with those large brown eye and she said "Thanks." I relaxed and we both laughed.

Liz wanted to try some famous Frontier steaks, so we ordered filets, medium rare, and later topped them off with a Wild Turkey liqueur.

She took another sip of her drink, set it down, and touched my hand. "And what else have you been doing these last fifteen years, besides hunting down the enemy and making lumber?"

"Exciting things. Do you still like to dance?"

"Yes. Love to."

"I know just the place, out on Warm Springs, only a snowball's throw from here, so to speak. We *are* in Sun Valley," I said, signing off on the dinner tab, over her protests.

"The rest of the evening will be on me," she said.

"Let's go. We can talk about that later."

As if on cue we both glanced around the screen toward the bar to see if Hanson the Golden Boy and his friends were there. They were, seated halfway down the bar with the other merrymakers. Hanson was talking to a young woman, barely twenty-one, wearing expensive faded shredded jeans and a low-cut paisley blouse. He was telling her how he skis the glades, if only the snows would arrive. Fauod Saeed and his bodyguard were at the bar on the other side, looking bored. I suspected they didn't like American women. Maybe they didn't like women.

"We can't let them see us. Hanson is going to want to dance with you."

"Fat chance." Liz laughed. "That big guy will want to dance with *you*. He was watching you. You can speak their language. He'll find that sexy."

"Sexy? Yes, he was watching me. He's a bodyguard, has a gun under his jacket. Forget them. I know a back way out of here."

My little automatic was in the river. Stopping that guy could take a full clip from the .25. More than a decade after the wars my mind still worked that way. The next time I'd put a .45 in the center console of the car.

We made our way to the other end of the restaurant where the smell of grilled steaks was overwhelming, making me want to stop and order another one. I pumped my fist to the head cook and pointed to the door. He nodded "not a problem." We exited to the side street, leaving the Golden Boy and his friends to their own mischief.

The bar with the dance band was dark, lively, and jumping with good music, laughter and partying, the liveliest place in the valley. After ordering drinks, I asked Liz to dance and when I put my hand on her waist we moved to the music like we had danced before, and we had, years ago. Shortly before midnight the members of the band were getting restless and began putting away their instruments. I slipped them four twenties and asked for one more request.

"I can't remember when I had this much fun," she said, and her cheek moved against mine, and the subtle smell of her perfume was intoxicating.

After midnight we slipped into the car. The moon was bright above the dark ridges, and the damp smell of cottonwood leaves lingered along the creek. This was the best time of the year in the mountains of Idaho. When I escorted Liz to her room in the lodge, she said that she had more to tell me, and there was this thing with her marriage, and she was unsure of how far we should take our new friendship. "Come into the lodge on the Middle Fork. I hope you will. It's my turn for dinner. I make great ribs. You can tell me about yourself, your mysterious self, and if you like to ride, and I know you do, Clint our wrangler will saddle up the horses, and you, Alec and I will ride up through the breaks."

She used the words Alec and I. Of course. *I can't forget that.*

"After my meeting tomorrow and your speech, I'll buy you dinner," Liz said.

"I'd love that, seven o'clock in the lobby."

I leaned toward her and kissed her. The kiss on the lips was a short one.

When we drove back to the lodge, a black SUV was parked in front of the entrance. Both the car and the lobby were empty. The car had a Texas license plate.

Phantom Ranch

Liz walked into the lobby at seven sharp wearing tight black jeans and a white blouse, cut low. Stunning. She kissed me on the check. I suggested we have dinner in the lodge, and she said yes. I motioned to the maître d' for a table. Liz followed him like she owned the place. Maybe she did. She walked with a little tilt to her chin, like she knew something I didn't, and might tell me if I teased her. The effect on me was the same as it was when we first met.

We had dinner, laughed a lot, talked about skiing, hiking, and investing. I told her I'd expect the Dow Jones to jump after she returned to her office, then asked about her purchase of the ranch on the Middle Fork. I knew those river canyons and mountains well. Apparently, Fauod did too. That bothered me.

"Fauod Saeed was eager to lease or buy," Liz said. "Alec was in Nevada. Clint, our lodge caretaker, was with me, or I would have been uncomfortable. Fauod was flying a green Cessna. He landed at noon, the windiest part of the day to land on a river strip. He knows how to fly. Another man was with him. This man got out of the cockpit and stood next to the plane, while Saeed was talking with Clint and me. Saeed was not happy when I told him I wasn't interested." Liz sipped her drink.

"The lodge is in the pines, next to the river, at the end of a long grass runway. We call our place the Phantom Ranch, named after Phantom Creek, which flows into the Salmon River not far downstream. Alec and I keep six horses at the lodge. In the early summer Clint walks the horses along the river trail into the ranch from Cox's Landing on the Salmon River. I love the place and I'm going to spend the summers and falls there."

Liz continued. "The canyon is beautiful there. Steep timbered slopes and granite cliffs. Clint is our wrangler and lives at the lodge. He is sixtyish, a widower, has lived on ranches and isolated country his whole life. We met him at the Fall Creek Lodge five years ago. He told us his wife died, he was alone now, and not about to settle down to city life. We hired Clint as caretaker and general manager. He brings in an elk in the fall, butchers the meat in the barn, and we have great steaks for weeks. He can shoot a fly off an elk's nose at a hundred yards."

"I know Clint," I said. "Met him at Fall Creek when we had a project there one summer, between fires. He has a scar across one cheek, doesn't he? He told us the scar was from a fight with the Sioux when he rode with Custer."

"That's Clint," she said. "I *have* to tell you the scar on *your cheek* is the same."

"I believe it is," I said, ignoring the scar talk. "Back to Clint and the Phantom Creek country. I know it well. There's an old airfield there in a high basin, cut out of the pines near the headwaters. CCC workers built the airstrip in the forties and the Forest Service abandoned the field in the sixties. Still, the grass strip could be used in an emergency. When I fly into elk camp in a week I'll check it out from the air."

"Let me know what it looks like now. We could ride up there and explore that country."

"I'll fly over and check out that country with Whiskey Bravo."

"Your plane, of course. We charter a plane to fly into the lodge. What kind of a plane is that?"

"A tail-wheel with a large engine and big tires. It'll go anywhere."

"Then you can come in to see me," Liz said.

"You *are* married, right?"

"I can explain our friendship," Liz said, and took a sip of the Tanqueray.

"That might take some explaining. Your husband will know."

She said nothing, leaned forward, and placed her chin in her cupped hands. She was looking directly at me and smiled. I could smell her perfume.

Her husband was older than Liz. I suspected that marrying an older man might have some trade-offs. "Does your husband like the backcountry?"

"Alec is tied up in his balance sheets, spends most of the time at his desk with his laptop. He's good for a week at the lodge, then back to Nevada. I could stay on the river forever."

"Yes, I know. How about Sun Valley? Do you come here often?"

"What a line. Do you and the other college boys use that in singles bars?" Liz laughed.

"Years ago. Now I'm serious."

"Sometimes, for the summer business meetings. I first came here looking out for my own investments, then added several clients, and the business grew. I can work from a computer in Nevada, or from the ranch on the Middle Fork. Let's go outside for a cigarette."

I slid her chair back and we walked past the lobby and down a hall to a side entrance. Outside the night wind swirled past the alcove and around the spruces. The sound of cars pulling up to the entrance was muffled.

Liz lifted a pack of cigarettes from her handbag, nudged one out and gave me the matches. Like the first time. I remembered the drill, cupped my hands, protecting the match from the wind, and lit her cigarette. She was looking at me, there in the darkness. She took a long draw, handed me the cigarette, and I did the same.

"I don't do this often," she said.

"Don't do what?"

"Smoke."

"Right."

"Only on special occasions."

"Like with an old boyfriend," I said.

"A very special boyfriend. The boyfriend who was more than that. Would you like a cigarette?"

"Thanks, but I quit."

"Start again. We all smoked back then, didn't we?"

"We did a lot things then, especially you and I."

Liz turned toward me, like she was waiting for those words. She dropped her hand with the cigarette, then flipped it into the darkness. "Happy now? Do you still do things?"

"Yes," I said, and kissed her then, there in the doorway, under the dim lights of the alcove. A solitary person, walking across the lawn, with his head down in the wind, glanced up and smiled.

The kiss was a long one, and she broke the spell.

"I love you," I said. "I always have."

"We loved each other once. But I'm married now."

"I know. You told me."

"Our journeys might have been different."

"If I would have stayed."

"Yes," she said. She kissed me again. Lightly.

"If we don't see each other for another fifteen years, we'll always have Paris."

"The Bogie thing is dating you." Liz laughed.

"Saw *Casablanca* on TV last week, for the fifth time."

I left her in the lobby, as she waited for the elevator. Three middle-aged men, at the hotel to attend the lumber meeting, having started early in the bar, all of them old enough to know better, laughing, talking loud and staggering somewhat, bumped shoulders with each other as they entered the open elevator.

She followed them in. One of them said "sorry" to Liz. Before the doors closed she smiled and winked at me. She mouthed "Middle Fork." Her eyes were larger and browner than I remembered.

The only access to her lodge in the backcountry was to fly, or spend two days riding the trails on horseback. Fly in, she said. I told her no because she was married.

A wise man once said there was no such thing as a coincidence. There was something between Liz and me. Always was. The long kiss in the alcove proved it. She invited me to her lodge on the river. Maybe I could do that—fly in for a cup of coffee. There would be time. Link and Jammer weren't coming into the backcountry for three or four days. Our camp was only twenty-five air miles from Liz's landing field on the river.

A devil voice was telling me there was a way, back there in the mountains, to accept her invitation.

Take-Off at Owyhee Crossing

The timber plant was located hard on the south bank of the Snake River at Owyhee Crossing. The Snake started as a snow-melt creek 300 miles to the east in the Yellowstone country. Ten miles downstream from the plant, the river, now wide and free flowing, turns to the north and enters Hells Canyon, the massive gorge separating the states of Idaho and Oregon. The mill was strategically located for manufacturing. Timber and lumber came inbound from the forests to the north, and long flatbed trucks carried the finished wood products on the interstate highways to the markets in the east.

The manufacturing buildings were positioned on one hundred acres, all asphalt paved, making it easy for the forklifts to operate in the dusty summer days and the rainy winters. The buildings were constructed for a straight line of production. Three separated manufacturing plants could operated independently, depending on the product mix, and the lumber market. This diversification was the secret of success of the company, and was the theme of the speech I presented to the lumberman at the Sun Valley Lodge. The talk went well; two large distributors signed on as customers, which was amazing because my mind was on Liz, Fauod, and the black SUV. Mostly on Liz.

The wood operation was running well. Six fully loaded semis rolled out of the shipping yard every day. Tony and Ellen managed the company. Both had been with me for ten years and had quickly become pros in the timber and lumber business.

Tony Mendez, the plant manager, supervised the crew. Tony was Hispanic, early forties, six feet plus an inch or two, and weighed in at 250 pounds on a good day. Tony could have been a movie star if he'd wanted to be.

I first met Tony when he'd been supervising a ten-man crew on a fire in Oregon's Wallowa Mountains. Mike and I had parachuted into the forest from Idaho, but we couldn't hold the line when the winds pushed the fire uphill through the big pines. Tony and his crew hiked in and immediately went to work on the flare-ups. When the fire burned to the top of the ridge, they followed it along the edges and stopped the flames. "Well, that was easy," Tony said, his face blackened by ashes, when he came up to me on the fire line.

I asked him, "Why don't you come over to Idaho and sign up for the smokejumpers? You'll get to the fires faster."

Tony took my advice and signed on. He passed the first year of training, even weighing in at 190 pounds, but several years and a steady diet of tacos caught up to him. When he came to work as my right-hand manager in the plant he was much heavier but still as fast as lightning. No one messed with Tony.

All was under control at the business and I knew I could leave the operation to him.

Link and Jammer were still busy. Link was trying to locate the hostiles, and Jammer was finishing up the fire season. I'd leave early for scouting, set up a spike camp, take the longbow and look for elk in the timbered draws. Joe Hooker, a friend and outfitter we used if we needed him to haul equipment or meat, had a camp and horses up on Indian Creek. Hooker wasn't far if we needed him.

I was at my desk, reviewing the sales and production reports, when thoughts of Liz overwhelmed the numbers—meeting her again after fifteen years. Her dancing was so smooth, always was. *Damn, she's an attractive woman, her cheek against mine, the smell of her perfume. Stop. Get back to business.*

Tony came into the office and sat heavily in a chair near the windows. Outside, two forklifts were moving lumber. Tony glanced at them, particles of sawdust spread over his massive shoulders. He had been working with the production crew. He didn't bother to shake his denim shirt when he sat down. That was okay. I was glad we had sturdy chairs.

"The plant is running well. Orders are up and we have lots of lumber, so go out and have fun in the mountains and don't get lost." Tony laughed.

"You take care of everything. I'm not going to worry about costs, but you'll probably drink all the booze in the guest house."

A ranch house where I lived in the nearby desert hills was also called the guest house. Customers from the East Coast loved to visit the Wild West, tour the manufacturing operations, talk prices, have a margarita or two on the deck, view the mountains to the north in the sunset, and stay the night at the house.

"Hey, boss, the customers do that. I make sure they don't fall off the deck and kill themselves."

"Cook your chicken wings and rib eyes," I said. "They love your barbecues."

"I'll do that. If you get stuck back there in the woods, start a forest fire. I'll get Jammer out of the smokejumper unit and we'll jump in."

"Jammer has the fire season behind him, and some fires ahead of him. It's still dry in the mountains. Are you ready?"

"I was born ready," Tony said.

I believed he was. *When we get some time I'll tell Tony about jumping on the fire on the Yellowstone, seeing Baker Brindell again, and saving a couple of injured firefighters, but he might think I was making that up.*

"Anyway, back to work. The second shift is starting up," Tony said. "We have a new lead man." He opened the office door, and there was the high-pitched whine of the timber planer, throwing off fir shavings through the blowpipe. A good lumberman could tell by the sound of the planer how the plant was running. I figured I'd be out there in the mountains soon and thinking about the elk moving through the aspens. Tony could worry about the lumber moving through the saws.

"What time do you lift off?" Tony asked, looking back at me.

"Seventeen hundred hours."

"There you go with that military stuff. Call me if you need anything."

"I'll have a satellite phone, but why call you? You going to drop in?"

"Sure, I'll call the Forest Service, see if they will loan me a chute."

"You'll need their plane. They'll give you a weigh-in." Tony was the only person on the management team I bugged about his weight.

"Okay, I've gained sixty pounds, but I'm still good looking."

"When you hit the ground, do an Allen roll, look for a swamp, or you won't be good looking for long."

"Have fun." Tony turned and walked down the hall and into the plant.

At that moment I made a decision. I'd fly into the backcountry now, set up camp, explore some ridges, and with weather permitting, fly Whiskey Bravo down the Middle Fork, land at the Phantom Ranch and visit Liz. What the hell, Link and Jammer wouldn't be coming into camp for another week.

To the west of the plant, a mile over a one-lane road, parallel to the river, was an airfield, 2,900 feet long. The river was wide there and made a slow bend so that each end of the runway overlooked the water. In the hot summer afternoons the winds from the desert to the south pushed the temperatures to the hundred-degree mark.

When flying onto the runway, the coolness of the river created a sink. A pilot had to touch the throttle on final, countering the sink, use the rudder on the crosswind coming over the trees, then back off the power as the summer heat from the asphalt came up to lift the wings. The sink on the approach kept your mind in high alert—good practice for landing on short runways in the backcountry.

Whiskey Bravo was waiting, tied down near the end of the runway, next to its hangar. The weather was changing. The plane seemed to know this, and if it could talk, would say, "Let's fly out of here."

The wind came across the river from the north, stirred the willows, and rolled over the wings. Swirls of dust along the edge of the blacktop danced along the fuselage and the wings began to shudder. The plane was tied down off the end of runway one-three. The white runway numbers were painted large on the black asphalt, so a visiting plane at 2,000 feet in the sky above knew exactly where to land. Whiskey Bravo was an Aviat Husky. With its nose in the air and the tailwheel on the ground the plane possessed a haughty look, even snobbish. It sat there, red, beautiful and shining in the last of the afternoon sun.

I lifted the longbow and the pistol from the front seat of the truck and walked down the runway. The wind kicked up dust around my boots. "Be patient," I said to the airplane. Behind the front seat went two boxes of food, a tent and sleeping bag, a large frame pack for carrying meat, and a small camouflaged daypack. On top of this was the most important item: a wood longbow, sixty pounds at full draw, with an attached leather quiver holding six cedar arrows, each tipped with a steel hunting broad head. A stout plastic box containing six more arrows was added for practice—and for good luck. The rifle season was three weeks off. The .30-06 stayed at home. Instead, I'd pack a pistol.

A leather belt with a hunting knife, sharpening stone, and a .45 caliber Army Colt semiautomatic pistol with a seven-round magazine were placed loose on top of the gear, an extra loaded magazine secured to the belt. There are wolves back there in the high country. Everyone knows that wolves don't prey on humans, but I wondered if the wolves know that, especially if they are hungry and their quarry is limping through the forest with a broken ankle, or bleeding from a mis-aimed axe swing. Those beautiful animals can drag down a half-ton moose or a five-hundred-pound elk. After years of packing armament on my belt in the Army, the extra weight of the pistol gave me a feeling of comfort.

I walked around the plane, checking the propeller, and sighting along the edges of the wings and tail assembly, inspecting all three tires, the tread, springs, and mounts. Next came the engine compartment; even if it had been inspected the day before, another look was necessary to ensure no birds or packrats had come in during the night and built their nests below the cowling. I've seen them do it. I could picture the excitement when the plane climbs to altitude, the engine heats up, and the grass stuffed around the engine by the packrats catches fire.

I never rushed the preflight inspection: it provided a feeling of security. In the cockpit you can concentrate on the fun part—the flying—keeping eyes outside the plane and watching the countryside. That's what flying was about. The instrument-watching boys can have all the gauges they want. The side windows of the plane were snapped open, exposing the cockpit and the cabin to the wind. In flight, with the weather mild, the left window open and the right panel fastened up, I'd be mesmerized by the rolling rhythm of the engine and the whistle of the wind in the cabin, and think back to the days with the jumpers on aerial fire patrol. Mike was with us on those days on patrol, looking constantly for smokes in the forest, wanting to jump.

Whiskey Bravo carried a maximum load of nine hundred pounds, including fifty gallons of aviation fuel, and at seven pounds per gallon, this left a balance of five hundred and fifty pounds for the pilot and gear. I prepared a flight plan and prepared to land at Soldier Bar, an airstrip off Big Creek in the Salmon River country. Several alternate fields were added to the plan, should the first destination be obstructed by fog or fallen trees.

The red airplane was getting impatient. Silver wavelets walked over the water from one bank to the other. The wind blew across the runway at ten knots, but the plane could handle it. This was October in Idaho, an Indian summer late afternoon, but the weather was changing. North of the butte, twenty miles away, gray clouds gathered. The windsock next to the runway rolled around on its post, trying to find a direction. With the weather coming in I decided to change the flight plan, take off, then fly east to Twin Falls, spend the night in a motel, and depart before dawn when the airport lights were still turned on. From there head north and time the two-hour flight into the Middle Fork country to watch the sunlight catching the top of the mountains. The air would will be like glass, unless those clouds turned into something big.

Turn the key and start the engine, warm it up for take-off. Roll to the end of the blacktop, line up with the white line and the numbers one-three, take one last look around the sky for traffic, and push the throttle forward. All earthly thoughts were forgotten—business, cash flow, ringing phones, crowded offices, coach seats on commercial flights, and weak coffee.

I keyed the radio: "Husky November Zero Niner Whiskey Bravo, departing runway one-three, to the east." There was no response. Not unusual, planes were few and far between, out along the Snake.

Baker Brindell

North of the river an inverted mass of rolling gray cumulus, punctuated by patches of black virga, was rapidly closing on me and Whiskey Bravo. The smell of oncoming rain filled the cockpit. Whiskey Bravo and I were thirty minutes from Twin Falls and flying three hundred feet below the clouds, closer than the regulations allowed for visual flight rules. The drone of the engine was comforting, but a squeeze was beginning between the clouds and the terrain below.

I rotated the engine mixture control as the altitude decreased—there was still time to do a one-eighty and turn back where the sky was a little brighter, but not much brighter. The avenue to the west was closing off.

Elevation at the Twin Falls airport was over four thousand feet. I could still see the ground below the plane. This was not a problem. Not yet. Be prepared—that was the old Scout motto. The airport was on open farmland five miles south of the city of Twin Falls and the Snake River. This river in the high elevation of the southern Idaho plain has over the eons carved out a majestic canyon with well-defined rock walls, a giant slash in the flat terrain, which had compelled Evel Knievel to attempt to jump the chasm on a rocket-propelled motorcycle, and he majestically failed. I had flown into Twin Falls before and was always mystified as to why a blacktop runway out there in the open was so damn hard to see.

"Twin Falls Approach, this is Husky Whiskey Bravo, twenty miles west. Inbound. Advise VFR, over."

A female voice came back with the authority given those in aircraft control. "Husky Whiskey Bravo, Twin Falls Approach. Ceiling is twelve hundred feet. Use right downwind for runway two-five. Approach airport at eight hundred feet. Advise when five miles out."

I repeated the instructions back to the tower.

The field was becoming difficult to locate in the dimming light. A silver twin-engine plane with red and green wing lights flashing passed five hundred feet below me in the opposite direction heading west. Did that pilot know something I didn't know?

The winds coming across the plains from the river buffeted the wings. I was moving the stick and touching the rudders more than I liked for a landing in the coming darkness. The running lights on the wings had been activated, and I turned on the landing lights. A moment later lightning flashed to the north in the approaching cloud bank. The airport runway lights and the rotating tower beacon flashed a moment later. Some daylight remained but I thought the woman tower operator turned them on just for me. Hardly.

The cloud ceiling was dropping and pushing the plane down. I kept some space below the clouds, and thought this was pushing the FAA visual flight rules. The plane was losing both air speed and altitude. The details in the terrain were more distinct now, even in the gray of the evening. Checkerboard fields of corn, beets, and wheat looked soft from the cockpit, but if a pilot had to land there, and keep the wheels parallel to the rows, the landing would be more than exciting. The throttle came back a quarter inch on the arc, and the airspeed dropped to one hundred miles per hour. The GPS showed five miles to the airport. As the controller requested, I keyed the mike for the tower.

"Twin Falls Approach, Husky Whiskey Bravo, five miles west at eight hundred feet, over."

The female voice came back, "Whiskey Bravo, clear to land runway two-five." This time there was humor in her voice.

"Whiskey Bravo, two-five."

I was on downwind, parallel to the runway, which stretched out to eighty-seven hundred feet. *This baby can land in three hundred feet.* I touched the throttle back, bringing the airspeed down to eighty miles per hour, pulled two notches of flaps, and turned to base leg.

"Whiskey Bravo, you have traffic to your left. Do you have the traffic in sight?" the tower woman asked.

"Negative on the traffic. Confirm clear to land."

"Confirmed two-five. Are you aware of the displaced threshold on two-five?"

Now she had my attention. I couldn't see a painted X, a plane wreck, a truck, or a front-end loader anywhere. Not a damn thing on the runway ahead that indicated a problem to land on the near end.

Displaced threshold indeed! The plane was fifty feet from touchdown. The windsock pointed toward me solid down the runway at a forty-five degree angle. The wind from the approaching storm was bumping against the wings. Lightning flashed to the north. I had no choice but to land, and I wasn't about to do a go-around. I added some power, kept the wings level, the nose of the plane straight with the rudder, then flew ten feet above the blacktop for two-thirds of the runway. The pilots call it air-taxiing. The tail wheel and the mains came down together when I cut the power and touched down on the asphalt.

"How was that, Flight Control?"

"Beautiful, Whiskey Bravo," the woman answered. "What is your destination tonight?"

"Tie down and stay somewhere."

"Use the next turn-off, tie down, then come up to the tower," she continued.

"Copy that, do I get a prize?"

"You'll see."

Baker told me on the Yellowstone she was accepting a permanent position with the FAA. *Now it's coming together.* I rolled the plane over a set of tie-downs, turned off the engine, used some nylon ropes to secure the plane from the storm, then unlocked the door to the cockpit, turned on the radio, and keyed the mike. "Twin Falls Control, this is Whiskey Bravo, over."

"What are you doing back in the plane? There is a storm coming. Besides, I want to buy you a drink."

"Well, well, Baker. I thought it was you. What a surprise!"

"Got you, Casey. Come up to the tower. My day ends in ten minutes, and you aren't flying anywhere tonight."

When I first met Baker, Tony Mendez and I were in a sleaze-bag bar and she had just come off work from a Forest Service ground crew. She was having a beer, when two old locals sitting next to her, drunker and smellier than the proverbial skunks, began to verbally insult her. Their comments, which we could hear, were nothing less than lewd. Without offending real skunks I stood up, walked over to the bar and asked her to join us at our table. She didn't know me but with a look of relief, picked up her beer and walked to our table. She gave me a big smile and slid onto a chair. A woman you wanted to protect. The two locals didn't like this idea. Both of them started, wobbling some, to get up from their bar stools, took one look at Tony, and changed their minds. Lucky for them.

Baker buzzed me through, and the elevator went to the top of the control tower. The door opened. Two men on the left were watching a radar screen. Baker came around from the right. Her long blonde hair was tied up in a loose bun, with glasses on a strand hanging from her neck. She said "Casey," and gave me a kiss, full on the lips, in front of the two controllers, who smiled and nodded hello. I'd like to hear her explain to her colleagues how she had spent many days in the mountains with me.

She introduced me to the FAA men. "Until last month I hadn't seen Casey since he went off to the wars, leaving me to knock down the forest fires in Idaho single-handed."

"She did a great job, didn't she?" I added. "Haven't seen any trees burning all day."

"Only smoking sagebrush in this country," one of the FAA guys said, laughing.

"You checked out my tail number on your computer when I first called in, didn't you, Baker? You knew it was me from the start."

"Thought it was you. Only an ex-smokejumper or an idiot would fly into Twin Falls on a night like this."

"Why do you call her Baker?" the other controller asked. "We call her Lorraine."

"Long story. She can fill you in."

"What brings you into town?" one of the FAA guys asked.

"I'm in the lumber business." I smiled, being as friendly as possible.

"That is what he wants everybody to believe. He's a former Green Beret and he spends his time flying his airplane around the state harassing air controllers," Baker added, then said to me, "Let's get out of here before these guys want me to work overtime. Traffic is light tonight and they can handle the planes." She pushed the elevator button.

We stepped inside and when the elevator door closed behind us she turned, put her hands on my shoulders and kissed me lightly on the lips. "This is for the nice touchdown."

"I knew there was a reason for coming to Twin Falls."

"You handled that landing like a champ," Baker said.

"You had me air-taxiing halfway across the state of Idaho, just because of a displaced threshold on runway two-five, the reason of which still eludes me."

"There was a commercial coming up on your tail, a ways back, and if you would have landed where I think you were going to land—on the runway numbers—you'd have taken a half hour to taxi down the field."

"But what if I had diverted, landed on the grass, and crashed?"

"You wouldn't have crashed. I've seen you put a parachute down in a thirty-knot wind on a patch of grass on the mountain with only twenty feet between boulders."

"I remember a couple of those."

"You won't need an airport car," Baker continued. "Get your duffel from the plane. That's my Cherokee over there. I am going to buy you a drink. I know a great cowboy bar."

The night and the sky had turned black, with thunder rolling across the hills. I walked to Whiskey Bravo, pulled on the ropes, and double-checked the tie-downs.

"Beautiful plane," Baker said. "The color red fits you. Air controllers like red airplanes."

A green Cessna 206 was tied down next to a commercial hanger one hundred yards west. The plane was equipped with large tundra tires, and there was mud splattered on its undercarriage. A real working bush plane.

"That 206 came in just an hour before you," Baker said. "The pilot was trying to get into the backcountry but the storm diverted him here."

"Where did he come from?"

"He didn't open or close a flight plan with us. He did say he departed the Hailey airport at Sun Valley. The weather was closing in up there. He had an accent. Said his name was Fauod."

Rustlers Noose

I threw my duffle into Baker's Cherokee. The five-mile drive into town went fast. We were almost breathless, talking about the fire on the Yellowstone.

Baker pulled into the front parking lot of a western dance joint. "Rustlers Noose," I said. "My kind of place."

"Lots of action here. Small band most of the time. Dancing tonight. Great booze and nice people. Mostly cowboys and farmers."

"And line dancing, I'll bet."

"Sure, if you like that kind of thing."

"I'd rather hold you close," I said, glancing at her, checking her reaction. Baker gave me a smile.

We found a booth not far from the door. The band was warming up. Baker ordered a Sapphire martini with two olives. I had the usual, Maker's neat.

I told her my plans: archery hunting in the backcountry, spending several days scouting solo, and then joining up with Link and Jammer on the Middle Fork of the Salmon. When I mentioned Jammer she gave me a long look. At one time they were a pair. And then China Brown came back into town.

"The weather from the north was closing in, so I thought I'd make a diversion to Twin Falls, and take off in the morning."

"And I thought you came over to see me." She laughed.

"If I had known you were here, I'd say yes. As it turned out, the stars made me do it."

"Or the weather. At least we aren't star crossed," she said.

"Never were."

"Of course not," Baker said, then added, "You'll be flying over the ridges where the two of us dug fire lines."

"I'll be thinking about that."

"That, or me?"

"You. Shall we dance?"

"We shall." Baker was a smooth dancer. I remembered that from the nights at the Yacht Club, when the gang was together and we partied the nights away.

We got caught up on the past years in Idaho. I stayed in touch with many of the old guard. The jumper clan kept together, like no other group I'd ever been a part of, even the military units. Baker knew of Mike falling in Afghanistan. She also knew Tony was working with me in the lumber business. Jungle drums.

Baker told me of splitting up with Jammer. Baker said she had been married for five years to a good-looking guy who was a manager for a small bank near the Forest Service jump base. They'd split up, and afterwards she was offered a seasonal job with the FAA, and now worked a full-time job in Twin Falls.

"He went home to his mother every weekend," she continued, "and as you know, I like to party, dance and raise hell once in a while. It didn't work out. We stay in touch as friends now."

"Did he ever land on a displaced threshold?" I asked.

"He might have, but I never knew about it."

We walked to the middle of the darkened dance floor. I held Baker tight and moved my right hand to the small of her back. "You and I went on several two-manners together, didn't we?" she asked. Her eyes were serious.

"We went on four together. One was for three nights on Telephone Peak."

"You kept count?"

"I did."

"You never made a move on me. Why not?"

"Was concentrating on putting the fire out." I smiled. "Besides, you were Jammer's girl. Furthermore, you were sweaty and had ashes all over your body."

"As if that would have stopped you. I remember you were sweet on a cute chick from the valley named Liz, but then you up and joined the paratroopers and I lost touch of your love life."

"We drifted apart. It took me years to figure it out, but I think she didn't want to get serious with a soldier. She wanted to settle down in a nice white house with a patio, raise children and join women's clubs."

I didn't tell her I had met Liz in Sun Valley. I also didn't tell her Liz was married to a rich businessman and had invited me to her lodge back on the Middle Fork. We moved back to the table.

"Liz didn't seem to be the PTA-and-white-picket-fence type," Baker said. "She would have followed you anywhere."

"Fifteen years later and here we are."

"The two of us. Let's toast to that."

"Yes, but I have to fly north tomorrow to the backcountry, weather permitting."

"The weather and I will not permit you. You will need official permission to take-off, and the flight controller may not assign you a runway."

"The flight controller being you. Hoo-rah. If you don't give me an official runway I'll do a short field departure, using a taxi turn-off. I have a friend who flies a Super Cub and when he's showing off he uses a taxi turn-off instead of the runway and lifts off. Seen him do it."

"That's unauthorized. I'll call the Air Force at Mountain Home and they'll assign two F15s to take you out."

"It might take two. Those jet jockeys would never find me. I'd get low enough in the canyons, fly below the tree tops." I pretended to move the control stick back and forth.

"They would find you—a red plane like yours. I know you fly below the treetops. There were pine needles stuck in your tail struts."

"Blown there from the storm, I suspect. Our smokejumpers pilots were great. When we needed a cargo drop on a fire, the pilot would come in across the ridge below the treetops. Remember?"

"Yes, they did. And do you do that? You lost a pilot and a jumper that way, before my day."

I didn't say anything to that; no reason to bring back memories of friends long gone. "Baker, before we get too buzzed, I need to check in at the Holiday Inn."

"No, you are staying at my place tonight." Baker's voice rang with the authority of an air controller. "I have a house out on the road to Devil's Lake. There's a nice guest room, and two steaks we can throw on the grill. The steak will go great with martinis and bourbon."

"You always wanted to be the cook on the two-manners, while I scouted the fire."

"Scouted! You were *asleep,* you mean." Baker nodded, pretending to look grumpy.

"Okay, I was asleep, and your cooking consisted of opening a can of spaghetti."

"Hey, that took skill."

The Rustlers Noose was getting active. She stopped now and then to say hello to her friends.

"Half the cowboys here would like to take you out," I whispered in her ear.

"Only half? What about the other half?"

"They haven't met you yet."

The waiter had brought another round without asking. I nodded to the two cowboys sitting next to us. Two cowgirls came over and sat with them. The girls wore wearing brightly colored short skirts and designer boots. The cowboys nodded back but their attention went to the girls.

"Excuse me," Baker said, without sitting. "I need to check the powder room."

I was watching the crowd, fingers around a cold glass of bourbon. Friday night and the party was in full swing. I was thinking maybe I should have asked Baker out after she broke up with Jammer. But I had been on another continent.

Baker and I were great friends. We worked on forest projects and parachuted to fires together, but she had eyes for Jammer Deming. Jammer, our friend with the wind-blown blonde hair, forty-eight inch chest, and rock-hard biceps. Fraternization was frowned upon in the unit, but nature will take its course. Baker and Jammer soon became an item.

After I was in the Army a glitch developed in the alignment of their stars, which I heard about from Tony. Tony told me Jammer was secretly in love from his early years with a local girl named China Brown, a rich and attractive brunette who spent her summers at her parents' cabin on the lake. China and Jammer went together, waterskiing, drinking martinis on her parents' deck, and partying on the weekends. Then China went back east to school, and Jammer lost her to a Washington lawyer. About that time Jammer met Baker.

China had a two-story house in the Washington suburbs, a maid, two cars in the garage, hobnobbed with the rich and famous people in the legal and diplomatic circles, and was bored to death. China divorced the lawyer, and moved back to Idaho.

About this time, according to Tony, Baker and Jammer were getting serious. When China came back to town, Jammer and Baker split up. Whether China had any direct part in this was anybody's guess, but I'm sure she did. I lost track of knowing how it all ended because I had other problems, finding al Qaeda hostiles in the mountains of Afghanistan.

I found out later about Jammer's romance. When I returned to Fort Benning he sent me a letter. Jammer wrote that he was still jumping. He was a squad leader now, but the Forest Service was having trouble knocking down the fires without Link and me. Could we come back? He also said he married China Brown.

My fingers were making circles on the wet side of the bourbon glass. I was unconsciously watching the door of the ladies room, and missing Baker already. I thought when she and I were discussing Jammer, the adventures we had together, and more recently the fire on the Yellowstone, her eyes got a little brighter.

While I visualized Baker applying more lipstick, four men walked into the saloon, stopping briefly behind the hostess station. They were rough, with unshaven faces, and looked menacing. Two of them got my attention because they were dark complexioned with unkempt beards, long black hair, and blue work shirts untucked outside dirty jeans.

The hostess led them to a corner table. A couple of cowboys looked up and then went back to their beers. The newcomers appeared uncomfortable, as though they didn't belong here. They also looked as though they didn't give a damn. A male waiter stopped at their table and took their drink orders. For more than five years I had seen guys like them in the Middle East, and asked myself what they were doing here. I caught myself staring.

It was best to avoid eye contact but I was close enough to hear the dark-haired men speaking in Farsi to each other, ignoring their white companions. Definitely Middle Eastern. And I could speak Farsi.

Baker came back to the table. I stood up and held her chair for her, putting me several feet closer to the group of four. Baker had put on lip gloss. The top button of her blouse was open.

"Thank you," she said.

"Shall we dance? I want to ask you something."

"If you want to drive across the state line to Nevada and marry me tonight, the answer is no." She laughed. "This is our first actual date and I hardly know you."

I ignored that, smiled, and at the same time slowly swung her around so she was facing the four newcomers at the corner table. "Don't stare, and don't even make eye contact, but have you seen those four men at the corner table before?"

"No. Why do you ask?"

"Just curious."

"You are never just curious."

I was intentionally leading Baker closer to their table. Two of them were drinking beer, the other two, coffee. They continued to speak in Farsi, and I picked out words like "plane" and "mine."

Baker and I kept our distance on the dance floor, my hand moving up higher on her back, touching her neck, and for a moment ruffling her hair. I put my cheek next to hers and she moved her body closer to mine. We were two people having a romantic good time. Then all four of the men at the table stopped talking and looked at me. One of the dark men held his gaze for a second; maybe he caught me paying too much attention to them, then he dropped his eyes. I danced Baker away from their table, looking in another direction, trying to hide my curiosity. After a moment they all went back to some serious conversation.

I led Baker back to our table. "There is something bothering you about those four men," she said. "They don't look like the high-school cheerleading squad."

"When I see men of Middle Eastern descent my antennae go up. Spent too much time in their countries. Shooting at some of them. Not saying it's right, but I can't help it."

"Racial profiling."

"Maybe. Might be military training. Sometimes there's a good reason for it."

"Forget about those days." Baker lifted her martini, looking straight at me, trying to swing my attention back to her. "This is our night," she said, and smiled, with a hint that it might even get better. I tried not to stare at the button.

"Of course. Can I have the next dance?" I smiled at Baker, but I was glancing at the other table.

I found myself looking into the eyes of the man I had met in Sun Valley: Fauod Saeed. He and his bodyguard had joined the table with the other four. Saeed wore the same black sport coat and white shirt. Before, I categorized him as a businessman, or a pilot. Now he looked militant and there was danger behind that stare. He sat taller than the others and his presence showed he was their leader. The bodyguard was big, husky, and was scanning the crowd. He was armed no doubt; the loose jacket he wore was oversize.

The four men were deferring to Saeed. He was the expert. The four of them were looking at him. Saeed and the big man were watching me.

Saeed could have nodded. He didn't. People like him didn't scare me, but it was an alarming look. I hadn't had this feeling since the days in the Afghan mountains, when our team was talking with the locals, then got ambushed, and we had to shoot our way past the Taliban riflemen. I put those thoughts behind me.

There is something going on up here in Idaho. I've been trained for this, for God's sake.

My hand was on the lower part of Baker's back. I turned her, my cheek next to hers. To anyone who might be watching I was whispering sweet talk into her ear. She seemed to like that part. "I'm going to talk to the man who just arrived. I've met him before."

"You can't get your mind off those guys, can you? Be careful."

The band started a new song, couples left their tables and filled the dance floor. A cowboy and his attractive partner with a short skirt and bright orange boots bumped into me. They laughed and apologized. "Not a problem," I said. Everyone was laughing, except the six men at the corner table.

I walked up and extended my hand to Fauod Saeed. "We've met before. Sun Valley?"

"Yes. You were at the bar," he said.

Saeed extended his hand. Strong grip. He didn't smile and didn't stand. I didn't offer my name.

"What brings you to Twin Falls on a night like this?" I asked. There, it's out. The other five men were now watching me.

"Real estate," Saeed said. He didn't like being questioned.

"Fly in? Hell of a storm out there."

"Yes—landed here," he said.

Saeed has a plane at the airport. The green Cessna, the pilot who landed without contacting the control tower.

Saeed ignored me, took out a pack of cigarettes, and slipped one out: the big man produced a lighter, and Saeed inhaled. He didn't offer a cigarette to me or the others. The bodyguard unzipped his black parka. The white guys looked me over; they looked dangerous, but not too smart. I wasn't armed, they were thinking. What the hell.

"Should be some good opportunities around," I said. Liz told me he flew into her lodge on the river. Was he looking for a remote location for clandestine activities?

"What do you do?" Fauod Saeed asked. His dark eyes were unsmiling.

"Lumber."

"Lumber?" He blew cigarette smoke toward the ceiling, picked up his drink and took a swallow.

I knew what he was thinking. Why would a man in the lumber business come up to six strangers in a bar and start asking questions?

"Your name is McConnell."

"Excellent memory."

"I think you do more than lumber, Mr. McConnell."

"Real estate, if you got any hot deals." The other men continued to pay more attention to the conversation. The big man's stare was unflinching.

"There are no hot deals," Saeed said.

"Then good luck on finding some. Careful of the weather on your flight out. Which direction you heading?" They didn't offer me a chair. Damn unkind of them.

"North."

"Do you fly a green Cessna? The one with the white stripe on the fuselage?" There was a perceptible movement to Saeed's head. "Tied down next to mine."

The big man looked at Saeed, waiting for his answer. I was asking too many questions.

"Yes. Is yours the red tailwheel, the back country plane with the big tires?" There was the beginning of an accent to his voice. The businessman's manner was fading. He and the big man took a drink. I took the bodyguard as an Egyptian.

"That's the one."

"You fly the mountains?"

"Yep. As soon as this storm clears, I'm lifting off. Going to be chasing some big game back there in the mountains." I looked at Baker, who was watching the conversation. She was getting impatient and not smiling.

"Not many people back where there are no roads. Where do you hunt?" Saeed asked. The others looked on.

"In the Middle Fork country." I said.

"Big area."

"It is at that—lots of canyons."

"Specifically, Mr. McConnell."

"Wal' now, a real hunter doesn't tell his secret spots, ya' know," I said, trying out my cowboy accent, smiling at the others, who were concentrating on the conversation. They didn't smile back.

"I'm from Texas. Give me a hint." Saeed didn't look like a hunter, but he could easily handle an RPG.

"How about Phantom Creek or Soldier Bar?" I said. His shoulders made another perceptible movement.

"You good enough to land your plane on those fields?" he asked. *He knows about those airstrips.*

"It's tricky, but I do."

"Good hunting, Mr. McConnell. Don't hurt yourself."

This guy from Texas is telling me about the Idaho mountains. He's also giving me a warning.

The big man's expression didn't change. He turned in his chair and glared at Baker. That I didn't like.

Saeed looked down and reached for his drink. He gave a commanding glare at the others at the table. The conversation was over. I nodded to him and walked back to Baker.

"Well, detective, what did you find out?" Baker asked. I'm glad she wasn't alone for long.

"I found out the head guy in the white shirt is Fauod Saeed and the green plane at the airport is his. I suspect they are up to no good. The people with him sure as hell aren't cowboys or lumberjacks."

"Forget those people. This is our night. Let's get out of here before you get into a fight. We can have the next drink at my place."

"A great idea."

I paid the tab, in spite of Baker's protests. We walked toward the door of the Rustlers Noose and I glanced at the corner table. Two of the men—the white guys—were watching me. The others had their heads lowered, but I knew they were aware of something going to happen. Saeed and his bodyguard were gone. Where would they go on a night like this?

A squall was coming through the valley and the rain started again as we climbed into the Cherokee. Baker was behind the wheel and activated the wipers. I glanced behind us as we drove from the Rustlers. Sixth sense it was called. We drove a mile in the rain, and I checked behind us again. There were no headlights. But then I didn't expect to see any.

Baker lived three miles east of town in a modest ranch house on five acres. A well-manicured lawn in front blended with the juniper shrubs and hardwood trees in the back. Behind the trees was a fenced-in pasture. A white barn-garage combination stood out at the end of the driveway. She didn't have any livestock that I could see around the barn. Baker turned off onto a gravel driveway. The blacktop road continued out to Devil's Lake, a local favorite for swimming and sailing.

Two cars had been behind us now and they kept going. Not many people went on to Devil's Lake at this time of night.

The squall increased in intensity, the wind picking up with the rain. In the morning the weather would be clear and I could get an early start. "I have to lift off at first light."

"*If* the storm has passed," Baker said, "and *if* I give you permission from the control tower. With you, I'll emphasize the word *control*."

"Tomorrow is Saturday and you said you weren't working."

"We'll see. Let's make a dash for the front porch. I want you to meet Otto."

"Who is Otto?"

"My live-in. You'll like him."

"Should I be jealous?" I asked, and faked a laugh.

"Not at all."

Otto Takes a Hit

Otto was an eighty-five-pound Doberman, blue black with patches of tan on his muzzle and paws, four of which were firmly planted on the floor, blocking the doorway. His tail was long, not docked, and neither were his ears. I was hoping he was the friendly type, because those black eyes were focused on only me. Then with a glance at Baker and with the authority of a well-trained dog, he came over and sniffed my jeans and boots.

"This is Otto."

"Your live-in! I love dogs. Especially big ones like this."

"Were you jealous, thinking Otto was somebody else?"

"Of course. Does he bite?"

"Only if I ask him to."

"Don't ask. I'll stay on your good side. Worship you forever."

"Oh sure." Baker laughed. "Throw your duffel in the guest room. It's at the end of the hall. I'm going to freshen up then mix us a drink. Will you build a fire? It's chilly in here with this storm. The kindling and firewood are in the wood box."

Her home was clean, well furnished, the walls accented with splashes of colorful art. A floor to ceiling full-wall stone fireplace was the focal point of the living room. A large, brown leather sofa and a low oak table faced the fireplace.

I checked out the guest room, took a quick glance in the direction of the main bedroom, dining room, kitchen, the third bedroom, and the doors—trained reflexes from entering houses in hostile country, looking for clandestine material or dangerous people. Otto stood in the living room, watching me. You don't make sudden moves when a big dog's eyes are on you. Outside, the wind splashed the rain against the windows. The lights of a car went by, going east.

"Baker, do you keep a firearm in your home?"

"Should I?" she answered from the bathroom. "This is a quiet town."

"Do you?"

"Several. There is a twenty-gauge double-barrel shotgun with a box of shells in my closet. Sometimes I go after pheasants in the back forty. Why?"

"Just asking."

"You never just ask. I know you. Thinking about those men at the Rustlers."

"Old habits die hard."

"There are no terrorists around here. For God's sake, they don't even know where Idaho is."

"I wouldn't be too sure about that. Link Barrett said the FBI was tracking some in this direction." I thought about Fauod, the man who had met Hanson Porter the Third, in Sun Valley, of all places. An envelope exchanged hands. The distance between Sun Valley and Twin Falls was seventy miles. Fauod Saeed was flying the green Cessna parked next to mine.

"We're here," Baker said. "Just you and me. Let's have some fun. You can start by building that fire."

I watched Baker walk into the bedroom. She looked as terrific from the back as she did from the front. What did she think was fun? I had my own definition. "I'll get right on it," I said.

Baker went into the bedroom and I investigated the fireplace. With some pine kindling a fire was crackling. The atmosphere turned cheery, the logs popping and sending sparks against the screen. The wind and the rain continued. Weather like this was unsettling to dogs. When a gust hit the window Otto answered with a short bark.

Baker walked out of the bedroom a few minutes later. She had changed into a yellow blouse, a fresh touch of make-up, and had switched from Western boots to sandals. Her toenails were painted bright red. We walked together to the wall cabinet, picked out a bottle of Bombay and a bottle of Jack, selected some ice cubes from the refrigerator, and set everything on the table. When she leaned over to reach for the jar of martini olives the top trim of her black bra was showing. The light aroma of a perfume she was using was heady.

"We are together again, Baker, and this time it's not a fire camp." My mind was back there in the past, when it was only Baker and Jammer, and Liz and me.

"It's been too damn long, Casey. You went off to war and the gang fell apart."

"We still get together. Tony works with me at the plant. Link is with the FBI. Mike is gone, and I see Jammer from time to time. We go hunting together every year in the backcountry. After the fire on the Yellowstone, I suspect the Forest Service will need more journalists like me to help dig fire line."

"Together again," Baker said. "How did you ever talk Jammer into letting you jump on that fire."

"My persuasive skills. Lori helped by telling Jammer to get me the hell out of her office."

Baker laughed. "Let's move to the living room—the fire is nice in this stormy night." Otto was occupying the sofa, filling his half of it. Instead of staring into the firelight like most dogs do, he was watching me, wondering what the next move was going to be. Baker solved the problem, pointing to the carpet in front of the fireplace. Otto, brooding, moved his body closer to the fire, putting his head between his paws, and keeping his eyes on me.

"This was my last summer with the Forest Service. The FAA put me on permanently in air traffic control."

"You had a great career with the jumpers. The whole damn Forest Service rewrote their parachuting requirements for you, from a minimum weight of 125 pounds down to 120 pounds. Just for you. Approval had to be cleared by the White House."

"And well they should have," Baker added, and touched my glass to hers. "We need to catch up." Then she moved closer to me on the sofa.

"Catch up on what?" I asked, trying to conceal a not-so-subtle smile.

"Maybe that, some day, you animal. I want to hear about your adventures with Mike and Link—what you did in Afghanistan."

The rain on the windows pounded and dropped in streaks. The blackness of the night was pierced by the blurred lights of a car on the main road, on the other side of the driveway, and for a moment the car came to a stop. The vehicle then slowly moved again through the rain, east out of town, in the direction of Devil's Lake. Otto's ears went up, his head motionless, his lips curled, showing teeth, and a low growl came from his throat.

Maybe I was paranoid. "Baker, let's put Otto outside. He is growling at something out there. And pull your shotgun out of the closest, with the box of shells."

"My, my, are we getting suspicious. You were in the mountains with the Taliban too long."

"That was over ten years ago. Some of those people still don't like us."

Baker opened the front door, pointed, and motioned for Otto. He jumped outside, still growling. The front door slammed back from the wind.

The rain continued to whisper against the windows. The wind rattled the eaves of the house. Baker looked exceptionally pretty with the firelight on her face, the blue eyes, and her blonde hair off her shoulders. She mixed another round of drinks, and I reminded myself that I would be flying tomorrow. One more bourbon and I could sleep outside in the rain.

A screech coming from the window interrupted our conversation. The screech turned into a rasping noise. Otto was standing outside on his hind legs, nose against the wet window, his front nails moving precisely from the top of the pane to the bottom. He looked formidable, a wet, shiny, black aberration. His eyes were large, watching, menacing. He was telling us something.

"You've trained him well," I said.

Otto dropped out of sight and disappeared. I went to the window again. A car with its headlights off was parked a hundred yards away on the far side of the road. That car had not been there when we turned into the lane to Baker's home.

I moved back to the sofa, turned toward Baker and switched off one of the table lamps. She moved closer to me and reached for her drink.

"One moment," she said, stood up and went into her bedroom.

The boom of a shotgun came through the noise of the rain and the wind. Pellets rattled against the siding. The sharp yelp of a dog in pain penetrated the night.

Baker dove across her bed, turning out the lamp with one hand, and in the other hand stood up holding a black automatic pistol. I grabbed the twenty gauge and slammed two shells into the breech. Baker went through the front door like a sprinter.

"Baker! Stop!"

The car was gone. Baker came back inside dragging a bleeding and whimpering Otto.

"They shot him! The bastards!"

"Let me look at Otto. I'll take care of him. He's still walking. Get me your first aid kit, then call the sheriff. I'm going outside and look around."

Baker slipped the pistol inside the waist line of her jeans.

I did a short recon—carrying the twenty gauge—checked the tree line on the dark road, walked around the barn, saw no one, returned to the house, and went to Otto, who had stopped whimpering.

"He's okay, Baker, what did the sheriff say?"

"I got the robo voice." At that moment the phone rang, the night deputy on the line calling back. Baker's voice was getting louder. I heard her say "Bullshit." Then she hung up.

"He said the shooting was probably a bunch of boys hunting coyotes. They've been doing that at night around here. He said they would send someone out in the morning."

"Damn good thing we're not in a firefight."

"It was those men in the bar and they followed us," Baker said.

"Saeed was sending me a warning. I apologize for bringing you and Otto into this."

"Keep the lights off. I don't think I can stand anymore gunfire. Let's have one more drink—in the dark," she said.

Coyotes, hell, I knew that Fauod Saeed and his people were close. That shotgun blast was a warning.

Baker gave me a kiss on the check and walked into her bedroom. I checked on Otto, who was on the rug, licking his leg. I had applied antiseptic and a bandage over the pellet wounds. We'd take him to the vet's in the morning.

The loaded double-barrel was leaning against the sofa. When the last log settled in a shower of sparks, I rolled over on the sofa, and regretted that I wasn't keeping a vigilant watch. The storm blew to the east, and the wind dropped, but it was an uneasy night.

I was still awake. At three in the morning Baker said from the bedroom, "Casey, come and sleep with me." She had thrown the covers back. She was wearing a short pajama top and bikini panties.

I put my arms around her shoulders and held her.

The morning light was touching the bedroom curtains when we both heard a thump from the direction of the kitchen. I rolled back the covers, picked up the twenty gauge and walked past the fireplace into the kitchen.

Otto had fallen off the sofa and was licking the bandage on his leg. The bottle of antiseptic was on the floor. I petted his head. Otto wasn't alarmed, so the shooters must be gone. I picked up the double-barrel and returned to the bedroom.

Baker was lying on the bed, her eyes questioning me. The smell of her perfume lingered on the pillows. The automatic was only five inches from her hand.

"Otto knocked over some bottles," I said. "Are you feeling better?"

"Yes. It's almost daylight. Come back to bed."

Baker had unbuttoned her pajama top. I rolled back to her side of the bed and kissed her. She reached down with both hands and slid her panties down her legs to her ankles. With her toe she flipped them into the air. The panties disappeared somewhere in the dark part of the bedroom.

"Are they gone?" she asked.

"The thugs?"

"No, the panties."

"Yes, they're gone," I said. "You won't need them."

North of the Slot

Morning sunlight streamed through the trees by the fence. I was in the kitchen. "Are you dressed?" I asked, glancing toward the bedroom, hoping Baker wouldn't be. "I made some coffee, strong and black, just the way you like it." I walked into the bedroom with the coffee.

"You remembered—from our fire camps in the mountains. Yes, I'm dressed enough. Come in. I finally got some sleep." She gave me a devilish smile. "I dreamed there was a shoot-out and I fell asleep in your arms."

Baker was sitting at her bedroom table wearing black bikini panties and a black brassiere, the bra low on her breasts. She was facing the mirror and applying cherry-red lipstick.

"That was no dream," I said. "Among other things."

"What a night. The last half was great."

"It was very romantic," I said. "We were wired waiting for the bad guys. For all the years we've known each other, we finally—you know."

"It was lust," she said. "We're both crazy." She turned from the mirror and smiled. "You're terrific."

I couldn't comment on that and set the coffee in front of her. "We were ready for the hostiles if they returned. Otto will be fine. We'll take him to the vet this morning."

"I've got to brush my teeth," she said.

"Don't bother," I said. I slid the coffee away from her, leaned over, lifted her long hair with my hand and kissed her. The black bra dropped to the floor and I took her hand and led Baker back to her bed.

An hour later we were in the kitchen. I was stirring scrambled eggs in a black iron frying pan, and singing in my best tenor—"Up, up and away, in my beautiful balloon."

"My, aren't we happy this morning," Baker said. She had taken a shower and dressed in a white blouse and blue jeans. "You never sang like that in the mountains. Thank God."

"You would have hit me with an axe."

"That's messy. Maybe the shovel."

"I remember the day you said you wanted to be a smokejumper," I said.

"The best day of my life, I had no idea it would so exciting. Gun play and all. Do you always attract danger?"

"It was a great day for the Forest Service. Four of us were talking to the district ranger. You walked through the door of his office, introduced yourself as Lorraine Baker Brindell and said you wanted to jump out of airplanes and fight forest fires. You could have heard a pin drop. The ranger was shocked. Tony and I said we knew you. We told the ranger about the night we saved you from the drunk jerks in the hole-in-the-wall bar. The old rules had been changed, the Forest Service encouraged the unit to hire women. We told the ranger we'd personally escort you to the jumper office to fill out the necessary papers. We'd be references."

"You guys? References? God help us." She laughed.

"Of course. We were the heroes."

"Sure you were." She took a sip of coffee. "You're improving on your coffee making."

I ignored the jab. "Back to that first day. The ranger, not trusting us with the skills to get the paperwork straight with you, our new woman applicant, said he'd escort you to the parachute loft."

"He knew you guys."

Otto came limping into the kitchen, dragging a bandage behind one foot.

"Go on with your story," Baker said. "Some of it is believable. I'll check out Otto."

"After you and the ranger left the office, Tony said if you were hired he'd volunteer to be your jump partner."

"I'll bet."

"We said Lorraine Baker Brindell wasn't a smokejumper name. Your hair was blonde, had some dark streaks, and we called you Baker Brindle. We dropped the Brindle later."

"Damn nice of you," Baker said, and rolled her eyes.

"Jammer was there. He said if you and Tony were jump partners on a two-manner you weren't big and strong enough to carry him off the mountain if he broke his neck. Was he ever wrong? Tony said, Didn't matter—he'd break out the tequila and die happy right there in your arms."

"Assuming, of course, that I would hold him in my arms in his suffering. I never did jump with Tony."

"Just as well. Tony's a hot Hispanic. And you went with Jammer for five years."

Baker said nothing. That subject was closed.

I walked to the window, and glanced at the sky.

Baker was watching me. "So much for taking off at first light. Or even second or third light. Stay another day. It's Saturday."

"It's a tight schedule, and I've already missed a day. I'm joining up with Jammer and Link in three days, then we'll meet Hooker. Hooker is an outfitter—has a string of horses on the Middle Fork, should we shoot some elk back in one of those canyons. He's a friend I see every year. My plan is to fly back up the Middle Fork for thirty miles."

"For Christ's sake, Casey, you haven't changed." Baker got up from the kitchen stool and walked toward the window.

"The storm is moving east," I said. "Take-off can't be later than noon, which will put me at Soldier Bar at two o'clock, one hundred and eighty air miles from here. I want to scout some ridges for elk, and there will be daylight still along the river. The winds may be starting to settle by then."

"Give yourself some time. It gets dark damn early back there in those canyons, and we are into October. Will you camp there tonight?"

"Yes, and tomorrow I'll solo hunt in the Middle Fork drainage before meeting Link and Jammer. The satellite phone will be in my pack. The Husky will be tied down at Soldier Bar."

"Call me when you're out there, so I know a bear hasn't eaten off your leg."

"It'll be damn hard dancing with you with one leg."

"Among other things."

She continued in a more serious vein, keeping Otto quiet on a pad. "Remember, most radios won't work along the river. You will have to be at flight altitude in the Husky before you contact FAA control, and that includes opening and closing your flight plans."

"I have a satellite phone, but that's hit-or-miss, depending on the position of the satellite and where a person is calling from, preferably an open ridge or field."

The sheriff's van pulled up in the lane, two deputies came into the house, and we told them the story of Otto and last night's shoot-out, including conversations with the six men in the Rustlers Noose.

"They likely weren't teen-age coyote hunters," the deputy said. "We'll keep alert for hostile people around town and suspicious activity at the airport." And with that they were gone.

Baker and I drove Otto to the vet, where the doctor removed three shotgun pellets. He said he'd keep the dog for two days for observation. Baker had work commitments and I was leaving for the backcountry.

At eleven o'clock Baker drove me to the airport. I unlocked the side door of the plane, then placed the overnight bag in back, and the longbow on top. The green Cessna with the large tires was gone. Saeed's plane. Saeed might have directed his tough guys to follow Baker and me back to her home.

Whiskey Bravo sat waiting for its pre-flight inspection. I checked the fuel level, opened the cowling and measured the oil level. The oil was okay, everything around the 360 Lycoming looked good. I swung the propeller several degrees, checked the edges for nicks, caressed the spinner, moved the ailerons, the rudder, and the horizontal stabilizers. All responded to the touch. Time to go. I unfastened the tie-downs, wiped a few pieces of dried grass from the wing surfaces, stuck there from last night's storm, and then taxied to the gas pumps. No gas stations existed in the Idaho backcountry. The plane held fifty gallons of aviation gas. At ten gallons per hour that was enough for five hours of flight time—a conservative calculation, but adequate, unless an emergency came up.

Baker walked to the side of the taxiway to watch the take-off. Pilots and smokejumpers did that. Maybe she was already becoming nostalgic about summer days when she climbed aboard the Twin Otter with a heavy jumpsuit and two parachutes.

This was where the excitement began. Call it what you will, but it was the feeling of independence, of control, of flying to the heavens, above the mountains, above the clouds, on to the top of the world. Alone.

On the phone from Baker's home I filed a flight plan with FAA. Using the card I kept inside the cockpit, the steps were covered for departure. I snapped the window down on the right and waved to Baker. She waved back. Twin Falls tower gave me clearance for departure.

"Twin Falls control, Husky Whiskey Bravo departing two five, right turn to the north."

I gripped the control stick lightly, dropped the flaps, tested the foot brakes with my toes, moved the rudder left, then right, glanced down the runway for last-minute traffic, and with left elbow on the edge of the open window, pushed the throttle down. The take-off was the best part of flying. A ten knot wind, the last of the storm, was blowing down the runway, out of the west. The engine sounded solid, powerful, like three over-zealous Harleys racing together on the freeway. The air blast from the prop pushed the tail up. With some back pressure on the stick, the plane lifted off on its own. At two hundred feet above the runway, I dropped the pitch of the nose by ten degrees, preventing a stall, then brought back the power. Below, Baker was leaning against the roof of her car. I dipped each wing a couple of degrees. She waved back.

The plane leveled off at fifteen hundred feet. The sectional chart showed a magnetic heading of 355 degrees to Soldier Bar, and the compass was lined up to that number. The red Husky, trimmed out for the light crosswind at altitude, purred north to the Idaho wilderness.

Ahead of the plane's nose was the Frank Church River of No Return Wilderness, two million acres of untouched primitive country: no roads, few trails, isolated grass airstrips, and only the canyons of the Middle Fork and the Salmon Rivers to break up the steep, mountainous terrain. The Frank Church was huge but was only the central portion of the wild expanse of ridges and timber that stretched from the Snake River Plain north to the Canadian border.

I settled in for the ride. The plane was flying smoothly at 6,000 feet, with the constant-speed propeller holding the airspeed at 140 miles per hour. The village of Fairfield appeared off to the left, and the ski slopes of Sun Valley were coming up on the right.

The skies were crystal blue in the wake of the storm. Galena Peak, at 11,200 feet, loomed in front of me. With a touch of power and a change in the fuel mixture the Lycoming engine steadily climbed without missing a beat. Off to the left was the mountain village of Stanley. Their long grass airstrip extended a comfortable 4,300 feet. Stanley, Idaho, was a mecca in the summer for hikers in the Sawtooths and river floaters on the headwaters of the Salmon River. In the winter this mountain village also had the distinction of being the coldest place in the lower forty-eight. The daily temperatures often dropped to thirty below—only the hardiest remained in Stanley through the winter.

The Salmon River originates in these mountains. The Middle Fork comes into the Salmon River from the south, starting as a small creek just west of Stanley. Now quietly cruising at 11,000 feet, I could see the headwaters of both rivers. The Salmon River and the Middle Fork drain the most beautiful and wildest mountains in the United States. It is a region that God made and few mortals know about.

I adjusted the compass heading north-northwest to fly across a mountain pass called Profile Gap, then down Big Creek, fifty miles as the creek winds, to the Middle Fork. The Big Creek drainage is a vast canyon itself, its steep, isolated timbered slopes the haunts of bighorn sheep, elk, mule deer, mountain goats, and wolves.

It was midday, and at an altitude of 8,500 feet over Profile Saddle the air turbulence arrived, making the ride more bouncy than usual. One wing tip went up, the other down, then they reversed, and at the same time the plane dropped like it was in an elevator shaft, hitting a level in the air, then falling to another level. Luckily there was plenty of spare air below the plane. I brought back the power setting, lowered the nose to prevent a stall, and lost more altitude to enter the Big Creek valley. Below in the canyon the turbulence ended.

A plane was flying toward me, coming low on the left, and climbing to clear the pass Whiskey Bravo had passed through. The plane would hit the turbulence and the pilot and passengers would get a bumpy surprise. The plane was the green Cessna. Baker had said the pilot was flying into the backcountry. Not many planes in this part of the world. I remembered the transfer of the envelope between Saeed and Hanson Porter. Why would he be coming back into this country? He didn't look like an outfitter, hunter or backpacker. Why did he want to lease Liz's lodge?

Below the canyon walls, the air calmed and I kept the same heading to Soldier Bar, another forty miles. The engine was humming beautifully, as if it were at home in this mountainous country. The landing field, on a bluff above Big Creek, was four miles upstream from the junction with the Middle Fork. My flight plan was to be over Soldier Bar at 1300 hours.

Before settling in for the night along the edge of the airstrip in the woods, I planned to fly over a nearby ridge and try to spot some wildlife. From Soldier Bar a trail dropped down off the airfield to Big Creek, crossed the creek and switch-backed its way up through the ponderosas and the firs, then entered an old burn of dismal black tree trunks, the weathered snags scattered among the boulders and man-high brush. The trail crossed the top of the ridge in a narrow, rocky profile. I had viewed the ridge with binoculars from across the canyon last year, and I nicknamed it the "Slot." A wildfire ten years before had swept along the summit, sparing the green timber below in the creek bed. The elk might be on the edges of this timber, a good place to hunt with the short-range longbow.

The old Luddendorf mine, a hard-rock tunnel operation, was up near the ridgeline, its timbers weathered and years before fallen into disrepair. The ore, when the mine had been active decades before, was hauled by mules down an old trail, now blocked with fallen trees, to Big Creek, then over several mountain passes on the pack trail to southern Idaho. A gray, dilapidated clapboard shack, its roof long since fallen inward from the snows, and an old outhouse, well positioned back in the trees, sat on a down slope from the old shanty.

A high grassy flat lay below the burn, a half mile from the old mine, and a mile below the Slot. I figured if I had enough nerve one day I might drop the plane in there. The weather was clear, and the plane clock read 1400 hours. There was still time to explore the ridge, check out the grassy flat, fly up and over the notch, then north to the Middle Fork, and fly back up the river to Soldier Bar—a full circle.

The air was bumpy flying back up the canyon. I added power to gain enough altitude to safely look over the Slot, then banked to approach the ridge at an angle, allowing several hundred feet of altitude, should the winds be spilling over the top.

Then the needle of the oil pressure gauge began to bounce.

Earlier in the summer I had flown over this high grassy flat, and on that trip noticed wheel tracks from a plane in the grass. Somebody had been landing on that bench. Maybe geologists checking out the mine; those guys continued to prowl around the old mines, analyzing the tailings for gold and silver, as the prices changed on the world markets. Must have been that. But now, buzzing the strip, I could see that the grass was flattened from several landings and take-offs. Up the slope at the end of the bluff were two tents, set back under the pine branches. At the end of the flat I banked, pointed the nose in the direction of the canyon, banked again to turn downwind to the field. Two men were hustling out of the old mine. Tracks in the dirt from the mine to the trees appeared to be made by a small motorcycle, like a trail bike. Motorized equipment of any type, except for airplanes, was prohibited in the wilderness. Didn't these guys know better? Were they new to this country?

The oil gauge on the instrument panel went to zero and stopped. The gauge and the throttle were not connected but I added maximum power anyway and the gauge jumped, then went back to zero. That was unusual. Maybe oil was draining out below the firewall to the tail, and I couldn't see it.

Two men stood near the tents, one carrying a rifle. Big game hunters? I doubted that. No pack horses or mules—outfitters' stock—could be seen. The Forest Service would raise hell if they found these men were using trail bikes to move around.

The oil gauge continued to flutter around the bottom. Power was normal, or was it too starting to slow? My imagination was working overtime. Big Creek was off to my right, its canyon deepening in shadows.

I decided to land on the grass bench. The sunlight was still bright on the pines on the ridge and the scree slopes above me, but dark was coming in the canyon. Without the help of a windsock I judged the wind direction, thinking the touchdown would be crosswind, as the air movement at that time of day was coming upslope. Landing uphill takes priority over wind direction, so I banked the plane for the near end of the grass, pulled two notches of flaps, kept the engine revved until the plane had enough power to make the landing. Then the feel of the wind came, full flaps and the plane's air speed dropped to fifty-five miles per hour.

Slowing down on the base leg of the landing, I thought I heard gunshots and a snap near the tail section. *What in the hell?* Somebody was practicing for the elk hunt, or some illicit miners were trying to warn me off. Anything could happen back in these mountains.

The plane was going to land. The oil gauge had again dropped to zero. No turning back. *Don't look over the propeller—eyes ahead, watch for ditches, rocks, and marmot holes.* The landing tracks in the grass were below and ahead of me. Then came three flashes at the edge of the woods.

Gunfire. *They're definitely trying to warn me off.*

Whiskey Bravo bounced in the grass then went into a bumpy roll out. But just for the moment. Flashes of automatic rifle fire came from the direction of the old mine, the bullets cutting a jagged line in the grass in front of the plane. The rounds ricocheted and two of them thumped against the undercarriage. The tail came up, the prop down, just missing the dirt, and I violently pressed right rudder and veered into a space between the pine trees. That was no warning.

Whatever this hornet's nest was, it was serious. I was a sitting target. *Get out of here fast.*

The plane stopped under some high, pine branches. I pulled the key, the propeller shuddered and stopped. Several bullets had gone through the fuselage, one destroying the satellite phone and a slug had ripped through my pack. The longbow, pistol, and binoculars were behind the rear seat. I grabbed them—wishing I had brought my rifle—had to move fast, grabbed the camouflage vest from atop the pack, and left the pack behind.

Four men armed with automatic rifles, AK-47s probably, were coming toward me. Two broke off and entered the pines on my side of the field. Two on the left dropped into the trees and brush below the edge of the flat. I could see one man moving ahead, the other crouching behind boulders. These guys weren't dressed like miners or hunters. Didn't matter; they'd already shot at me. Did they think I was some airplane jockey dropping in for a cup of coffee?

The two men below the field, long dark hair, ragged blue shirts, who looked like Arabs, were blocking an escape downhill to the creek and the thick timber. The two on the uphill side had disappeared into the brush.

Something big was happening. Were these people expecting another plane and I surprised them? Nobody in his right mind would land on this bluff unless he had a damn good reason. The oil gauge problem had given me the reason. They had other objectives.

There was only one way out of this, and that was to move uphill. This was like the Hindu Kush. But now there was a difference. A big difference. This was my country, not theirs. They had the advantage in numbers and firepower but I knew these ridges and canyons. I'd climb to the Slot, a mile above me uphill, watch these people, try to ambush them, then cross the ridge and drop down to the river. Somebody would have a radio or satellite phone. If I went down stream far enough the only ranch there belonged to Liz. Liz Hollis and her husband.

An old Forest Service trail went up and over the top. When I got to the trail, I moved uphill. They would see my tracks. I was counting on that.

The trail was built for horses, with switchbacks zig-zagging to the top. The flatter sections weren't too steep and I could jog on parts of the path. A plan was taking shape.

Where the trail went across the top, the place I named the Slot, the timber was smaller, scattered, most of it short, blackened fire snags. The bear grass after the fire was starting to regenerate. The deer brush was as tall as a man: perfect place for an ambush. On the north side of the ridge—the river side—the terrain dropped off fast. Two hundred yards of granite scree gave way to a scattering of short firs. There wouldn't be much cover until I could get below the rocks into the trees. The timber was tall and dense toward the Middle Fork, and hiding out would be much easier near the river.

If they followed me uphill, I'd know they meant business. I stayed on the trail, went up and through the Slot, then fifty yards farther down the other side, making certain my boot tracks were clear in the dust. Huckleberry bushes grew near the rocks and I hid the longbow and arrows under them. Then I walked across the rocks, doubled back parallel to the trail, found some bushes between two boulders, lay down, and prepared an ambush. Twenty-five feet in front of me the path turned, and the point man would be fully exposed coming around the turn. I blackened my face with charcoal from a burned stump and pulled the camo hat lower. The camouflaged vest was a plus.

The ambush would be at close quarters. We had Special Forces soldiers setting up ambushes in the timber where you couldn't see them two feet away. This hide would be better than that. The two boulders and the small bushes between them were on the military crest of the mountain, just off the trail and facing the turn.

I lay on my stomach behind the brush, the .45 in my right hand, out in front, a round in the chamber. The safety was off. The extra magazine was lying within inches of my left hand. I slid the binoculars out and glassed the terrain. There they were, three of them, coming up the trail in single file, the point man forty yards ahead of the other two. Was the fourth man out there, climbing around the rocks and timber, trying to flank me? He could be a problem.

The first man moved closer. His beard was black and scruffy, and his dark eyes were looking out beyond me. He was wobbling, not in good shape, his chest heaving in the high elevation. His rifle was in his right hand, hanging low, and pointing in my direction.

A horsefly joined the ambush. It buzzed under the bill of my cap, landed on my nose, then walked around to my ear. The little son-of-a-bitch was ticklish. I couldn't swat him. He jumped to my lower lip at the same instant the badass came to the straight part of the trail, twenty-five feet in front of my brush.

When the point guy got closer, he had the two-thousand yard stare, looking beyond me. His chest was heaving and he was panting. He was tired. He was also dangerous.

Close enough. I ignored the horsefly, moved the barrel and the sight picture a fraction of an inch to the right and squeezed the trigger. The .45 roared once, twice, and the 230-grain slugs hit him in the chest, knocking him backwards. Booming echoes bounced back from the crags in this high country. The other two men disappeared into the brush. So did the horsefly.

Death on the Switchback

Three bullets hit the rocks above me, snap-snap-snap, whining their way into space. Three echoes boomed from the crags. The flanker was shooting: he had spotted me. I thumbed the pistol on safe, crawled and slid like an animal backwards through the yellow leaves and branches, turned between the two boulders, went into a crouch and ran up and through the notch and down the trail, making foot tracks in the dust for a hundred yards.

The flanker was on my right, climbing up to the top of the ridge. I left the trail again and went over the rocks and into the brush. A thirty-foot cliff below put me into a skid. I went back down, rocks rattled below me. *Dammit, too much noise.* My legs went out and I jumped again, across rocky ledges, over weathered, burned logs, around rocky outcroppings, and reached the edge of a line of stunted firs. The shots had stopped.

The last jump was to the top of a flat rock. It see-sawed over a small rock, and my left ankle twisted. *Pitch forward like a parachute landing. Take the weight off. Pray it's only a sprain.* The pain was sharp. I went to ground and slid under some pines branches, then stood up and walked several steps. The ankle hurt, but I could walk.

The two hostiles on the trail would be coming this way. Now I had become the hunter again, a good feeling. I topped off the pistol magazine with eight rounds and put the other four in my pocket. When those were gone, there would be the longbow and the hunting knife. One or two of these people needed to be taken out before dark. Now they'd be ready.

I pulled the binoculars out again and crawled in the direction of the trail. A copse of wind-stunted firs offered better cover. The trail ran off to the left, not far, and was covered with late-summer dust. I jumped the trail and after a hundred yards climbed back up to the ridge. A movement higher on the mountain: two of them sneaking around the granite outcroppings, using the rocks and brush for cover. They didn't want to be ambushed again. The flanker was off to the right, shadowing in and out the trees near the top of the ridge. He was moving slowly, cautiously, like the point man had been doing, but the point man was dead. I had to reduce the odds.

The flanker disappeared. He had seen me, and more rounds cracked through the aspens. The shots were random. Shooting wild. The river was down there, far below. The line of the sun climbed the side of the canyon. White water was visible below, reminding me of the size and strength of the river.

The men above me again fired in the blind, muzzle flashes bright against the dark rocks. Tracers! They were shooting tracer ammunition. In the infantry we set fire to the woods and the fields at Ft. Bragg and Ft. Carson when we fired tracers. Those bullets will start a fire here: early October in the dry forest. The first to arrive would be the smoke-jumpers, trained as firefighters, not infantrymen, and they'd be killed. It could be Jammer himself, and some of his men. *I'll lead these guys to the river.*

First I had another idea. The flanker would expect me to move downhill. The top of the ridge was above me, not far. *Double back, move uphill through the trees and ambush the flanker.* He was moving north on the ridge when I last saw him, and if I could beat him at his own game, I'd lower the odds.

The pain in the ankle made me wince but I couldn't stop, not here. In the alder thickets off the ridge were game trails where the elk moved. I suspected the flanker would be following these trails, not wanting to be sky-lined. He'd be coming along the crest where he could watch the valley below. I'd be there.

There was a concealed spot next to some elephant-sized boulders, and I knelt down, the .45 in my hand. Here he came, sooner than expected.

He was Caucasian, dirty faced, heavily bearded, and wore a torn gray sweatshirt and a military vest. The pockets bulged with ammunition. The short carbine he carried looked vintage. He was tired, tripping twice on small logs lying across the game trail. *You were shooting at me, you asshole. You made the wrong choice, Mister.*

I quietly exhaled, winded from the climb. Thirty feet away he stopped and looked down into the valley. Damn, I hoped he didn't move downhill off the ridge. Bad luck for him, he continued on the game trail toward me.

At twenty feet he saw me. A flicker of recognition appeared in his eyes before I touched the trigger, then I fired another round. He fell backward. I ran to him, the .45 in front, unwavering, pointed on his body, thinking he was grazed, and might shoot back from prone. There was no need. One slug went through his neck, and the other bullet tore through the wood stock of his carbine and ripped into his chest.

Two of the four hostiles were now down. The other two would have heard the shots, but I had to take that chance, to gain more time, to plan the next attack. I checked the man's pockets. He was carrying two old-style hand grenades, and two cans of sardines. The carbine he was carrying was an Army carbine M1A1 .30 caliber with an automatic fire selector. The Army had long since quit using them. Six cartridges remained in the magazine, and the wood stock was shattered from the pistol slug, so I threw the carbine into the brush, along with the ammunition. My pistol would be a better weapon, faster and more accurate at short ranges. Easier to point. His group had stolen the old carbine and grenades from an Army depot somewhere. I could use the grenades. He had a cell phone. Much the better. I pocketed the sardines and left the cell phone.

Another idea came to me—move back to the grassy flat on the other side of the ridge where the plane was and make booby traps with the two grenades. Enough daylight remained. I knew how to do that. I leaned over the body and cut six strips from the bottom of the man's shirt, enough to secure the grenades for the booby traps. He had no rope or tape. Then I carried his bloody vest and hat with me for decoys.

Going downhill off the ridge through the small timber was easy. The bad ankle wasn't giving me trouble. At the edge of a small clearing I stopped and glassed the field, the tents under the pines, and the old mine. Nothing moved.

Whiskey Bravo sat parked where I left it, between the big ponderosas. I moved slowly, cautiously toward the plane. Seventy-five yards away, near the field, I found a tree with a branch stub protruding out at eye level. This is where the first grenade would be attached. I tied the cloth strips together and wrapped them around the grenade and the tree trunk, with the spoon facing out. These were old grenades—no safety clips on the spoon. I wrapped a short piece of the vest cloth over the spoon and around the grenade. I tied one end of this strip to the vest and hung the vest over the stub. I carefully pulled the pin and put it in my pocket. I did the same thing with the second grenade, found another broken branch and used the hat as a decoy. That made two grenade pins in my pocket.

I'd taken too long setting up these explosives. My luck wasn't going to hold forever. I moved back toward the mountaintop, taking a third route to the ridge near the Slot.

Over the ridge and then downhill again in the canyon, hobbling to take the pain off the ankle, I followed the small benches and obscure game trails. Copses of firs and pines were thicker here, providing more cover. I hadn't seen the other two men, but going downhill to the river put elevation and distance between us. They would be traveling more slowly, wary of another ambush. Two of their buddies were already dead.

A thin column of smoke broke the skyline at the top of the mountain. A lookout would spot it and call the Forest Service fire base and a jump plane could appear by early morning. I'd have to find a phone or radio somewhere on the river and warn the jumpers, then call Link's FBI team. Until then I was going to lead these guys as far away from that smoke as possible.

Along the river the pines, firs, and aspens grew larger, providing more cover. The question kept returning: what were these people doing in that old mine up on the ridge? What were they hiding? If the oil gauge hadn't malfunctioned they'd still be up there. Whatever it was, they thought it was worth killing me to keep that secret.

The timber was thicker now, but there was still enough light for another ambush. The only weapons were the .45, with eight cartridges, and the longbow, which I had retrieved from the brush. No ridge to climb over and escape. I had to find a place for a fire-and-fall-back-attack. The terrain wasn't cooperating. The trail from the top veered to the right and I jumped it in one leap, favoring the good ankle. I turned the binoculars upslope, and in the dim light saw the two hostiles on the trail, walking slowly like infantrymen with fifty yards between them, rifles ready, expecting another ambush. In the next moment they disappeared into the darkness of the woods. The ambush idea was risky.

The best option would be to drop lower on the mountainside and hole up in some thicket, then move to the river in the morning and find an outfitter's camp or somebody with a satellite phone or a radio. Liz's ranch was another five miles downriver.

Travel in the darkness was getting difficult and dangerous. A jay squawked back in the timber. The moon would not come out until the early hours, if then. The canyon walls were steep and deep, with shadows everywhere. The only way to move was on the open lower slopes between the ponderosas. These clearings could also be places to get ambushed. Though more hazardous, walking in the dark, were the thickets of aspen and firs—where the elk hide from the wolves.

A horse trail followed the river. I planned to stay two hundred yards above the trail and the river, then follow both downstream until I could find an outfitter's camp, or in the worst case, go as far as Liz's lodge on the Middle Fork. I kept coming up against small cliffs and rock slides, then dropping to the trail, and trying to determine the best way to move around them. Darkness was settling in the canyon and now was the time to hole up.

The two hostiles were out there somewhere. How much did they know about the mountains? *Hunter and hunted.* Which would it be, them or me? *Think positive, very positive.* Two of them were dead and no quarter would be given. I slid the .45 into the holster, and used my right hand to hold away the low branches in the thick timber.

The moon had not risen above the breaks. The darkness was complete when I stumbled into the next aspen grove and made the decision to stop and sleep. A small brook trickled through the trees. A black log lay beside the dark water and a makeshift bed could be scuffed out next to the log with leaves and moldy branches. This wasn't the Hyatt but who cared? Then I waited. And listened. The pistol was in my hand, the safety off.

The forest was deathly quiet. The only sound in the night was the gurgle of the brook. I rolled in the aspen leaves and pulled more of them over me, but the dampness and the cold crept in. *I didn't die in the mountains of Afghanistan and I'm not going to die out here.* Mike was gone, and I couldn't save him. Son-of-a-bitch. The war and the dream came back.

We were below the snowline. Link was on my left and Mike to the right. I was the team leader. The three of us were the point. The rocky ridge we were climbing was narrow. The other soldiers of my team waited five hundred yards below, concealed, behind rocks, so we thought.

For two days we'd been watching with spotting scopes six Taliban fighters moving supplies to an arms cache. Our helicopters were limited at these altitudes and the enemy knew this. At dawn on the third day we made an attack with the three of us in the lead. The rocky hog-back ridge was narrow. Moving laterally across the mountain was not an option.

Sergeant Mike Romano stood six feet tall, weighed one hundred and ninety-five pounds, had shoulder and neck muscles strong enough to carry a 130 pound combat pack and a weapon all day and all night through the Afghan mountains. His long black hair that morning was tied in the back with a camouflaged doo-rag.

You're too far to the right, Mike. Get back in line! He held two fingers in the air and pointed above, then moved farther right, under the rock ledge. I shifted my rifle to my left hand and made a return motion.

You're in the open, you dumb ass!

The smell of their campfire smoke was stronger. Mike nodded, touched his nose with his hand, pointed his finger in the direction of the smoke, made a little roll of his M4, first left, then right, then turned and made a goofy face at me. I had also smelled the smoke.

I made another return motion. *You're not a one-man army, you crazy Italian. Get back over here.* That accomplished nothing. I saw him bring his M4 into a firing position.

The grenade came over the top of the rock wall. I wouldn't have seen it except the high arc of the lob caught the morning sun for an instant. Mike dropped his rifle, caught the grenade, and threw it back, but the hostile, a trained infantryman, had held it two seconds longer, and the grenade exploded twenty yards in front of Mike, knocking him backward.

Mike tried to stand, picked up his rifle, turned, looking for me. He dropped his rifle, put his hands behind him and sat down. From the top of the ledge two hostiles came, following the grenade, their black coats flapping in the wind, looking like giant bats, their Kalashnikovs firing, and Mike, sitting there, took three rounds in his stomach.

Link shot the man on the left and I shot the one on the right, his hat flying off into the rocks

—My dream in the leaves was fading. I rolled and bumped against the log. Wake up—they're coming—back to sleep—.

Four Taliban were behind the rock wall, trying to flank us. Link and I expected more grenades. We split up, putting thirty yards between us. We ran up the slope, sliding in the shale and jumping over rocks. Backing up was not possible.

Link was trained in hostage recovery. He could shoot an assailant at twenty paces in a dark room, or an airliner cabin, if the hostile showed an inch of his body. The M4 was in his left hand, the nine millimeter in his right. Two turban heads appeared above the rocks. The pistol bounced twice in Link's hand and they were dead.

Mike was hit hard. A crunching sound in the cold air of people moving on the rocks above came with the wind. Two hostiles were running for the saddle below the snow line. Link shot one in the back, and I dropped the other with a three-round burst.

Wake up—something's out there! Twigs snapped on the other side of the log. The cold crept in through the damp leaves.

Link checked the bodies and I ran back to Mike. The rest of the team came up and I radioed for a Medevac. An hour later the helicopter landed below the ridge in a flurry of dust and dried grass. Two medics came over and Mike died in my arms. I put my chin on his forehead and told him he was a bastard for leaving.

"You'll be sitting in the open door of the Otter," I said, "in the high sky over the mountains, looking for the greenest jump spot on the ridge. I'll be right behind you."

The medics, kneeling next to Mike, wanted to be out of there. "Wait one," I said, and made a hand motion to the pilot.

"Mike, you wanted this. We could be out in Idaho, drinking whiskey and raising hell. I'm glad you were my friend. Take care of yourself, wherever you are."

The medics covered Mike with a poncho, then slid him through the door of the helicopter. I stood there, cursing the fact that I wasn't God, came to a position of attention, saluted Mike and the helicopter as the rotors began to wind up. The two medics glanced at me. I heard a sergeant say, "Those special ops guys do what they want. Don't piss them off."

A journalist, jumping down from the Medevac, came over, said "What a fight," and asked what we did with the prisoners. "What prisoners! The hell with the prisoners," I said, picking up my rifle and moving back from the rotors. The journalist was the first man inside. The helicopter lifted off, gained some altitude, then dropped into the valley below for Asadabad.

That was the last time I saw Mike. Now it was just Link and me.

The leaves stirring in the aspens woke me. Something or somebody was out there. The only movement was my finger, feeling for the trigger guard of the pistol, then the trigger. The gray light of morning came filtering through the branches. Was it the wind? A twig snapped. The sound came from the other side of the log. I carefully moved the muzzle of the .45 across the top of the log.

Another twig cracked, closer. The forest was silent. Were people out there? My patience ran out and I looked over the top of the log.

A cow elk stood on the other side of the log, close enough to touch, her big brown eyes staring at me. She looked huge. The elk was trying to make sense of this creature covered in leaves behind the log. I exhaled and the elk walked away, without a care in the world.

I brushed off the dirt, leaves and branches, waited ten minutes, heard and saw nothing, then slowly stood, working the kinks out from the damp ground. The comforting smell of the pines was in the air, and the sun touched the high slopes of the canyon walls. Two small birds chirped to each other while they hopped from one tree trunk to the other. The forest in the canyon was idyllic, but it had turned into the backdrop of a deadly game. I gathered my weapons, the longbow and arrows, the .45, and a hunting knife. Time to move.

An outfitter's spike camp was downriver three miles. When flying up the Middle Fork I had seen the canvas tents and the horses from the air. They might have a satellite phone or radio, and maybe some better weapons than a pistol. Now it was a race to get there before the hostiles did. The disadvantage was mine, because I'd be above the river and the trail, moving cross country, moving slow, navigating every open ridge, rock slope, and brushy ravine.

Daylight was in the gorge when I heard the distant rattle of gunfire. Automatic weapons, the echoes repeating themselves in the canyon. The shots came from the direction of the outfitter's camp.

I moved from aspen thicket to aspen thicket, above the river trail. The river flowed below, changing from plunging white water to stretches of brilliant blue, down beyond the orange bark of the large pines.

From the next rise I could see a white canvas tent belonging to the outfitters. Off to the left in the trees and below the trail two horses were tied to a high-line rope. Nice-looking stock, a gray and a chestnut. I stopped behind a boulder at the base of some pines and centered the binoculars on the roof of the tent. The only movements were the horses snapping their tails at the flies. The metal stovepipe protruding from the top of the tent looked cold, as if it hadn't seen a fire for some time.

The binoculars moved from left to right, continuing a regimented scan like the pattern our snipers used. Never could sit in a tree stand all day watching for elk, or work with the sniper teams for more than a couple of hours. Wasn't how I was wired. But this was a deadly matter. The eight-power binoculars continued to move from left to right and back again. Nothing changed at the tent, the horses, or on the trail. Two hours passed.

Time was approaching noon, the temperature mild but climbing. The camo vest was getting warm. On the open meadows the grasshoppers jumped in the sun. Horseflies buzzed in the maple brush. Two horses still tied to the high line looked restless, stomping their hooves and snorting. The smell of death hung over the camp. Nothing moved at the camp except the horseflies and I feared the worst.

Those bastards could be waiting in the tent. I doubted they were, but circled the camp and the horses, keeping thirty yards back in the trees, and feeling uncomfortable with minimum ammunition. The sun at high noon warmed the grass in the meadow. Then I heard the flies: many flies. The humming that comes from a warm-blooded kill in the mountains, when the day's heat increases and a breeze moves through the grass.

The cowboys lay behind the horses, dragged there and left to the elements. I walked up, checked for booby traps—an old military habit—then rolled the bloody bodies over. The wranglers never had a chance. They were probably drinking their morning coffee when the killers walked into their camp with automatic rifles.

The gray horse whinnied, followed by the chestnut. The horses had seen me. I slipped behind a tree. If the guys were in the tent they'd come out now. My pistol was leveled at the canvas tent door. No one appeared. I had to see inside that tent. I was damn hungry and maybe there would be a can of beans inside. And a radio.

Time was up. I opened the flap. The tent was empty. The radio was gone, probably destroyed. There were some canned goods. I slipped two cans in my vest pocket—baked beans and corned beef hash.

A pot of cold coffee, half full, on the camp stove, confirmed my suspicions the wranglers had been taken unawares, murdered while they'd been getting a start on their day. Two streaks of blood on the dirt floor showed the wranglers had been dragged out of the tent. As good as that coffee might taste, I didn't want a cup from that old porcelain pot. It was time to move.

The horses stomped and whinnied again. I couldn't stand knowing the horses might starve on the rope line or cause havoc to get loose. I untied them and slapped their rumps. They made a straight run to the river. The bodies of the two wranglers would have to stay where they were.

Back on the river trail, old horse tracks dented into the dust, and on top of the hoof prints two sets of footprints, two or three hours old, came from the camp and heading downriver. Downriver to Liz Hollis's lodge in the canyon.

The sound of a plane came up the gorge. The rumble echoed back and forth along the ridges, the sound louder as the pilot flew across the river canyon and began to make circles over the timber on the highest ridge. The plane was the Forest Service's Twin Otter and it was circling the smoke in the high timber. They'd kick out four jumpers then drop their cargo bags at a lower elevation, just over the tree tops. If any terrorists from the old mine were waiting for them, there'd be no contest. I had to find a radio or phone soon.

The hostiles were in front of me. Where? I decided to follow the tracks on the trail downriver and take my chances on an ambush. I was heading straight to Liz.

From the Treeline

Boot tracks were deep in the trail dust. The two terrorists were moving fast toward the lodge. Were they tired? They weren't expecting another ambush. Or they were setting me up, hiding behind the rocks somewhere. At this pace they would reach Liz's lodge before I did. Domestic radicalized terrorists, and some from foreign countries. Here in the backcountry of Idaho. They think they can hide in these mountains. They killed two innocent wranglers and tried to kill me. I had seen their kind before in the Middle East. They showed no mercy and I had none.

The horse trail followed the river, over and around rock outcroppings, dropping back to the water, leading through stands of cottonwoods and pines. It was a wide trail, dusty from the dry summer. A pack bridge crossed the river a mile downstream from Liz's ranch, and if the hostiles were taking that route, I could gain some time by swimming and crossing the river above.

Moving on the trail was quiet. The dust went puff with every step.

The sound of a short burst of automatic rifle fire came up the canyon, and the echo bounced back from the rocks above.

Oh God, they've already killed the wranglers. Please, not Liz.

To hell with caution. I waded into the unknown, the dark water where the shores spread and the river looked deceptively shallow. The ford was easier than expected. Halfway across the river my feet left the rock bottom once, and after clumsy strokes with one arm, holding the bow and quiver high with the other, I waded into the shallows and climbed the other bank. From the flat above the river, the lights of the ranch were visible a half mile away. It would be smarter to move to the edge of the airstrip, keep some timber between me and the grass, and come out behind the lodge.

I was in the trees fifty yards above the back of the ranch. Lights showed in the downstairs windows. The front deck was empty. A small barn and bunkhouse were off at an angle near the airstrip just short of the tree line. The smell of fresh hay, horses and the corral came to me on the breezes from the river.

The light was dimming in the canyon.

Move closer to the lodge.

With binoculars I could see people walking back and forth through the window. Liz's silhouette appeared for an instant. She was alive. Were Clint and her husband alive?

My first instinct was to kick in the back door, and charge in with the pistol. But that might get me—and Liz—killed in the firefight.

The Army taught me to wait. I didn't want to wait. The longbow was in my left hand, right hand fingering the first sharp hunting arrow in the quiver. The arrow would be easy to pull out. The bow was silent. If I could take them one at a time, that would be the plan.

A wolf howled up in the timber. A haunting answer came back from across the canyon. Ravens squawked in the trees down by the river. The wild creatures of the forest were alive, the sounds in the coming darkness rising to a crescendo, to some ancient law of the mountains. They were telling the netherworld that evil was going to happen.

The canyon became ominously quiet. *Move slow. Don't even breathe.*

A metallic screech of a door being opened came with the night breeze, then scuffling and cursing, and three people came through the kitchen doorway, dragging a body. One was Liz. A man had one hand on the back of her jeans, jerking her through the door, his other hand on the ankle of the dead person. Liz looked limp, like she was barely struggling, unable to stand. Was the body Liz's husband? *What had she told me about him?* He was a businessman, trying to fight armed men.

One of the men, the dark one, stopped dragging and went to the table on the deck. A bottle of whiskey sat on the table, and the dark one lifted it and took a long drag.

I was close enough now and circling. Their voices were clear.

"Bass, here's some whiskey!"

"Drop that damn bottle and grab his leg!" For a big man Bass had a high-pitched voice. He stepped over the body and shouted to Liz. "Get this cowboy into the trees. It's dark now and sleeping with the enemy is bad luck."

I stepped another ten feet toward them in the soft pine needles.

Bass jerked again on Liz's waist.

"No. He was my friend. There is food for you, beans and bread." Liz was sobbing. "In the kitchen."

The body must be Clint. The man called Bass grabbed the back of Liz's blouse, ripping it, and pulled her to him. She snapped back by reflex and Bass punched her on the arm.

"You're going to help!"

"You bastard."

Liz was an athlete. This was her ranch and she knew these forests. She could break away from this man and disappear into the timber and he couldn't find her. But she must want to stay close to her husband, whatever might happen. Bass had one hand on Liz's wrist.

"Makdur, drop that bottle and grab a leg. We'll drag him into the trees, then we'll tie this woman and her husband—the dumb bastard—to a tree. We can sleep in their goddamn bed tonight."

I could see Bass hauling on one ankle and the dark one on the other. Makdur held the whiskey bottle in his free hand. Bass had one hand on Liz's wrist, jerking her with him.

The darkness in the canyon was complete. I circled inside the trees, moving closer to the struggling pair. I pulled the first hunting arrow from the quiver. The arrow was cedar, perfectly straight, armed at the tip with a two-bladed, steel broad head, honed razor sharp. The pistol sat loose in my holster, a round in the chamber. The .45 was my last resort. Forty yards separated us. The two of them were struggling with the body, dragging it to the trees.

Move closer for a kill shot with the longbow.

I was warmed up, but my bow arm was not. I prayed it would do the job when the moment came.

The man in black was giving Liz orders. They pulled and jerked the body toward the trees. I moved between the big pines to intersect them. The forest floor was covered from years of fallen pine needles, muffling my footfalls.

Stay behind the trees and freeze. Remember the reflexes and the memory are still there. Like Mike, who didn't have a chance, who caught the grenade. There were no prisoners.

"That's far enough," Bass said to Makdur. "Me and this woman can drag the cowboy back in the woods. Go back to the house."

Makdur was happy to leave the edge of the forest. He was gripping the whiskey bottle tighter, putting it up to his face, looking at the label in the dark. A real find.

Liz knew what Bass was up to, the dreaded outcome. She pulled back, and Bass grabbed her arm. He dropped the leg of the dead man, and groped for Liz's blouse. I could hear the cloth tear. Liz turned and hit the man in the face. For a second he was stunned, then he said something. They moved apart by several feet.

I moved closer between the trees.

The wooden longbow had a sixty-pound pull. Holding a full draw for more than two seconds takes some strength. This would have to be fast and precise.

Twenty-five yards separated us in the darkness. I stepped out from behind the tree and shouted, "Liz!" I was counting on startling Bass, and hoped he wouldn't drop to the ground, like a soldier.

Both of them turned. Liz stepped back, away from the man. My left foot was down hard on the pine needles, the bowstring came to my cheek, the tips of the wood bow arched back, and the arrow released. For less than a second, the bow quivered, hummed, then silence.

The big man jerked, coughed, and sat down. I nocked another arrow in the bow, ready for the second draw, when Bass rolled over on his side.

"Liz!"

"Good Lord! Casey?" She could not see me in the trees.

"Here, Liz. Over here." She rushed toward me in the darkness and threw her arms around me. She was trembling, terrified. Then she kissed me on the mouth. Twice in one month. I put my arms around her and held her.

"That's Bass," she said. "Is he dead? There's another one inside. He'll be coming."

"I know. Wait." I pushed her away and stepped over to the fallen man. He was gasping, then went quiet. "Get down, Liz."

A shaft of light came from the kitchen door. I knelt down, put my arm around her, quietly pulling her to a crouching position next to me. We were inside the tree line. "Don't move an inch."

The bow with the nocked arrow on the string was in my left hand, the .45 in my right. The lighted door was forty-five yards away, too far for an accurate pistol shot.

"Alec is inside. He's badly hurt." Liz's voice was breaking. "We have to help him before he dies."

"Is that Clint?" I pointed the tip of my bow at the body they were dragging.

"Yes. He was trying to defend us with his rifle. God, Casey, what is happening?"

"These people are terrorists. They started shooting at me up at the old Luddendorf mine."

"Terrorists?"

The back door of the lodge flew open. "What ya doing, Bass? Are you fucking with that woman?"

"Makdur," Liz whispered. She was difficult to see in the darkness.

Makdur went inside, slamming the door.

"He'll kill Alec if we don't do something."

"Stay here in the trees."

Makdur would be back. I ran forward, staying low, staying balanced, and was near the back door when the kitchen lights went out and he came slowly through the door. The target was a dim silhouette. This time Makdur was carrying a Kalashnikov. The distance was twenty-five yards.

I lifted the bow again, pulled the string back to my cheek, and released the broad head. The string hummed and the path of the arrow was lost in the night. Makdur screamed. He pulled the trigger of the Kalashnikov and fired a long burst wildly into the trees. He screamed again and cursed in another language. It would take a second for his eyes to adjust to the darkness, and I dropped the bow, took a two-handed hold on the pistol and fired five rounds in the direction of the rifle flashes.

The gunman was silent.

Do not move. Fifteen minutes passed. The ravens near the river were quiet. The wolves were silent. Waiting. A sliver of moon breaking above the rim of the canyon came through the pine branches and scattered patches of silver light over the grass. Was Makdur dead, or was he playing possum? Three rounds remained in the pistol.

My watch showed two o'clock in the morning. *Do not move.* The leaves in the aspens were silent. The smell of the horses in the barn drifted through the night air. A horse snorted and stomped, a noise of fear. They had heard the gunfire. *Be patient.* My clothes were wet from the river crossing, and the night air of the canyon held a chill. Shivering in the moonlight was only a small discomfort.

Someone in the house turned on the kitchen lights. A man opened the back door, came out on the deck, lurched against the porch post, and collapsed.

The light from the open lodge door revealed the body of the first man, down on the grass, his body twisted into a crumpled fetal position. He looked dead, but I approached the body from a position behind his head. If Makdur was playing possum he would have to turn to shoot me.

There was no need: he was indeed dead. An arrow protruded from just above his crotch. Blood soaked his dirty pants. The broad head had hit an artery. Both of Makdur's hands gripped the bloody yellow feathers—he was trying to withdraw the arrow when one of the slugs from the .45 took off the top of his head.

Damn, I keep shooting high.

The man slumped against the porch rail was holding a towel over a bullet hole in his thigh. The towel and his jeans were blood-soaked. He looked bad. It was the first time I had seen Alec. It wasn't a great introduction. He was tall with curly gray-blonde hair, well built, but now had turned pale and gaunt, and was going into shock.

"Who are you?" he asked, as I walked over, kicking the dead terrorist in the back as I passed the body on the grass. The arrow in his body was sticking straight up, its yellow feathers like a cross over a grave. The .45 was still in my hand, the barrel pointing toward the body. Just in case.

"McConnell, from Owyhee Crossing. The shooting is over. We'll get some help in here for you, some first aid."

Then I turned toward the trees and shouted, "Liz." She had hidden behind the pines as I told her, and she was already running back to the lodge.

"How many of them were here?" I asked. Liz had made her way onto the porch, stopped and leaned against the rail to catch her breath. She glanced at the dead terrorist, looked at me, then at Alec. "God," she said.

"Both of the bastards are dead," I said. "Get the sheriff on the radio. I'll work on Alec." I threw his arm over my shoulder, put my other arm around his waist and dragged him to the sofa near the kitchen. He was helping with his good leg.

"They used the radio and talked to someone at a mine somewhere, and they ordered him to bring a plane in here at daylight," Liz said. "They had us trapped in the house. One of them called someone on the radio, and that person said a plane would be here this morning to pick them up."

"They're up at the old Luddendorf mine. I know exactly where." I told Liz what had happened during the last two days in the mountains and along the river trail.

"Call the sheriff on the radio right away. I'll talk to him. We need to get some security in here before daylight, because Alec can't be moved. We still aren't safe."

Liz went immediately to the radio and began turning dials. "The sheriff's dispatcher is on the radio," she said. "Talk to her. I'll make coffee."

I told the night dispatcher we had a gun battle in the mountains and I suspected the hostiles were domestic and imported terrorists. There were a half-dozen fatalities in the mountains and along the river, and more hostiles still out there. She said she would contact the sheriff immediately, and I repeated the request that she also talk to the FBI. I also asked for the FBI number and she said she was not authorized to give me that contact. I told her I knew the regional special agent from our days in Afghanistan, and the terrorists were planning some kind of a serious international attack. She should call him, give him my name, and confirm. I'd give her ten minutes. Link Barrett was an old friend, I repeated, and we needed firepower.

"Will you give me the FBI number?" She did.

I tried the radio call sign the dispatcher gave me and got nothing. Then I called for anyone who received this transmission to call FAA Flight Control in Twin Falls, and ask them to call back to this number, as this was an emergency. I was praying the terrorists weren't monitoring the radio. In a matter of seconds Calvin, a ham radio operator in Alabama, called and said he would do just that. I told him I was back in the wilderness of Idaho and there had been a gun battle and the FBI was needed and I couldn't call out from the canyon. I needed him to relay the message to the FBI through FAA Flight Control.

In a matter of minutes Baker was on the radio. "Is that you, Casey? What kind of trouble are you in?"

"Big trouble," I said. "Those people we saw in the bar came out here, and I had to kill several of them. There was a gun battle, with fatalities, and we have one injured man here. I need to talk to Link at the FBI, and have him bring in a combat team as soon as possible. We're at Liz Hollis's lodge on the Middle Fork. It shows on the chart as the Phantom Ranch. Link knows where it is."

"Well, you didn't waste any time finding your old girlfriend," Baker said, with a touch of coolness.

"It's a long story, and I'll tell you the details when I get to the office."

"You were right—about those men. Big trouble, Casey." Baker was more earnest this time. "I'll find Link right away. Remember, you're not in the Army anymore. If I can't find him, I'll send in the Special Forces."

"Send somebody. Soon. I expect a terrorist plane to land here any moment. We can't take to the hills, because Liz's husband is severely wounded."

"I'm on it."

"Did you record the tail number of the green Cessna at the airport? I suspect the Middle Eastern man I met at Sun Valley was flying that plane, diverted to Twin Falls, then flew his friends to a remote field I found off the Middle Fork."

"What kind of an air controller do you think I am? Of course it's been recorded."

Damn, Baker was efficient.

"We have talked to the sheriff's dispatcher, but we need more firepower than the sheriff has. Also give that tail number and the name of the pilot—Fauod Saeed—to the FBI."

"I'll call Link right now. He has multiple radio channels, as do we. Casey, your instincts were correct again." She keyed off.

Ten minutes later a radio call came through from the FBI. A polite young woman began speaking. After some formalities, I said, with the firmness of an infantry officer, "Please put me through to Mr. Barrett."

A commanding voice came on the line. "Casey, I just hung up with the sheriff. What in the hell are you up to at eight o'clock in the morning?"

"I've come across a terrorist cell, believe it or not. There is one severely wounded man here. I'm out on the Middle Fork, in the wilderness area, and need some combat troops and a medical extraction immediately."

"Is the wounded man a hostile?"

"No, the wounded man is Alec Champlin, Liz's husband."

"As in Liz Hollis?"

"Yes, the Phantom Ranch."

"Are the hostiles wounded?"

"No, they are dead. Four of them. There are more out here, storing material, and probably planning some nasty activities."

"For God's sake, Casey, did you take them out?"

"I'll tell you when you get here. Bring in snipers or a SWAT team."

"I'm already working with the sheriff. Explain."

"I landed my plane on a grassy bench just off a ridge north of Big Creek, when the oil gauge was acting up, near the old Luddendorf mine, if you know where that is, and some bastards started shooting at me."

"You do attract gunfire."

"Whatever. Then they came after me. I am on the Middle Fork now at the Phantom Ranch. The wounded man needs to be airlifted out of here right away, and the hostiles are scheduled back here at this airfield along the river."

"We are aware of a cell in the Rocky Mountain region, but have not located their exact position."

"Well, I have."

"How many are there?" Link asked.

"I counted six to eight, maybe more. Now four less."

"You did say four less?"

"They killed two outfitters and the ranch manager here. They've been shooting at me," I said.

"And you have been shooting back. Tell me more when I get there. I'll bring in the Blackhawk with two SWAT teams. An EMT is coming in after the airstrip at the ranch is secured. A plane will pick up the wounded man. I'll confirm with the sheriff."

"Link, there's also a forest fire up near Stoddard Peak—started by their tracers, when they were shooting at me. The Forest Service has some smokejumpers on the fire now. They could be in danger. Call the Forest Service and have them extracted right away. The hell with the fire. I'll try to reach them from here by radio. The jumpers could include Jammer."

"If we get there first we can pick them up with the Blackhawk."

"These guys are armed with automatic weapons. They shot at me and they'll shoot at you," I said. "By the way, my red airplane is there on the field, between the trees, near the mine. Don't shoot any more holes in it."

"Casey, keep in mind that we'll have to authenticate this. We can't just go in shooting."

"Authenticate all you want, but if the bad guys come back here Liz and I will take to the hills. If she will leave her husband."

"Stay put. We will be there. Oh, Casey?"

"What?"

"When I get your ass out of this one, you owe me a whiskey."

"More than one."

"Roger, wait." Link keyed off.

At ten hundred hours the distinct whomp-whomp-whomp of a helicopter filled the canyon. An alien noise in the cold morning air, powerful but vulnerable, bringing with it an instant wave of memories, but this was no time to think of other days. Over the tall pines it flew in a hurry to do its work. The Blackhawk came straight down in a cloud of dust fifty yards from the ranch house. Both side doors opened before the skids touched and eight well-armed, camouflaged officers dropped out, split up immediately, and moved at a run to both sides of the runway: a practiced tactical move. In a moment all were concealed, but I knew that eight rifles were covering 360 degrees of the terrain. Link was in command, and a moment later he jumped off the helicopter and headed my way. The pilot remained in the craft, and an EMT, carrying a medical bag and a stretcher, followed Link.

In the years since the Army days, Link had grown more mature, even better-looking than before, with a touch of gray showing in his black hair. He was fit, as usual, and he said it was from running marathons. After the campaigns in the Middle East the two of us left the Army and our paths diverged. I went into business and Link into the FBI. He had worked his way up the ladder to special agent. I called him the director. He was packing a 9mm automatic in a shoulder holster. He was a deadly shot with a handgun. Some kind of a radio device was attached to his collar.

Link and I shook hands. "Casey, tell me the whole story." And I did.

A single-engine plane flew down the canyon and circled high overhead. When we identified the plane, Link radioed the pilot, told him the FBI was here, the field was secure and said it was clear to land. Link and I went out to meet them. Liz came with us, momentarily leaving Alec's bedside.

"I'm Quentin Bronski, the county sheriff," the first man said, looking us over, not shaking hands with anyone, looking official, his eyes taking in the helicopter and then sweeping the sides of the canyon, hesitating a moment wondering, if he was the boss here or Mr. Barrett. "The deputies are Reynolds and Thorpe, out of Cascade. They brought some M14s from our arsenal." Sheriff Bronski turned to me. "I know Mr. Barrett, and he gave me some of your background. Said he knew you from the Special Forces."

The sheriff had hard eyes. "In the meantime, you have a lot more to tell me—to tell us."

I think he was going to ask me if I thought I was a gunslinger.

John, the medic, with Liz, went immediately to Alec, who was not in the best of shape. I related to Bronski the sequence of events and that three bodies were out behind the lodge: the ranch manager the terrorists shot, and the two terrorists. He gave me a fierce look.

"How do you know they are terrorists?"

"They sure as hell aren't choir boys."

Then he gave an order to Reynolds to secure them, put them in body bags for a flight out. "Protect them from the rodents," the sheriff said.

"Evan!" Bronski barked to the second deputy. "Help him with the weight. Then take up a position on the front deck."

"Holy smokes!" Deputy Reynolds said, as he approached the first body. "What are we going to do with this arrow sticking out of him?"

The sheriff looked at me, not so pleasantly, then turned to Reynolds. "Cut if off and put the feathered end inside the canvas," he said.

Sheriff Bronski gave me another long look. "You have a lot of explaining to do," he said.

Link nudged me on the arm. "Do you have an archery tag for that?" he asked quietly, then smiled at me behind the sheriff and his deputies. There are still hostiles out there, he was thinking, then slid his pistol out of its holster and re-checked the magazine.

"Four miles upstream you'll find two more bodies near some tents. They are two outfitters these guys killed. The rest of the hostiles are up at the old Luddendorf mine, probably storing materiel there. They still may arrive here in a plane, or on foot, to pick up those two out there. They don't know they're dead. I suggest you put your men in a defensive position."

The sheriff didn't like being told what to do. He went to the window again and looked at the airstrip, hoping, I think, that more cavalry would arrive.

"We have eight men out there. You can't see them," Link said, "and they are pros."

The sheriff took his radio, called somebody and ordered roads closed at Yellow Pine and Elk Creek, should the hostiles somehow make their way out of the wilderness area on foot, or by vehicle. He picked up the Kalashnikovs on the deck and handed one to me. "You know how to use this?"

"I was weaned on an AK47," I said, grasping the rifle like a baseball bat, checking the number of cartridges remaining in the magazine. Bronski nodded and went back to the window. There was no plane in sight. The sunlight was working its way down the west face of the canyon.

The deputies carried Alec on a stretcher to the Cessna, which was equipped with a specialized side door. The EMT, Dan the deputy, and Liz climbed in with him, and the pilot wasted no time starting the engine. Liz gave me a wave as the sheriff fastened the cabin door and moved away from the plane. The Cessna made a noisy 180-degree turn on the ground, throwing a dust cloud into the pines and over the deadly looking Blackhawk. Then it roared and bounced down the field and lifted off.

The sound of the plane and its echoes were soon lost in the canyon.

Link turned to me. I was looking over the Kalashnikov and counting the cartridges in the magazines that once belonged to the dead terrorists. "Well, Captain," he said. "It's you and me again."

Fight Below Stoddard Peak

Link spread a Forest Service map on the table. "The Luddendorf mine is sixteen miles by trail, up the river, and the trail switchbacks to the grassy field and the mine," Link said. "That was the old mule trail used when the ore was brought out of the mine at the end of the eighteen hundreds."

"I know it well. It's at least that far," I said. "I ran up to the ridge from the mine, shot two of them up there on top, then crossed the ridge and dropped to the river. That's where the two dead wranglers were lying outside their tent."

"Son of a bitch." Link shook his head and gave me a long look. "You told me two more hostiles, maybe more, are at the mine, and someone is flying down here tomorrow at this airstrip to pick up their people, who you took out last night. Damn, this is another Afghanistan, isn't it? We'll leave two men here with the sheriff and his deputies. You and I will take the rest of the team to the mine in the Blackhawk. Once the mine is secure and the lodge is safe, we'll sweep the trail along the river to the top of the ridge."

"There's another body near the top, where the trail comes across the ridge, at a place I call the Slot. And there's another one on the trail near the top of the ridge."

"You did say four less." Link jerked his head away from watching the SWAT team climbing into the helicopter. "You've been busy."

"Self-defense. They were shooting at me when I was landing."

"Of course they were."

"I'm glad you agree."

"You must be about out of arrows."

"I used an Army .45 for the two up there on the mountain. I *am* about out of ammo. Do you or your men pack any .45s?"

"No, only cartridges for the nines. The sheriff will send some men to the outfitter's camp, and then up the trail to the top."

"The jumpers on the fire on Stoddard Peak need some security. These people chased me all over the mountains for two days, and they might go after the firefighters, thinking they'll compromise their location."

"You've already compromised them. We radioed the Forest Service. They're planning to extract them by helicopter today."

Link gave me an extra 9mm pistol and two magazines. We adjusted our pistol belts and followed the snipers into the Blackhawk.

The pilot lifted the big bird off and powered up the side of the canyon, staying several hundred feet above the treetops. The trail from the ridge zigzagging through the rock scree was easy to follow. There was no sign of the fight that took place there two nights before. When the helicopter cleared the top of the mountain, the pilot came back on the power and we flew aft of the field on the flat below the tops of the big firs. Wheel tracks in the brown grass from several planes were prominent at the far end on the upward slope to the old mine. One set of those tracks had been made by my plane. A patch of red behind the pine branches halfway up the field was Whiskey Bravo. I pointed out the plane's location to Link.

"I see it. You get closer to the enemy every time you're in a firefight."

"They find me attractive."

"I don't know why."

The pilot, following Link's direction, set the Blackhawk down at the far end of the bench, keeping some large firs between our team and the open field. We advanced through the trees, trying to remain invisible until we came to the edge of the field. I pointed out the old mine to Link and the pilot. Timbers at the entrance were falling in disrepair from their original positions. Using binoculars, we could see signs of tracks, trampled grass, old water bottles and fresh dirt at the mine entrance. The timbers around the mine opening were at an angle, had slid over the years; loose rocks covered the rusty rails leading to the darkness inside, but we could see where some logs had been placed for shoring.

"Do you know if there are any other tunnels or lateral shafts?" Link asked.

"No, but we can call the sheriff, and he can find a geologist who knows the history of the mines in this country."

"We don't want any hostiles to come out of a side tunnel and surprise us." He called the Blackhawk pilot and asked him to radio Sheriff Bronski and request some research.

Link gave field commands to the six members of the team. Link knew most of them, and nodded to those he did not know. He split the team into two sections and picked two team leaders. Each team was to take a side of the field, staying undercover, moving in cover off the edge of the bench for the downhill section, and staying in the trees for the uphill team.

"Advance to within fifty yards of the mine entrance. One member of each section is to keep continued surveillance in all directions, specifically behind you. They may have prepared ambush points. They also may have emplaced land mines. Walk on the grass and not on fresh dirt. Do not fire unless fired upon," Link continued. "There may be hostages or noncombatants in the mine or the cabin."

A disturbing thought entered my mind. The hostiles could have moved out to the forest fire and taken the firefighters as hostage. The distance was only four or five miles overland, off trail. Jammer, if it was Jammer, and his men would put up a fight. But with what? Shovels and Pulaskis?

"You're the shooters and the pros. Keep in touch with me here," Link said.

"Wait one," I said to the camouflaged men, who were locked and loaded, eager to move out. "The red plane you can barely see there in the trees is mine. Try not to shoot any holes in it."

"We'll watch it," one of the section leaders said.

"We don't want to make you mad," added another SWAT officer, his face blackened, his hands firmly holding an M16. "We heard what you did out here with a bow."

"Somebody did." I gave them a smile. "One more thing," I added. "And this is important. There are booby traps around that field. Explosives—hand grenades—are under a camo jacket and a hat hanging on two trees. Do not touch those clothes. I say again, do not touch."

"How do you know this?" Link asked, those serious eyes focused on me.

"Because I set them myself. Found two hand grenades on one of the bodies."

"A jacket and a hat hanging on pine trees! Do not touch!" Link repeated to the SWAT officers. Link was looking at me.

"You taught the booby trap course at Ft. Bragg," I said. "Remember? 'Improvised Munitions' you called your lectures. I happened to be in one of your classes."

"Improvised Munitions? You remembered. I thought you were asleep."

"Not for everything you taught," I said, then turned to the SWAT officers and in a first sergeant's tone of voice said, "Once again, any jackets or hats hanging from trees are rigged."

Some of them nodded.

"Okay, we got that," Link said. "Move out."

In less than a minute the camouflaged teams disappeared into the woods. Not a branch moved.

"We will give the teams thirty minutes to secure their positions around the mine," Link said. "Let's take up concealment here in the trees. You have the Kalashnikov. How many rounds?"

"Two full magazines from those dead guys."

"Okay. I'll get my hunting rifle," Link said.

"Hunting rifle?"

"Yes, if you can use a wooden bow with arrows, weaponry outmoded by two centuries, I can shoot my old Savage." Link unzipped a canvas case and slid out a battered scoped lever rifle, its bluing long worn off from years of use.

"Are you still packing around that old Model Ninety-Nine? That is, by the way, a Model *1899.*"

"Hey, don't knock it. These .300 Savages have brought down more elk than all the magnum boys combined. Grew up with this rifle in Montana. I brought it along because after this adventure we may go back to our hunting camp. I know you have more secret haunts. Like this one. Just hope it will be quieter."

I could tell from those dark eyes watching me he was going to needle me more after this adventure was over. "You can take the long shots," I said.

"If they get within twenty feet, use the Kalashnikov or your bow."

We got in position behind some weathered gray logs at the edge of the trees. The Blackhawk was in a secure location in a small meadow two hundred yards behind us. Link was on his radio to one of the section leaders.

"The tents are clear," Link relayed.

We were watching the action around the mine with binoculars. Motorcycle tracks in the grass led up to the entrance. Link and I speculated the hostiles were storing munitions in the mine, probably C4 or ammonium nitrate. Explosives required arming devices and detonators. They'd be included. Just great. *This whole damn mountain could blow up.*

Link and I were in position at the other end of the grassy flat, a thousand yards from the mine entrance. The SWAT men had moved up to the entrance, in cover behind the trees.

Automatic rifle fire erupted from the mine entrance, staccato bursts pounding loud in the trees. The SWAT team held their fire. They had cleared the woods around the old cabin and the mine. We saw a camo-clad man drop over the timbers at the top of the entrance and throw a grenade into the blackness.

"CS grenade," Link said. "Nonlethal, but it should bring them out, unless they keep going deeper into the tunnel, or there is a side shaft."

The morning wind coming up the slope from the bottom of the canyon was increasing. Smoke from the grenade swirled against the sides of the mine entrance. With our binoculars we could make out the outline of a man behind the timbers of the open doorway. A flash of automatic rifle fire came from inside the smoke where we had glimpsed him, and bullets went in all directions over the grassy field.

"See him, Link?"

"I see him."

"Think that old Savage will shoot that far?"

"The range is a thousand meters."

"The SWAT guys are hesitant to shoot."

"Unless they are being shot at."

"They have been now," I said, looking over the open sights of the Kalashnikov.

The sharp bam-bam-bam of an M16 broke the silence. A SWAT member ran down the hill through the brown brush above the mine and threw a second CS grenade into the opening. He rolled to one side and sprinted back to the trees. The grenade exploded.

We could hear the team leader in the trees using the megaphone to order the hostiles to come out.

A hostile with an automatic rifle in the mine fired again, the bullets hitting the branches above us. "So much for giving up," Link said.

CWO Dawson, the helicopter pilot, came up through the trees behind us with a message from the sheriff at the lodge. "A couple of old-timer geologists from the valley told Sheriff Bronski there was a cave-in near the entrance, and the tunnel is accessible for only two hundred feet. There are no side shafts."

"Thanks. Take cover near the Blackhawk. This could get nasty."

I was positioned behind some rocks ahead of Link and off to his left. Link pushed a loaded magazine into the Savage. "When the badasses were cornered in Afghanistan, what did they do?"

"Attacked and died," I said. On the hand-held radio Link relayed the sheriff's message about the mine tunnel to the SWAT leaders.

The time was high noon. Smoke covered the mine entrance. The sky was deep blue above the granite peaks, a scene that God hadn't intended as a setting for death. But they were there, wanting to kill us, and we were here, and our military instincts had taken over.

The high-pitched whine of a motorcycle came from the direction of the mine. A black apparition appeared out of the smoke at the tunnel entrance and a man riding low on a motorcycle burst out from under the sagging timbers, revving a trail bike to maximum power, racing downhill to the flat between the scattered pines, the back tire skidding over rocks, catching itself, throwing dirt. The motorcycle was pointed in the direction of the SWAT officers spread out in the trees.

Three separate shots cracked near the entrance, followed by automatic rifle fire. An explosive blast of orange fire and black smoke blew out laterally and engulfed the rider, the motorcycle, and a large portion of the end of the field. We watched with binoculars as flame, smoke, and dust rolled over the edge of the trees.

"What a bunch of fanatics," Link shouted at me. "They got close to our men in the trees. Maybe got them."

Small arms fire erupted in the pines uphill from the mine entrance. The M16s were banging away, then came the snapping bursts of a Kalashnikov. Link was motionless: only his eyes and the binoculars moved. He scanned the brush around the mine, the trees where the team was, then uphill to the timber.

A burst of rifle fire, then another, broke the silence.

I pulled my head down, checked out the left flank, then the right. These guys could be anywhere.

Link didn't move, but I knew his eyes were scanning anything out of place on the hillside.

The flat crack of a .308 sniper's rifle broke the silence. Link had the discipline of an infantryman during the firefight. He tilted his head and keyed his radio. The woods were quiet except for his commands to the teams. He turned to me. "A hostile was hiding in the trees above the mine. They got the bastard with the .308. He took out one of our guys. Pete."

"Pete?"

"Pete's gone—took a round in the head." Link's eyes and binoculars were back on the side of the mountain.

"Son of a bitch." I kept my eyes on the perimeter.

Ten minutes passed. Nothing moved, except for two vultures high above in the thermals.

"Here comes another one!" I shouted.

Out of the smoke and dust at the mine entrance another motorcyclist came at full throttle. The rider was big and ominous and hunched over the handlebars, a lunatic on his last ride. On his head was a shiny metal round miner's helmet, outdated by a century. He was wearing a bulky explosive suicide vest. The motorcycle was coming straight at us.

Link levered a cartridge into the chamber of the Savage. I was twenty feet from Link and heard the smooth sound of the lever closing on the first round in the old rifle.

"Six hundred yards and coming this way," I said. The barrel of the AK47 was resting on the bark of the old pine log. Link shifted to settle his rifle, laying his cheek over the old wooden stock, his right eye behind the scope, just above the trigger housing.

"Four hundred yards and closing." *Shoot him, Link. Shoot him.* I tensed up on the trigger of the Kalashnikov.

"Three hundred." Link triggered the first round. Dust jumped behind the rider, and the rider jerked at the same time. The bullet grazed him but he kept coming. In a fraction of a second Link levered another cartridge.

At two hundred yards Link fired the second round. A small, white spot appeared on the edge of the windscreen above the right handlebar. The bike skidded, and the rider went off in a series of somersaults. The man stood up, stumbled, and then came running directly toward us. At one hundred and fifty yards Link was settling in with his third round, his head steady and unmoving, low, just behind the scope.

He's still coming. Shoot him, Link, shoot him now. I've seen you do it. He's under a hundred yards. I dropped my head behind the open sights of the AK and started a trigger squeeze of my own. Link beat me to it.

The Savage bucked, and the man exploded in a sheet of flame. We dropped behind the logs as pieces of clothing, dirt, blood, and brush flew over our heads. The metal hard hat he had been wearing rolled on its edge towards us, bumped over some small rocks, then fell against the log in front of me. The inside with the headband was scorched black.

"Let's hope that's the last of them," I said. Link was pushing fresh cartridges into the Savage.

The report came in on the radio that two officers were down, both stunned. One had rock fragments and pieces of branches embedded in his face and shoulder. Link ordered the uphill team to cover the mine entrance. There could be more of them.

"Let's get up there. The officer will have to be evacuated." He stayed on the radio with the two teams. "Keep the tunnel entrance covered and a three hundred and sixty degree vigilance. The hostiles could be anywhere."

The explosion of the second suicide biker had blackened a fifty-yard circle in the dry grass, and flames and smoke rose near the pines. The wind pushed the fire into the brush and the conifers. "Now we have a new problem," I said to Link. "My plane is there in the trees. We also might have a major forest fire on our hands."

"This whole mountain will be on fire in thirty minutes. You may have to get a new plane."

"I'm attached to Whiskey Bravo."

Link ignored me. "There may be more of them in the tunnel, even with the gas grenades."

"There's a shovel and an axe in the plane. I can get them and put out that grass fire now, before it gets into the trees. If you'll cover my ass. Spray the tunnel if anyone shows."

"Go ahead. It's your body." Link radioed the two teams to inform them of my intentions.

I went into the trees and ran straight to Whiskey Bravo. The Kalashnikov was in one hand should another firefight start. No shots came from anywhere. The SWAT teams had the mine entrance and the field covered. The shovel and axe were easy to pull from the plane and I had the grass fire smothered with dirt in minutes.

Link's Blackhawk pilot was in contact with the Forest Service ranger who was talking via UHF with the four jumpers on the fire near Stoddard Peak. The firefighters' last communication stated that they could see two armed men, unknown, approaching them in the open, crossing an old avalanche chute. Then the communication went dead, the ranger said.

"Those firefighters are in jeopardy," Link told the ranger. "If you make contact, tell them to break from the fire, go out into the mountains. Hostiles are moving in their directions. We have SWAT agents with us, and we will attempt to secure your people."

"I'll keep trying to make contact," the ranger said, and disconnected. Link immediately made the decision to take the Blackhawk, myself, and two of the officers to the top of the mountain.

A column of white smoke in the high blue sky gave us the direction for the next assault.

Jammer Swings a Pulaski

"Link, I know that country from the trail across the Slot," I said. "Rocks, open chutes, and patches of thick timber. We should stay on this side of the mountain, find a meadow for landing, and then move up through the trees and over the top. We need surprise. If they have captured the firefighters they may kill them if they hear us coming. It will take longer, but it will be safer for everyone."

"All right, Captain. You always had a sense for ground combat."

The helicopter set down in a small forest clearing a half mile below a low saddle on the main ridge coming off the mountain peak. The fire, now controlled, was on the northern slope in the trees. Faint trails of white smoke faded into the sky on the far side of the ridge. The jumpers had done their job. The four of us climbed up and over the mountain and came out to the edge of a rockslide. Below us was timber, the black of the fire, and smoldering logs inside the burn. We could not see the firefighters. Link said to stay high and circle above the burn.

The high afternoon sky was a deep blue and crystal clear, but a snap came in the wind, forewarning of the coming winter snows, touching these peaks first. The aspens were shedding their leaves in the park-like glades. The climb up the ridge was starting to get to me; must have been the night before without much sleep. Link looked like he could keep going; he was tireless. I first learned that when we were smokejumpers together, fifteen years ago. He runs marathons.

We took cover behind the deer brush and glassed the black ashes of the burn, and the timber around the edges. The quiet was deadly and ominous. Maybe the Forest Service had somehow extricated the jumpers, or had given them the word to get the hell out of here.

The two SWAT officers, trained for mountain work, had bolt action sniper rifles in the .308 caliber, equipped with variable scopes. Black combat knives were attached to their belts. In the helicopter ride to the top, Bittner and Carter had applied new stripes of black and olive-green camo to their faces. Just the whites of their eyes showed. I wouldn't be able to recognize them later in a bar to thank them. They were ultra-alert and I felt a big comfort knowing these two guys were with us.

"There they are," Bittner said. He let his binoculars drop to his chest, turned and whispered to us. "On the other side of the burn." Four firefighters were sitting in the ashes, their hands tied behind their backs. There was no sign of anyone else.

"I see them," Link said. "They've been taken hostage."

We glassed the burned ground, the blackened snags, and the green woods on the edges, back and forth. Twenty minutes passed. The SWAT men were relentless, not dropping their binoculars for a moment, not even to brush bugs away.

"One of the hostiles just walked up to the prisoners," Bittner whispered. "He's armed."

"There must be another one from the tracks we saw in the trail leading away from the mine," I said.

"I figured for two," Link added. "We'll have to wait for both of them to be in sight at one time. Then take them out. Unless they start shooting the hostages."

"They just changed places," Carter whispered.

"Get into firing position," Link told the shooters.

Link was off to the left behind a shrub, and I was laying behind a large rock to the right of our team. "If they both appear together, Bittner, you count off, then you and Carter take them out at the same time, on the count of three."

"Roger," Bittner said.

"If they move, keep shooting, but don't hit the prisoners."

"The range is five hundred and fifty yards," Carter said, not moving his eye from his rifle scope.

We could see that the terrorists had forced the captives to take off their hard hats and yellow fire jackets, throwing them in a pile in the black ash.

"Both in sight," Carter whispered.

"On three," Bittner said. "One, two, three." Two rifles cracked together. I was watching with binoculars and saw both hostiles fall. Suddenly, one stood up and picked up his rifle. One of the captive firefighters leaped to his feet and jumped on the bad ass, who was far from disabled, and who was leveling his rifle at the captives. The jumper was struggling with the hostile. The hostile was putting up a good fight, even though Bittner must have winged him with the .308. We could see two people grappling.

"Get down there," Link commanded. "Run and spread out!" We ran as if the firefighters' lives depended on us. We leaped over logs, rocks, and clumps of brush, moving downhill as fast as we could run. The distance to the burn was five hundred yards. I held the Kalashnikov tighter, switched to automatic fire, and took the safety off. One of the jumpers in a gray T-shirt was swinging on the hostile.

When we got to the burn a smokejumper was standing at the edge of the black holding a yellow jacket, waving both arms. He looked familiar, and I knew immediately who it was—Jammer Deming.

"Link! Casey!" Jammer shouted, as we ran up to the hostages. "You saved our butts. How did you find us? We were about to eat these freaks for breakfast. The one over there went down fast. Nice shot. There's another over there, laying over that log. He's dead now. You winged him with the long shot." Vintage Jammer.

Link grabbed Jammer's hand, shook it hard, and then pulled Jammer down. I slapped Jammer on the back, then realizing other hostiles may be around, dropped to my knees, the AK pointed toward the trees. Carter took up a covering position behind a boulder. Bittner began to untie the other men.

"There could be more of them," Link said.

"Just like the old days," Jammer said, rubbing the bruise on his shoulder.

"We knew your ass was in trouble." I smiled.

"I had the ropes untied, and was trying to figure how to take out both of them, then you guys came out of nowhere and shot them. How did you know we were here?"

"It's a long story."

"I'll bet. We didn't know these people, or what they were up to, but they were going to kill us."

Link ordered Carter and Bittner out in two directions. "Stay alert. There may be more of them."

"We weren't this violent before," I said. "I'll tell you the whole story. But let's have some coffee. Did you bring any?"

"Of course," Jammer said,

Bittner and Carter separated and kept up the security. One hostile had a bullet hole in his chest. Another body was draped over a log. One of his arms was bent back where a bullet had almost taken it off above the elbow. Link prodded the hostile's chest with the end of the barrel of his Savage.

"This is the one Jammer was punching. For Christ's sake, Casey, look at this!" I ran over and helped Link pull the corpse off the log. "He's stuck on something," Link said. We jerked the body loose of the log and rolled him to the side. The axe end of a Pulaski was buried in his chest.

"A Pulaski! Who in the world would do something like this? Hoo—rahh!" Link said, and exhaled with a nervous laugh. He straightened up next to the body. The protruding wood handle of the fire tool was sticking straight in the air. Link stared at Jammer, and shook his head.

Knowing Link as I did, he wasn't worrying about the hostile, whose sternum was split wide open, but how he was going to phrase the after-action report.

"You showed up just in time," Jammer said. His blonde hair was straggled, his gray T-shirt ripped, most of it stained with blood. A red welt rose on his chest where the hostile had gotten in a blow with his rifle butt. "You guys are great shots. You winged him on the arm just enough to give me an opening."

"I've never seen a Pulaski used this way," Bittner said, keeping his eyes on the tree line.

"Been in tougher fights with loggers in bars." Jammer smiled at Bittner. "Should have joined the Green Berets with Casey and Link, where it was a hell-of-a-lot safer."

Link shook his head. "A Pulaski," he muttered.

The other three firefighters were untied and conversations were at the crescendo level. In moments everyone knew what had happened down on the river, and at the old mine tunnel.

"This action has made me thirsty," I said. "Let's see what the modern firefighter brings to the table."

Jammer was drinking water from a plastic jug. He passed the jug around.

"This is it?" I said. "No Kool-Aid."

"Just water."

Link shook his head. "We've got to move." He radioed the Blackhawk pilot behind the mountain and cleared the Forest Service helicopter to pick up the smokejumpers and their gear.

"What about those assholes we shot?" Bittner asked, to no one in particular.

"What about them?" I said,

"What will we do with the bodies?"

"Fuck the bodies," Jammer said. "Let the wolves eat them."

"The wolves won't touch them," I said.

Jammer—wildcatter, logger, and smokejumper—hadn't changed. Thank God. He saved his own skin and the lives of the other jumpers. Jammer was as tough as ever.

I told Jammer that after the fire on the Yellowstone I had met up again with Baker, and we saw some of these hostiles in a bar. Didn't think he'd care about Baker's romances. *He married China Brown, and I suspect that was going just fine.* He said he knew Baker had a permanent job with the FAA. He gave me a long look. Jammer was going to say something, then stopped.

The afternoon was waning. A steady wind rolled the top branches of the firs. The sun made the grass and the green buck brush too bright to look at without sunglasses. The four firefighters and Link and I were reclined behind logs, up on one or two elbows, keeping vigilant, but catching our breath from the lull in the action. Bittner and Carter were again on security watch, out from the perimeter in opposite directions, behind boulders and brush, impossible to see. The magazines of their sniper rifles were topped off. The side arms they carried could be accessed in a moment. I kept the Kalashnikov ready.

Two ravens landed on a burnt log fifty feet from our circle and began squawking. We had dragged the bodies of the terrorists into the shade under the branches of some low spruces. The ravens knew they were there.

"You think we got all of them?" Link asked.

"Good question. I'd answer with a no," I said. "These hostiles, domestic and imports, have been pressured in the cities and they've come out here where they think they're safe to store explosives and armament."

"We will have eight body bags after this fight," Link said. "You have a tally of four, my team has three, and Jammer has one. Our headquarters people have been following others around the country. The ones here may have escaped from the mine to the woods. After the Forest Service picks up the jumpers, we'll go back to the mine, and look around."

"You mean these firefights are not over. You and I should have left that action in Afghanistan."

"Don't kid yourself." Link laughed. "Next, the mine."

"My plane is there in the trees."

"Look it over for bullet holes," Link said.

We were at the edge of the burn waiting for the Forest Service helicopter to pick up the jumpers. I told Link about meeting Fauod Saeed, witnessing an envelope exchange between him and Hanson Porter, then seeing the two of them in a bar in Ketchum, and Fauod again at the Rustlers Noose. The man was flying the green Cessna. That had to be the same plane landing at the mine, although I didn't see it there, only tracks in the grass.

"Were any of these people the ones you saw in the bar?"

"The white guy at the top of the ridge on the game trail could have been, the one carrying the old Army carbine and the grenades. The dark ones who shredded themselves could have been them. There's not much to look at."

"I'll call Audra and have her check out Saeed." And he did.

"Domestic extremists linked up with Middle East jihadists," I said. "What a combination."

"The Middle East is full of mountains." Link continued, "Remember the eco-terrorist threats a decade ago. These people were extremists, pushing the environmental credos. They were spiking the trees in northern Idaho and Montana, driving six-inch spikes at four and five foot levels in trees on logging sites. The logs went through the head saws in the mills and sent pieces of steel flying like shell fragments around the workers. They finally did themselves in when they resorted to explosives and blew themselves to smithereens in the process."

"I remember that well. They weren't jihadists. They were domestic eco-freaks. Nothing compared to the present day terrorists."

Audra radioed back. "Fauod Saeed is a suspected terrorist the FBI has been watching in the South. His name is also an alias. He was last seen in Texas, and from there the trail went cold. He is supposedly wealthy with black market oil money."

"Well, I've seen him here. Did she check out the green Cessna? Baker has the tail number," I said.

"She did. The N number the pilot gave Baker is a fake. FAA in Washington says that tail number belonged to a Navion, long since dismantled."

"Not surprising," I said, "that both his name and tail number are aliases. Link, I think Fauod is out here somewhere. He looked to me like the type of guy who is tough enough to survive anywhere."

"Well, if you insist on going elk hunting," Link said, "get yourself something more powerful than a longbow, although, by God, you did well with it."

We heard an air-slapping sound and a helicopter came through a low saddle on the ridgeline. The aircraft was smaller than the Blackhawk and it landed in a meadow next to the burn. The pilot, dressed in a blue jump suit and wearing the customary Ray Bans, climbed out, came over and introduced himself. He announced that because of the elevation he could only take two fire fighters at a time, drop them off at the Phantom Ranch, and then make a final pick-up for the gear.

Link nodded. "Stay clear of the Luddendorf mine. There are FBI officers and possible hostiles still up there."

The helicopter climbed straight up above the black trees of the burn, then descended into the valley. I thought of the Medevac in the Hindu Kush, and of Mike, and wished he was with us in the mountains.

Link scanned the trees with binoculars. He looked like a combat fighter, even behind that streaked camo. *A Savage Ninety-Nine! He made some nice shots on the nutcase on the motorcycle.*

The 800-Foot Runway

The mystery plane did not appear at the lodge in the morning. Sheriff Bronski and his deputies were ready. Bronski requested more help from Cascade to guard the lodge and the outfitters' camp on the river.

Link radioed for the Blackhawk, secure on the other side of the mountain, to pick up our team in the meadow next to the burn. The pilot responded instantly, came down this side of the tall firs, kept the rotors moving, and we dropped our heads and ran for the open door. The SWAT officers stayed hidden in the brush until Link gave them the order to withdraw. Bittner opened the bolt of his .308, followed Carter aboard, and declared no hostiles were moving out there in the timber, or they would have knocked them down. He loved his job.

"Let's go back and clear the mine shaft," Link ordered, turning to the pilot. "Set the Blackhawk down at the far end of the field from the mine, behind the trees."

Rescue squads used robots to check out hostiles and booby traps, and I suggested this to Link.

"Keep your positions," Link radioed the teams. "We don't have the luxury of a robot so the uphill team will sweep the mine on foot. Clear first with more CS, then proceed to the cave-in. Check out the mine shaft for more hostiles, noncombatants, or bodies. Keep your eyes open for wires and booby traps. Paperwork and files may also be rigged. After the mine is cleared we'll take out Pete's body."

The two SWAT officers who had superficial face injuries from the first blast volunteered to throw CS grenades into the mine. They did, then backed away from the entrance. Nothing. Two officers from the team, their automatic rifles ready, were behind them. They waited ten minutes.

Stan, a demolition expert and the other two riflemen, advanced into the mine. Seventy-five yards into the mine Stan radioed back they had discovered several hundred pounds of explosives. The cache included C4, ammonium nitrate, detonating devices, sacks of steel shot, fuses, backpacks of rifle ammunition and incendiary delay bombs. They also discovered canned goods and water containers for a short stay in the mountains. Enough materiel was stashed in the old mine to create a lot of havoc and destruction.

The green 206, if it *was* the plane parked next to Whiskey Bravo at the airport, had been busy hauling people and munitions.

"Check thoroughly for non-combatants, dead or alive, in the mine," Link ordered. "Once you've made a complete inspection, call me when the mine is clear."

The forensic experts would investigate the site in detail, but Link wanted the explosives detonated or taken out of the mountains. The safer method would be to destroy the munitions in place. The hostiles might return and he didn't have enough manpower to post guards at the mine for a round–the-clock watch.

"Don't forget my booby traps," I said to Link.

Link turned to Carter. "Have you seen the grenades Casey rigged on the trees?"

"Saw them," Carter said.

"Let's see how good you are with that .308. Be sure everyone is off the flat, then go back a hundred yards and shoot the grenades. They're too dangerous to reinsert the pins."

"Piece of cake," Carter said. He set off across the field, took a sitting position in the grass at one hundred and fifty yards and hit each grenade, knocking it off the cloth wrap, and both exploded when the spoon was released by the bullet from the sniper's rifle.

"Blow the explosives and everything else in place," Link ordered Stan. The area was evacuated, and a huge blast collapsed the old mine. The concussion knocked me back into a tree. After the smoke and dust cleared, the mine entrance was a pile of dirt and broken timbers.

The red plane was still back in the trees near the end of the field, a safe distance from the mine blast. I checked it for holes. Two bullets, possible ricochets, had perforated the bottom of the fuselage, ruining the satellite phone, but hadn't severed anything that hindered flight. I patched one hole through the wing with duct tape. One of the SWAT officers was a mechanic and he inspected the oil gauge and the wiring. "No oil leaks, sir," he said. "Start it up. I think the gauge will work just fine." I did, and the gauge was operational. We pushed the plane out from between the trees onto the grass, both ends of the field now blackened by the suicide bomb blasts. I threw the Kalashnikov and the camo vest into the back seat and started the engine. The Lycoming kicked over immediately. All was working well. *Damn, what a nice sound.*

The midafternoon sun was bright and warm in the big pines. It had been a long night with little sleep. My thoughts were wandering.

If Mike had been with us he would have agreed with our plan of attack. Terrorists gave no quarter to innocents and combatants alike. He would have whacked the bastards, just as Link and I had done.

There were no prisoners, Mike.

Link was leaving these mountains in a government helicopter. I was happy flying Whiskey Bravo out. The takeoff on the grassy flat was going to be short, eight hundred feet give or take. Large pines off the end of the field were positioned like a line of sentinels. I closed the window of the airplane, placed my left hand on the throttle, and slowly taxied up the field to where the first suicide biker had detonated himself. Two magpies were jumping around over the scorched grass, screeching, and picking at shreds of bloody clothing.

The plane bumped easily through the grass. The propeller revolved slowly, flashing in the sun. The tail wheel and rudder responded smoothly to pedal movements when a marmot hole or two appeared in the grass. I had turned the plane to face the tall pines, ready for a short field power take-off when Link walked up. He circled his finger in the air, motioned with his fingers on his lips that he wanted to talk. I was the team commander in Afghanistan, but now he was my boss—that is, when it came to killing terrorists. Link approached the plane.

I dropped the side panel.

"You owe me a whiskey," he said.

"When we get to town."

"We will have to write independent reports on this adventure."

"After-action reports, we called them," I said.

"Come into my office tomorrow, and we'll do the paper work."

"I'll be there."

A strange expression came over his face, and he made that noise with his mouth. "There is something I want to ask you about," Link said.

"Ask away." I reached forward and adjusted the radio to the back-country frequency.

"The authorities are still working on solving the case of those two bikers found dead last month at a rest stop in Wyoming. What do you know about that?"

"Hell, I'm a business man," I said. "I don't travel in that dark world."

"It follows you around," he said. "Look what happened here in the mountains."

I had not told a soul about passing through Wyoming that night, but oddly enough, Link brought it up. I thought that criminal act would fall under the jurisdiction of the local Wyoming sheriff, but somehow Link was involved. He was the special agent in charge for the FBI and he covered that territory. More than drugs had been involved with the bikers down there in Wyoming. They could have been engaged in money laundering, or were under surveillance as domestic terrorists.

Why was he talking to me about this now?

"Yes, I heard about that. Read it in the papers," I said.

"The authorities reported the shootings looked like the work of a professional hit man," Link said, pulling the brim of his hat lower against the sun, and giving me a serious look. "Or a Green Beret."

"That bad, eh? Hard to believe." I smiled at Link, and then scanned the instrument panel. "The TV commentator claimed it was a shoot-out over a drug deal."

"What do they know?" he said. "The surviving biker testified that a front man came into the bar before the SUV arrived. He was driving a silver Porsche and carried a small automatic. The biker didn't see the license number in the dark. The authorities want to talk to the man in the Porsche."

"What authorities you talking about?"

"The Wyoming sheriff."

The lingering smell of CS gas and gunpowder drifted through the pines in the afternoon air. The smell was pungent.

"There's wind coming up the creek," I said. "This bird can't linger here much longer. This is a short field. You and your chopper can take off anytime. I think your pilot is asleep."

Link continued, ignoring me, adjusting the leather strap on his shoulder holster. He did that a lot. "The investigation showed the bikers were shot numerous times with a small-caliber pistol."

"Okay, so they were," I said, feigning impatience, going through an instrument check on the airplane panel. "Maybe they deserved it."

"You pack a little Beretta, don't you?"

"At one time I did."

"Just for the record, where is it?"

"For the record—gave it to a ranger down at Benning," I lied. "He was leaving for Afghanistan."

"Some of the hostiles we just encountered had small pistols." Link winked. "Could have been them that shot those bikers."

"Could've been."

"Just for the record, where did you keep it?"

"Now, don't put this in your official record, but in my car."

"Well, at least you're covered."

"That little .25 was for close-in stuff. Remember."

"Which you're good at."

"It's easier than carrying a goddamn longbow," I said, and gave Link a big smile.

The wind coming up the creek was increasing. The plane shuddered. Link noticed the shaking and moved back from the window.

"Keep those arrows handy," he said, laughing.

"Only you can laugh at that. That's in the same category as that old rifle of yours. I was worried you couldn't hit those bastards on a motorcycle. Put that in your report."

"That you were worried?"

"That you were waiting until they were close enough to shake hands."

Link laughed.

"Are you going to keep me here all day, answering your official questions?"

Link stepped back from the plane. "I'll call you tomorrow at your office. We have a lot of red tape to complete." He was using an olive-drab handkerchief to wipe the smeared camouflage off his face.

I moved the ailerons up and down with the control stick. "He's out there somewhere."

"Who?" Link asked.

"Saeed."

"We have our agents looking," Link answered, louder, over the rising wind, "for him and the green airplane."

"The green airplane is probably in a hangar on somebody's back-forty."

"Yes." Link nodded. "Get out of here."

"Clear the prop!" I shouted, looking at Link.

Link walked to the Blackhawk, and turned to watch my takeoff. I had my feet on the brakes. When the prop revolutions were high enough to bring the tail of the plane up, I turned in the cockpit and gave Link a big grin, then the V sign with my fingers, and released the foot brakes. Grass and pine needles blew back against the trees.

The plane cleared the pines by fifty feet. Whiskey Bravo banked into a 180-degree turn. I leveled the wings and flew back over the field on the flat. Below were two fire-scorched patches of grass, one downhill from the old mine and the other next to the boulders by the trees. That's the spot where Link and I made our last stand. Those idiots didn't stand a chance. I rocked the wings twice for Link, pushed the throttle another quarter-arc forward to gain elevation and took a heading southwest to Owyhee Crossing.

Three hours of daylight remained when I landed the Husky at the airstrip along the river. The weather was clear, winds aloft were light, and the oil pressure gauge was working just fine. Helped along by a steak and a glass of bourbon, falling asleep at my house at Owyhee Crossing was easy.

Monday morning at the office was anticlimactic. I called Liz at the hospital. She said Alec was in intensive care.

Link and I were to meet again the next afternoon to tie up loose ends. I radioed Joe Hooker at his outfitters' camp and told him I'd have to delay the rest of the hunt for two or three weeks. There were some details to wrap up with the authorities. Hooker had already heard about the shoot-out on the Middle Fork. Word travels fast in that remote country.

At my desk in the morning, I had just stirred up a strong espresso, and picked up the monthly operating statement when Tony tapped on the edge of the open door. Without waiting for a nod of acknowledgment, he came into the office and sat down.

"Heard the news. You and Jammer created quite a sensation in the backcountry. Don't know the details yet, but the badasses didn't stand a chance."

"You're just jealous you weren't there," I said.

"The story is out that Jammer dispatched one of them insurgents single-handed without a weapon."

"He had a weapon all right. He used a Pulaski. Some day when you have a stronger stomach and three tequilas in you, I'll tell you the details."

"That could be today after work."

"Could be."

Tony continued, "The plant is running well. We made some adjustments on the new timber planer. That damn thing is heavy, might have to take some down-time to put in heavier footings."

"Do that on the weekend. Don't lose any production," I said.

Tony nodded. He was a skilled manager—had a desk but didn't use it.

Ellen came into the office with some up-to-date reports and phone messages. Am I a good judge of people or what, I said to myself, thinking back to the day I hired her, ten years ago, when she walked into my office and said she was good, and wanted a job in accounting.

"You and Tony have been keeping this place humming."

"Of course we have. Here are the calls. The message on top is from a woman named Liz. I thought you might want to see that first," Ellen said, a question in her voice. "She was very nice." Ellen wanted to find out more. I gave her the knowing smile.

"Thanks."

At the doorway Ellen turned and gave me a questioning look. "Don't forget the call to Liz. That one sounded important."

"Yes, I'll take care of that."

My mind shifted from the accounting numbers to Liz. I thought about Alec and the shoot-out. But not for long.

The office window was open. A plane at full throttle was lifting off from runway one-three. The pilot had dropped the nose several degrees from a climbing attitude and was flying intentionally low over the plant and directly over my office. Steve, the mechanic, was checking out the oil pressure gauge on Whiskey Bravo. I had the feeling I was going to need it.

I paused for a moment thinking about more questions Link would have on the drunken bikers.

Hell, he might think I shot those guys.

The little Beretta and the biker's gun were rusting away in the sand at the bottom of the Snake.

Return to Phantom

Steve Mason dipped a small brush into a can of solvent. He was patching the bullet holes in the fuselage of Whiskey Bravo when I walked into his hangar. The odor of oil permeated the air, and the hangar had the cool feel of a well-managed shop. Steve, a certified FAA aviation mechanic, had been taking care of Whiskey Bravo, as well as other local planes, for years. Besides the Husky, two other planes were in the hangar: a yellow Super Cub and a Cessna 182. Randy, Steve's assistant mechanic, was on a short ladder, working on the engine of the 182. He had canvas tarps spread over the concrete floor below the engine. "Your plane looks like it went through World War Two," Randy said. "We'll wash it up for you."

"Thanks. I'll be flying back into the Salmon River country soon."

The hangar door was partially open and across the runway I could see the orange windsock stirring from the noon breeze. "You can take your plane up," Steve said. "The paint is dry. Just stay away from people with guns."

"You're telling me. Maybe the plane should be painted in camouflage colors."

"Then even I couldn't find you." Steve laughed, wiping his hands on a shop towel.

I walked around the plane, moved the ailerons up and down with my fingers, caressed the rubber tread on the oversized tundra tires, flexed the rudder back and forth with my hands, then the elevators, then knelt and took a final look at the tail-wheel springs, stood up and for the second time looked over the whole plane. *Can't be too cautious.* I wasn't asking for any more trouble, and someone might start shooting at me.

My cell phone rang: Link was on the line.

"Casey, can you come into my office? We need to write a report on the skirmish in the backcountry, especially the actions you took before the FBI and the sheriff got there. The authorities want to know in detail how those four people were taken out. About ten o'clock?"

Actions I took? They're calling them "people." I'd tell them exactly—two with a .45 Colt and two of the bastards with a longbow and hunting arrows. Let's hope no bleeding hearts would be reading about this action. "Sure, but I need to clear my desk again."

"If ten o'clock will work for you, this may take several hours."

"I know. I don't think we took out all of them," I said.

"And you think that why?"

"He's still out there."

"Who, Saeed?" Link asked.

"Yes, he wasn't in the gun battles, and I got that feeling again in my neck."

"The feeling you get from drinking too much bourbon?"

"No, the Taliban feeling."

"Okay, we have agents checking out Saeed," Link mumbled. "Do you want me to schedule a doctor to examine your neck?"

"Hey, that creepy feeling saved our asses more than once."

"I know. Just kidding."

"I think Saeed's the leader of the cell," I said, "and we know terrorists come here and use domestic nut cases to carry out their missions, and their mission is to kill Americans. Insurgents, call them that if you will, are slipping into this country as instructors. These people are experts in explosives and mayhem."

"We haven't located the green plane. And the tail number was bogus," Link said.

"Have you checked out Mr. Hanson Porter the Third in Ketchum?"

"We have. The money transfer you witnessed was from a real estate agent in Houston. Looks legit so far, but we are continuing to investigate the money laundering channels. We suspect these funds are profits from oil operations in the Middle East."

"What are they up to? We found a lot of explosives for a remote cave."

"We'll try to figure it out tomorrow," Link said, and hung up.

I pocketed the cell phone and jumped into the pickup truck, thinking I'd accomplish some business.

It was a mid-October day, a perfect sky with no clouds. The leaves on the poplars along the river were turning brown, and flocks of white pelicans paddled carelessly in the river eddies. Indian summer days. The snows and rainy weather along the Snake River plain were a month away.

The distance from the end of the runway to our plant was two miles. Inside the company gate, four trucks carrying lumber were parked, one behind the other, the drivers in their cabs, anxious to be unloaded. We didn't keep them waiting. That wasn't good business. From the large storage sheds two other carriers were moving lumber to the main plant, choreographing their movements for wood species, lengths, and widths for the production press lines.

In the shipping yard at the far end of the plant two of the largest lifts were loading eighty-foot structural fir beams onto over-sized flat-bed truck trailers, destined for a ski lodge in Colorado. These long-length high-stress laminated timbers were our specialty product, and their sales provided high-end revenue for the operation. Few other wood products plants were as diverse in manufacturing and sales.

Tony and Ellen were halfway down the hall to my office when the phone rang on my desk. Liz was on the line. "Alec didn't make it."

"Oh God, Liz. Where are you? I'll be right there."

"At the hospital. He lost too much blood. There was an infection."

"I'll be there within the hour."

I glanced at the yellow-noted phone messages on the desk, quickly stacked the business statements in a short pile, and slammed the file cabinet drawer with a metallic bang. Laura, the receptionist, swung her chair around and stared at me, looking for an exclamation.

"Alec just died," I told her.

She said, "I'm sorry." She didn't know who Alec was, and went back to her typing.

Another unarmed innocent American. Alec—killed at his lodge. *He's dead and it's my fault. I led them on that chase, down to the river, then to the lodge.*

In an hour I was at the hospital. Liz stood at the end of a hallway in the hospital. When she saw me, she ran up and fell into my arms. I held her. Neither of us said a word.

"I'm sorry. Really sorry," I said.

"They wanted to do an autopsy. I won't do it. Never. I know how he died.'"

Her eyes were red, but she had made herself up, and put on fresh lipstick. She was almost as tall as me, in heels, and even in a moment like this, I thought she looked great.

"It was my fault," I said. "I led them down to the river."

"It wasn't you. They were coming to the ranch anyway. They would have killed us all if you hadn't taken them out."

Now my eyes were watering.

"In a few days I'm taking Alec back to Nevada, Casey. He was raised there."

Those dirty sons-of-bitches.

Liz put her arms around me again. I held her close, tighter than before.

She moved away, her lips brushed my cheek, close to my ear. "Take me back to the river, Casey. Take me tomorrow."

"Of course, I will." I held her for a moment. It was happening too fast. She wasn't close to her husband when he died. Maybe they were drifting apart. Now wasn't the time to ask her.

"I need to pick up Alec's personal things, iPad, brief case, and some of his clothes." She was trying to explain something else to me. Had their marriage been coming to an end?

"We'll take the red plane. The oil gauge is working and the bullet holes are fixed. We can bring back one hundred pounds, plus our overnight gear, which we will be taking in. Shall I pick you up at the Boise airport?"

"I can be at your hangar at Owyhee Crossing at two o'clock," she said. "We can leave from there. We might need the extra time."

"Can I take you to dinner, Liz?"

"I'm exhausted. I need to get my head straight and make some phone calls. Let's meet at two o'clock at your hangar." She kissed me, and I knew she was thinking about the two of us, going off together into the Idaho backcountry. Again.

Tony Mendez called on the cell phone. I told him I could make it back in time tonight to the company house for a managers' meeting and margaritas. "Bring Ellen, Laura, and the shift supervisors if they can be there on the short notice." I was asking, not ordering, but Tony said they'd all be there. I knew he would get it done. Later, that evening, after margaritas and grilled steaks, with all of us sitting comfortably on the porch watching the sunset, I told them the story of the fire on Stoddard Peak, how it got started, the terrorists, and how Jammer swung the Pulaski. The looks of their faces showed how far I had strayed back into the military days.

The next morning I was in Link's office, sitting at a side desk, and working on my second cup of coffee. Link handed me a draft of the FBI report, and I shook my head over the amount of bureaucratic red tape. Outside his office, phones rang incessantly at the administration desks. The phones didn't ring that much in our sales department on a good day. I made a mental reminder to ask the sales people to pick up the pace.

Sheriff Bronski called three times in as many hours, asking for more details on the shoot-out at the old mine. He also wanted to relieve his deputies at the mine and the lodge on the river, and bring them back to civilization. On his last call, I advised the sheriff that a wrangler friend, Joe Hooker, was riding in from his hunting camp upstream on the Middle Fork, and he was looking after the stock, at least until Liz could make some plans. Could they stay a day or two until Hooker arrived, or until Liz and I flew in? He said they could.

"Link, I'm flying Liz back into the Phantom Ranch tomorrow."

He turned from the computer screen and gave me the kind of look your professor might give you if you forgot your assignment. "What?"

"She wants to collect Alec's personal belongings, and then make arrangements for services in Nevada."

"Be careful, Captain. You only have nine lives." Link's dark eyes were giving me a hard look.

Link had gained some wrinkles around his eyes from squinting in the desert sun. He was one hell of a shot with a semiautomatic handgun. The

Army taught him that skill, dispatching hostage-takers at short range, in the dark. Now I could add to his list of accomplishments, proficiency with an old .300 Savage at long range. He wasn't going to settle down to a life behind a desk. Not yet, that wasn't Link's style.

"Where's Fauod Saeed?" I said. "We haven't connected him yet to the guys we just took out, but he could be back in those mountains, camping somewhere, and fishing at my favorite lake."

"Don't be funny. He should be considered dangerous," Link grumbled, turning back to his computer. "You and Liz be careful back there."

I finished the paperwork with the law enforcement agencies in plenty of time to meet her at the plane.

Sheriff Bronski and his deputy from Cascade were also at the office to take my statement. "Assailant met death by a hunting arrow," Bronski said, attempting to record the correct word on the computer screen. "Self-defense, huh? That's the first time that's happened in this part of Idaho. Right through the heart."

"Anything else?" I asked.

"One more thing, Mr. McConnell," the deputy said. "Will you show me how to shoot a longbow? I keep missing elk."

Fightin' General Joe Hooker

Liz was standing next to the red airplane when I drove up. I was lucky to be with her again, even under these circumstances. When I walked up Liz put on her aviator sunglasses, touched her hand to her chin, smiled, and struck a jaunty Amelia Earhart aviator pose in front of the propeller. She was as pretty as Amelia.

White nylon ropes, attached to a ring at the end of each wing, held the plane to the blacktop. The tops of the long brown grasses between the tarmac and the yellow willows swayed back and forth from the wind coming up from the bank. Small waves on the water shimmered in the sun. The breeze was a crosswind to runway one-three, but not enough to be a bother on take-off. High white cumulus clouds covered most of the blue sky to the north, and the same clouds mirrored themselves over the Owyhees to the south.

I set my overnight bag next to hers on the tarmac. "Are you ready for this?"

"Of course. Do you know how to fly this bird?"

"I do. The weather is holding. We'll fly across Chamberlain Basin and the main Salmon River, then up the Middle Fork to Phantom Creek and your ranch. A flight plan has been filed with FAA Control, so they'll know where we are going. Link knows too. We can reach him from the radio at your ranch. I also have a new satellite phone, if I can get out from the canyon."

"Cross your fingers," Liz said.

I secured our overnight bags in the compartment behind the rear seat. We both brought light parkas, stowing them in the back. Weather was changeable in Idaho in October. A survival pack was a standard item in the baggage space. On top of the duffel went a pistol belt with the .45, this time with a magazine inserted in the grip housing, and two extra magazines on the belt. It was hunting season and I laid a scope-mounted .270 Browning bolt-action rifle on top of the gear. The wood longbow was stowed at the house for another time, another battle.

"Still thinking about the terrorists, I see." Liz watched me place the pistol and the rifle in the back of the plane. She gave me one of her infrequent serious looks. "I thought you and Link killed them all."

"I'm sure we did. An old habit. It's also hunting season along the Middle Fork." I didn't tell her about Fauod Saeed and the creepy feeling in the back of my neck. "We'll be flying across Lick Creek summit, over the South Fork, Chamberlain Basin, and Cold Meadows—beautiful country." I also didn't tell her I would be looking for plane tracks in the grass at Phantom.

Getting into the rear seat of the plane was equivalent to doing a chin-up on the inside overhead strut of the fuselage. The Husky had dual controls so a pilot could fly the plane from the back seat. Liz seated herself comfortably, her hand touching the control stick and her feet on the rudder pedals.

"Don't play with those in flight, or we'll be doing aerobatics. This plane isn't certified for loops, and neither am I." I handed her the headset. She placed the band over her head, smoothing out the ruffles in her hair, then adjusted the mouthpiece. I showed her how to change the channels and the volume.

"You've been doing aerobatics, certified or not."

The plane was equipped with a lap and shoulder safety harness for each seat. I reached over and pulled the webbing across her thighs and clicked it in place. She swung her shoulders to the left, tightening the nylon strap, and I noticed the top of her blouse had parted, revealing the top lace of a red bra. "You better button up, or we may have to land in the parking lot of the No Tell Motel. With this plane I can do that."

"Behave yourself, and lower your eyes," she said, and smiled, maybe knowing all along the buttons were open. She fastened them. "I'm ready."

I reached over her and tested the tightness of her shoulder harness. It was secure enough, and when I moved back, my cheek brushed against her neck.

"What is this, the shoulder-harness move?"

"You could call it that."

"I'm paying for this trip. Let's go," she said.

"You are not paying for anything." The propeller caught immediately and I felt the wind from the prop and the adrenaline rush.

The cockpit intercom was open. "It's just you and me again, kid. Just like Paris. Or was it Sun Valley?" My eyes were on the sky in front of the plane, watching for white pelicans. The pelicans loved the islands around the airfield.

"It was Sun Valley. You couldn't fly this plane to Paris. The next time we meet, let's fly this pretty plane to the Bahamas."

"We will. That will be our next adventure."

With one foot hard on the right brake pedal, still on the ground, I turned the plane in a 360-degree continuous arc, checking the sky high and low for air raffic. The southern Idaho sky was empty, except for a dozen pelicans following the river upstream.

I switched to the flight control channel, announced to the world we were taking off, pushed the throttle down, the wheels left the tarmac and we were in the air.

The altimeter showed four thousand feet, five thousand feet, then six thousand, climbing to clear the sagebrush foothills to the north. Liz was quiet, looking through the right window, watching the river and the farms receding in the distance. She looked relaxed, but there was a faraway look in her eyes. She glanced up, catching me watching her, then turned back to the window.

The GPS direction indicator on the panel showed a heading of zero-four-two for the flight to Phantom.

The Lycoming moved us along at a steady pace. We gained altitude and flew up and over Lick Creek Summit. Below the plane were dark green serpentine mountain streams, the water catching the sun's reflections and flashing back at us in the sky. The shadow of the plane on the ground raced across the meadows, jumping from log to log, from rocks and grass, keeping up with us, then disappearing in the forest, and coming back again on the sides of the basalt cliffs.

We crossed the pass and looked down on the weathered buildings of Brown's old logging camp on Zena Creek. In another ten minutes

Whiskey Bravo was flying over the canyon of the South Fork. I added more power, leaned the mixture and in front of us loomed the granite mass of Mosquito Peak, at eighty-eight hundred feet. I told Liz about a fire in the forest near there one summer. I remember sitting on a rock after the fire was out and watching a golden eagle making circles a few feet above me. The eagle, finding nothing below but a dusty firefighter wearing a silver hardhat and holding a short-handle shovel, dipped his wings, screeched once and disappeared into a distant canyon.

Liz and I kept up an intercom conversation about the beauty of the mountains, the rivers far below, and I told her about the secret lakes nobody visited, or even knew about, small purple-blue lakes surrounded by tall spruces, tucked below high rocky ledges and talus slopes where the noon sun barely touched. We flew over the airstrips at Chamberlain Basin and Cold Meadows. A white plane sat at the end of the runway at Cold Meadows, a chartered plane probably, bringing hunters into their elk camps.

We dropped to five hundred feet above the treetops, an altitude I was comfortable with. I couldn't feel any afternoon air spilling over the low ridges to push us down. We flew over a timbered basin, and came up on Phantom Meadows. There was an outline of an old airfield here once. I told Liz that the strip had been abandoned in the forties and pines were growing tall on what had been the runway. But there were a few small meadows here and there where a gutsy pilot could land. We circled the basin, but I could see no activity.

"What are you looking for?" Liz asked me over the intercom.

"Any tracks in the grass where a plane might have set down on these meadows."

"Haven't seen a thing."

"Nor I."

"Clint, rest his soul, some years ago hunted elk on Phantom Creek, where it flows into the Salmon. We named our lodge for the creek."

"That's rugged country toward the Salmon. You picked a good name for your ranch. We'll turn south over these mountains and I'll show you the field where the badasses were hiding explosives."

In twenty minutes we were flying over the two blackened patches of grass where the crazies on motorcycles had blown themselves to pieces.

Then I showed her the switchbacks on the trail below the Slot where the first ambush took place, and the second one on the old elk trail, below the top of the long ridge.

I banked the plane and Liz looked out and down from the left window. The plane was doing a slow circle in the sky.

"Oh, my God," she said.

I straightened the plane and directly below us was the trail the killers took to the river. She knew the awful outcome from there.

We dropped to the Big Creek Canyon, flew downstream to the Middle Fork, crossed above one timbered ridge after the other, as they all dropped steeply to the river. Ahead was the Phantom Ranch and we flew over it to check for traffic, horses on the runway, or maybe more intruders. We counted eight horses in the corral. Two were Hooker's.

I had called Hooker earlier on the satellite phone from the office, and told him of our delay in the hunt, and asked if he could ride to Liz's ranch and take care of the stock. He had already heard of the shootout on the river, and said he'd watch the ranch.

A faint wisp of smoke rose from the chimney in the main lodge. The runway was still in the sunlight, the windsock limp. I did a one-eighty in the canyon above the river and lowered the flaps for a landing.

It was a nice three-point touch-down with the Husky, and I stretched against the seat belt and shoulder harness to look over the nose and the spinning prop as we bumped our way over the grass for a tie-down next to the rail fence.

"Nice landing!" Liz said.

"Thanks." I didn't tell her it was one of my better ones.

"Someday, will you teach me to fly?" She was doing a chin-up on the overhead strut and I helped her swing out and step down from the back seat. Liz touched the top of her blouse to see if her buttons were holding.

They were.

"Someday."

Hooker came out to the plane to meet us. Joe Hooker was in his mid-fifties, a poster boy for a cowboy. His hat was stained from the rain and the wind and years in the saddle. A red neckerchief above a blue work shirt completed his outfit. Hooker could lift and tie an elk quarter to the side of a horse without breaking a sweat. He was suntanned, and looked strong and tough as he walked up to Liz and me. He shook my hand, cuffed me on the shoulder, and then extended his hand to Liz.

"The deputies left this morning on a chartered plane for Cascade. I'll trail the horses out to my camp, and you can make plans from there," Hooker said, directing his comments to Liz. "What a gunfight. The sheriff told me about the battle at the mine, and the fight up at Stoddard Peak. Damn, wish I could have been there."

Knowing Hooker as I did, I believed him.

"And I'm real sorry about your husband, Mrs. Champlin."

"Thank you, Hooker."

"Those dirty sons-of-bitches." Hooker was reading my mind.

"My feelings exactly," I said.

Hooker was getting a little agitated. He was a mountain man, a horseman, and a guide. He said his name Hooker was from his great-great-great grandfather, who was named after Fightin' Joe Hooker, the Union Civil War general.

Hooker said, "I'll grill some steaks and make some of my camp potatoes. You two just relax from your trip."

"The three of us can have a moment in the lodge for drinks," Liz said. "I'll make the martinis, if there's any gin left. Thanks for taking care of the cabin and the stock."

"We didn't touch the bar. I brought my own, I did."

"What a guy." Liz laughed.

"Has everything been quiet here? Seen any suspicious people around?" I asked Hooker.

"No, it's been quiet since the fight. The deputies kept their M16s handy. Haven't seen a soul. The sheriff flew back in to take pictures and write down what happened. We also cleaned the lodge up the best we could. I've got to feed the horses now, but I'll be back for one of those martinis."

Hooker returned and after a round of drinks he excused himself again. "I'll get started on supper." He was a true mountain man, a loner.

This was the first time I had a chance to take a serious look at the inside of the lodge. The deputies and Hooker had been busy. There was no sign of blood, inside or outside, from the skirmish. For a bunch of gunslingers, they had done a good job of tidying up the place.

A wood-paneled great room was the central attraction of the lodge, with wood roof purlins and heavy decking sloping upward to the ridge beam. Two over-stuffed yellow sofas and three chairs of the same design surrounded a coffee table in the center of the room. In one corner was Alec's office: an oak table with a ham radio in the center, a laptop with the lid closed, and numerous piles of business papers. A huge fireplace, built from local river rock, rose from floor to ceiling, and covered the entire north wall. Blackened stones above an iron screen showed that the fireplace was used often. Oversized windows on the other walls brought in the canyon light.

Above the fireplace, an old Kentucky long rifle rested on wood pegs. The octagonal barrel looked to be four feet long. The stock was curly maple, customized with brass and silver inlays. The rifle had a military design: a spiked bayonet was mounted at the end of the barrel. Light coming through the window reflected off the sharp tip of the steel bayonet.

"I've never seen an antique rifle looking that good," I commented to Liz.

"Actually, it isn't an antique. It was made by a custom rifle maker. Alec only fired it once."

A layer of dust covered the octagonal barrel. The rifle had a percussion cap ignition, instead of the old flintlock. A small leather bag, the type the mountain men carried, hung from another peg off to the side of the wall away from the fireplace. The bag contained lead balls, powder, and percussion caps.

"The rifle is beautiful."

"It's yours, Casey. Alec would want you to have it."

"I couldn't accept the rifle. He has family who would love to have it."

"Well, I'll twist your arm another time. I've pulled together Alec's personal items, his briefcase, business papers, and some cash he liked to carry. I'll send them down to Nevada with him. Then after the services I'm going to come back to the ranch for awhile."

"Alone?"

"I'm hoping you'll come back with me."

"I will," I said. "You'll want to bring in more provisions and take more out. We can charter a plane from McCall. My plane can't carry enough for a longer stay."

"Alec liked it here, but he was restless," Liz said.

"It's a beautiful place."

"Lately, he didn't want to stay more than a week at a time. He brought his company with him, his computer, his investments. He had been taking business risks lately. We had words about that. I don't know what he had been thinking. Some of that risk money he had inherited. He wanted me to transfer some of my investors' funds to his accounts. Of course, I said no. This is behind me now."

"A toast to Alec," I said, raising my glass. "He put up a good fight against the odds. He was trying to rescue you when he came out on the porch."

We touched glasses. "I know," Liz said.

I couldn't read her thoughts. Maybe her marriage was dissolving.

Hooker announced supper. We were starved. He was excellent at steak and potatoes. After dinner Hooker excused himself and headed to the bunkhouse next to the barn.

"Here is my room," Liz said, pointing to the first door on the left, off the living room, "and there is your room." Hers was the master bedroom, with a view of the river and the pines.

"Shall we have coffee on the deck?" I suggested. The fall evening was cool and we were both wearing sweaters. There was enough light in the canyon to see the trees on the skyline.

Neither of us spoke. When the evening breeze came from the north, just so, we could hear the rumble of whitewater downstream.

A throaty hum of an airplane at a high altitude came over the stillness of the evening. We looked up, searched the sky, and the black silhouette of a plane appeared far above us. It was flying parallel to the river and passing over the lodge. The sound faded, and the plane disappeared into the distance.

"That pilot is going to have to hustle if he wants to make McCall before dark," I said.

Liz said nothing, but I knew she was enjoying the quiet.

The quiet didn't last. The sound of the plane, instead of fading away, grew louder, and by the pitch of the engine, I knew the pilot had changed directions and was returning, this time lower in the canyon. A thought crossed my mind: where had I laid the .270? *Yes, in the great room, next to the door.* I picked up the rifle, pushed cartridges into the magazine and leaned the rifle against the deck rail.

For a moment the droning was static; then the airplane came around the nose of a ridge, in a crescendo of noise. The pilot was applying full power, coming down the river three hundred feet above the trees, and flying directly toward the lodge.

"Good Lord, he's low," Liz said.

The sound followed the plane down the canyon and then both disappeared around a ridge.

I was thinking of a plan if he came back. The canyon was quiet. Some ravens squawked across the river.

This place is getting dangerous.

Liz stood up, walked through the lodge, into the kitchen, and out onto the back porch. She stayed a moment there, then came back into the great room, where I was standing. I went back to admiring the long rifle on the rock wall. Alec had good taste in women and guns. At least one woman.

She stood behind me. "It's over, Casey. A big part of my life is over."

"Yes, it is." *Where is this conversation going?*

"Let's leave for Owyhee Crossing in the morning. Can we? In two or three weeks I want to come back and spend some time here before winter sets in. Will you fly me in?"

"Of course. I can't say how long I can stay away from the plant, although the managers are running it well. We can depart early tomorrow, as soon as we see Hooker off with the horses."

I walked out on the deck and with binoculars looked over Whiskey Bravo, tied down between the windsock and the lodge, then I swept the glasses over the runway and the trees above the river. Nothing was moving. An owl hooted behind the lodge.

Liz came out behind me. She put her arms around my waist and her head on my shoulder. I turned, and she said, "The day has been a long one. I'll see you in the morning."

"Yes—in the morning."

The light in the canyon was fading. I remained outside on the deck. The moon was behind the breaks. A coyote barked up on a rockslide across the river. Looking for marmots. I strained my ears to hear the noise of an engine upriver or down, maybe an airplane trying to make a last attempt at a landing. But nothing. I went into the lodge, found my gun belt and duffel, carried them into the guest room, along with the rifle, and threw them on the bed.

The plane that flew low over the lodge was the green Cessna.

The canyon was still in darkness when I made contact with the FBI on the third try with the satellite phone. I stood in the middle of the runway, the only place at the ranch where a person could line up just right with the satellite and call the outside world.

Link picked up. The FBI must have learned that when I called, they best damn well put me through. "Are you in another gun battle?"

"Not yet, Link. The green Cessna flew over the ranch house last night."

"We'll do another search of FAA flight plans, using the same faked tail number Baker gave us."

"Check again with Baker in Twin Falls. Saeed was there before, and they might have a semblance of a cell there."

"Could be. It's a small town, out of the way. We'll also check motels," he said.

"He's a professional, not the common fanatic who will blow himself up. He'll get others to do that. I've seen him; he comes across as an urbane businessman, who speaks good English, but he's a killer."

"We have some intel on a cell in Texas, using home-grown fanatics with imported instructors. Saeed might be part of that group. I'm telling you this because you know as much as we do about the backcountry terrorists, of which there are now eight fewer."

"If it makes you feel any better, Liz and I are flying out of here today, back to Owyhee Crossing. After she gets everything settled, and the services, she wants to return to Phantom for several weeks."

"She can't stay there alone. Will you be with her?" Link still remembered the summers Liz and I were together.

"I will. I won't leave her alone back on the river, for a number of reasons, not that I have any say over what she does."

"Yes, you do."

"She's a very capable and independent woman. Women do what they want to do."

"That they do."

"I'll take care of her," I said, and left the conversation at that.

The big sorrel stood patiently in the grass just off the deck. Seven other horses tugged at their lead ropes, waiting for the chance to move up the trail. The bottom of the canyon was in the shadows and the chill of an October morning frosted the air. Above the breaks the sky was blue and the day looked promising. Three hawks, high and quiet, rode the thermals.

Four of the horses were loaded with sawbucks and panniers, and Hooker and I made last-minute inspections and tightened the cinches.

Hooker put his foot in the stirrup and swung into the saddle on the sorrel. He had one hand on the pommel and the other holding the lead rope.

"It's twenty miles to camp," he said. "We'll be there by mid-afternoon. I'll try to get you on the satellite phone, if I can make the connection."

"Thanks, Hook, for your help." I handed him a check and some cash. Liz was in the lodge, organizing the kitchen after the large breakfast.

"No need for this, Casey. Just let me know when I can get into some of the action."

"Take it. That's for the nice job. Liz and I are flying out today, then coming back in later to bring more provisions, feed for the horses when you bring them back, and get the lodge ready for the winter. That will be after Alec's funeral in Nevada."

"Call me when you want the horses back," he said.

"Watch your top-notch," I said, imitating Robert Redford.

"I will, and you watch yours." Hooker pushed his sweat-stained cowboy hat back, rubbing one hand over his head, making sure his own hair was still there. "Take care of Miz Liz. She's a Miz now, ain't she?"

"Yes, she is." I looked the sorrel in the eye and rubbed his nose. The horse looked happy he was going to be doing something.

"Stories are that you and Miz Liz were a pair once."

"Those are the stories."

"She's a good-looking woman. I'd set my hat for her myself if I was her class of people."

"Don't run yourself down. I'll bet you had movie stars standing in line to see you when you got out of the mountains."

"Never seen any movie stars like her. I know you'll protect her. The deputies told me those terrorists looked like pin cushions with the arrows stuck in them."

"The deputies exaggerate."

"Maybe so, but I'm glad you're here. To help her, that is." He gave me a wink and clucked to the sorrel. "Call me if you need me. If the badasses return, keep in mind my great-great-great granddaddy was Fightin' General Joe Hooker," he said.

"You'll be my first call," I said.

The horses in the remuda turned one by one and soon Joe Hooker was in the pines above the river and lost to view.

The flight back to Owyhee Crossing in the Husky was smooth, with clear skies.

"I'll return to Idaho in ten days, Casey, after everything is taken care of in Nevada," Liz said, throwing her duffel into the back seat of the rental car. "Are you sure you will fly back with me to close the lodge for the winter? We'll need a large plane to take in provisions and bring out Alec's belongings."

"Of course," I said, and gave Liz a long hug. She got back into the car and turned left on Route 95 to Nevada.

I had asked Hooker to ride back and check the ranch in a week. He said he would. He'd be armed.

The Man in the Forest

Three weeks later Liz returned to Idaho and chartered Idaho Air to fly the two of us back into the river. Mac Alistyn, the pilot, flew the single-engine Otter De Havilland, a plane large enough to carry provisions for the lodge and feed for the horses. The plan was to fly to the ranch, stay the night, then return to Owyhee Crossing in the chartered plane with the rest of Alec's personal belongings. Mac came into the airfield at Owyhee Crossing to pick us up, and Liz and I loaded the food and gear into the Otter. We lifted off in mid-afternoon and flew north to the backcountry.

Ten minutes from touchdown, Mac announced over the intercom, "There's wind coming up the river, but the field is clear of wildlife. We'll go straight in." He lowered the wing flaps and we could feel the plane slowing. We closed on the field, five miles ahead, next to the pines. The winds were erratic, squirrelly, the pilots would say, and the plane bumped as the wheels hit the grass. The Otter rattled for several hundred feet before settling into a solid ride to the rail fence next to the lodge.

"Sorry about that touch-down," Mac said. Liz didn't give it a second thought; she was already looking for her carry-on.

"Hell, that was a nice landing," I countered. "Like they say, any landing you can walk away from is a good one."

Mac opened the baggage door, and the three of us carried gear and provisions into the lodge and the horse barn.

An autumn chill made us shiver, a contrast from the warm plane cabin. The empty lodge was cold when we walked in. I started a fire in the fireplace, and carried in dry pine from the covered woodshed. We sat around the fire, toasting to each other and remarking how lucky we all were. We also said a prayer for those less fortunate: Alec and Clint, the two outfitters, and the SWAT officer. Liz bowed her head for a moment.

The flames crackled and popped as the logs and the river stones of the fireplace adjusted to each other. It was the best part of the day, with the subtle smell of wood smoke, relaxing, with drinks in hand, and enjoying the quiet. Liz looked exceptionally pretty, I thought, and surprisingly calm, here at the place she now called home, considering what she had gone through.

"What else can I do?" Mac asked.

"Entertain us with flying stories," Liz said.

"My stories would be dull compared to yours. You had quite a firefight here on the river."

"Yes, something I would not want to do every day," I said.

"I thought you Green Berets engaged in this kind of revelry before breakfast, just for exercise."

"If we have breakfast. Our First Sergeant once said eating is a sign of weakness." I smiled at Mac.

I didn't tell him the Army and the wars were the reasons Liz and I never married. That was the reason I told myself. Hell, maybe she wanted to marry a secure, wealthy guy, and I had been kidding myself.

I suspected their marriage had not been that tight. She had told me he had been taking too many risks and losing not only dividend returns but invested capital. They had words about his new investment strategies. Recently, lots of heated words. Coming back to the lodge where I smoked the two terrorists and where Alec was shot didn't bother her. Liz was a lot tougher than I thought.

"I hope you and Mac like spaghetti."

Mac wanted to know more about the gunfight. "Who would have thought the terrorists were out here. How would they even know about these mountains and canyons?"

At dinner, we changed the subject, talked about other things. Liz had a lot on her mind, and I wanted to protect her by not discussing the fight.

Mac said he was perfectly happy sleeping in the bunkhouse next to the empty stables. I stayed in the great room, lounging on the leather sofa, finishing off a coffee, losing myself in the embers of the fire, and thinking about the events of the past three weeks. The logs in the fireplace cast a red glow, falling into each other.

In the quiet of the lodge with darkness coming on, something had put me on edge. The strange tingling feeling was starting again in the back of my neck. Where in the hell was Link when I needed him? *Where was Mike?* If Link was here, and Mike was back among us again, I would shout at them both, "They are coming! I can smell them."

Mike would say, "Smell them, hell, *Captain.* You need to take a shower!"

Damn it, Mike Romano, you were my best friend, a great NCO—and a crazy Italian. I wouldn't be edgy knowing you'd be spraying bullets over the hillside if you were here. *No, you'd be picking them off, one by one.*

I walked out to the front deck with my binoculars, restless from the thoughts. The remaining daylight was a pale purple above the breaks. The groves of tall pines along the river were dark, almost black, the grass of the runway barely visible. Near the far end of the airstrip two elk stepped from the trees and walked across the field. When they were near the trees they started running and disappeared into the forest. Elk moved that way for a reason, either startled by wolves, or by hunters. With the binoculars I began a systematic search around the edges of the airfield, then the scattered openings above the flat.

Someone was standing at the far end of the field. Vision through the binoculars was blurred, but the person walked from the trees onto the airstrip, and then stopped. I braced the binoculars against a porch post to steady them. The figure—I thought it was a man—appeared momentarily in the glasses. Then he, or the apparition, was gone. Was that a hunter, another terrorist, or a ghost? If it was a hunter he didn't have a rifle that I could see. I spent the next thirty minutes with the glasses searching the field, the open glades above the flat, and the edges of the woods, but saw nothing.

If the person at the end of the field was traveling along the river trail he'd see the lights of the lodge and most likely would stop and say hello, or share a coffee. But he was gone. The night sounds had stopped. I waited on the deck for an hour, but saw or heard nothing more.

Was it another terrorist? Some lone-wolf hostiles still out here? I wanted to think we had taken care of them all. Except for Saeed, who was flying the green airplane, which had returned, and flown over the lodge.

The loaded magazine for the .45 was on a belt in my duffel. I slid it out, snapped it into the pistol, racked the slide back, put the automatic on safe, and laid it on the nightstand next to my bed in the guest room. The time was after midnight, but I couldn't sleep and walked back to the deck. With the faint light from the stars, the tree line and the De Havilland were visible. At two o'clock in the morning on the second trip to the front deck, I kept walking and moved to the plane. The beautiful white Otter parked there in the starlight looked undisturbed. I inspected the locked side doors, looked over the wings and the tail assembly, then bent down and glanced at the underside of the wings. Was this being overly cautious? Hell, I was the one who had rigged the hand-grenade booby traps at the old mine, defensive learned habits from the Army, meant to keep a person alive. Next, I slipped behind the barn and walked around the back of the lodge, where three weeks ago, a deadly gunfight had taken place. I was hoping Mac the pilot, sleeping in the bunkhouse, wasn't trigger happy. He said he had a pistol in his duffel.

A flashlight was in my pocket. Turning it on would present an easy target if somebody was in an ambush position, hiding out there in the dark. *Where did the person go? Did he move up river, or down? Who was he? Were the terrorists out here again?* The green Cessna had flown down the river and over the lodge three weeks ago. The pilot had a purpose. Some of these people could still be here in the mountains, hiding somewhere, plotting more evil.

Above the canyon the Milky Way crossed the sky. The moon remained hidden. The stars provided a glow, enough light to move through the trees, to step lightly over river rocks, pine needles and tree limbs. Every dark bush and patch of woods was a suspect and held a danger. Any moment I expected the muzzle flash of a rifle.

I was the hunted again, an uncomfortable feeling, walking along the edge of the trees. I was meant to be the hunter. Don't push your luck, I thought. My instincts had paid off in the mountains at the Slot. The night did not know that, and the night was silent. Someone in the woods was watching me.

A raven down off the riverbank made a single harsh squawk. When I was a kid I read a story, "The Legend of Sleepy Hollow," where in the darkest of nights, a headless horseman came riding, a black ghost, who, the legends said, was a cavalryman who lost his head a cannonball in the war, and on his steed, just as black, came galloping down a foggy road in the woods and thundered across an old stone bridge. Was he coming again?

Along the river there was no headless horseman, no pounding hoof beats, nor a moss-covered stone bridge, only the eerie call of a single raven. What did the raven know? Was the raven talking to me? Was *someone* in the trees along the river?

Concentrate. I was standing motionless with my back against the trunk of a large pine, the tree at least four feet wide. *Catch your breath. Forget the headless horseman.* I took the .45 off safety, held it with two hands on the grip, and waited.

The sound of a twig cracking came from the direction of the river. Could that be a deer or an elk? Or a person? If a muzzle blast flashed in the night, there might be a chance for some cover behind a log. Twenty minutes passed without a sound. The lone big bird on the edge of the trees squawked again, this time farther down the river. The night wind stirred and the sound of the rapids whispered through the branches of the pines.

Parachutes Over Rush Creek

"You look like you were up all night." Liz handed me a cup of coffee in the kitchen four hours later.

"I was," I said, and told them of the man I saw at the far end of the airstrip, just at nightfall.

Mac looked up from the stove. "I thought you got them all?"

"I thought so—maybe a wandering hunter." *Saeed was there somewhere. Hunters wouldn't be in the trees in the night.*

Liz gave me a serious look. "You were moving around last night in the woods?"

"We'll be leaving soon. I'll tell Link about the possibility of someone still out here."

The October weather was holding with clear skies. This was the time of year the temperature could unexpectedly drop, the sky change rapidly, and an early snow hit the backcountry. Here, on the river, it would likely be rain. Mac said we should lift off by early afternoon, no later. I agreed. There was more to load in the plane than Liz anticipated, and we were both sorting and boxing.

The take-off was routine. Mac cleared the trees with a hundred feet to spare. The plane banked south over Monumental Creek with a heading for the airfield at Owyhee Crossing. Liz rode shotgun in the co-pilot's seat. I was again behind the pilot. The Phantom Ranch was well behind us and we climbed to one thousand feet above the highest peaks. Twenty minutes had passed and we were at cruising altitude, slipping between the gathering clouds.

The engine of the De Havilland suddenly sputtered, coughed, revved back, then coughed again. Liz glanced at Mac. He was instantly alert, leaned forward and adjusted the mixture control. The propeller revolutions went back to normal. Moisture in the fuel was causing the roughness. That was it. Mac moved some switches and turned some knobs on the panel, ones hidden from where I was sitting. The engine caught again, smoothed out, and Liz went back to watching the green forests slide past her below. Ahead was a light-blue haze marking the massive canyon of the South Fork of the Salmon where the river cut its way through the mountains.

Everything was under control when the engine coughed again, the propeller fluttering and flashing in the sun. "If this thing gets worse," Mac said over the intercom, "three reserve parachutes are behind the last seat. Pull two of them out and stand by."

Mac continued to adjust the knobs on the panel. The engine was running on two or three cylinders, and poorly at that. It sputtered, revved up again, and I could tell without looking at the panel that the Otter was losing altitude. Liz watched Mac and remained calm. The tallest granite peaks were now at our level and I glanced outside to see where in the hell we were. Rugged and rocky timbered country lay below us. Rush Creek or Monumental Creek. No emergency backcountry fields were close. We were south of the Middle Fork. The main Salmon was off to our left, over some rocky spires. I reminded myself that Lewis and Clark called the Salmon the "River of No Return."

On the emergency channel Mac issued a May Day. Then I heard him talking to flight control, telling them we were over the headwaters of Rush Creek, and if the plane continued to lose power he couldn't make it to land at Big Creek or any other fields and would try to set the plane down in the Middle Fork.

I pulled two chutes and two harnesses from a canvas container. The chutes were the 24-foot reserves we used in the Forest Service, the chest types with an orange release handle on the top of a green cover.

The engine coughed, then stopped. Mac adjusted something and the engine wound up, then stopped again. I opened the side door of the Otter, and snapped it against the side of the cabin.

The sound of silence in a plane in the air when the engine quits provides one of the most attention-getting sensations in the world. "That son-of-a-bitch sabotaged the plane last night," I said. "He did something to the engine."

"Probably unscrewed some of the spark plugs," Mac shouted, over the headset. "Must have missed that on the pre-flight."

I told Liz to move with me to the door of the plane.

"I radioed in the clear the two of you were evacuating the plane, gave them our location, five miles south of Rush Creek."

"We'll jump, Mac, but come with us."

"No. I've never parachuted and I think I can land this plane in the river. Go! That's an order."

As the pilot, he had command of the plane. I turned and looked at Liz.

She was spreading the chute harness. "I've always wanted to jump, but not this way. How do you work this thing?"

"We can't stay with the plane—we have to jump. You'll love it!" I shouted at Liz.

Liz shook her head.

Mac started the engine again and the prop turned over for a moment. We were flying in a high timbered valley and the tops of the highest ridges were now above us. Below the plane were rolling forests of pine and fir, open meadows, and a dark green stream snaking its way in and out of the trees. The winds appeared light. Off to the west, gray clouds gathered. The mountains and canyons would be dark in three hours. Liz and I pulled off our headsets and threw them on the seats.

Mac banked the plane to turn north, back toward the river. The wings were at an easy angle, not stalling, and he turned in his seat. "Go now!" he said. The quiet of the plane lent some urgency to what we were going to do.

I slipped the nylon harness on Liz, attached the straps around her thighs, pulled them tight, then the chest snaps, and the last step, fastened the chute to the D-rings. Liz had a parachutist's instincts; she took up the slack in the harness, and tugged again on the connections. I did the same for my harness and chute, then grabbed my red survival pack to throw from the Otter after Liz jumped. Not being a very religious guy, I made a quick Sign of the Cross, and asked "for a little help here," hoping that the two of us would be walking upright on the ground.

I yelled in the slipstream coming in the open door. "Are you ready?"

The engine coughed again, getting her to say, "Okay, let's go!"

"Easy. Place your feet on the edge of the door and look at the horizon," I shouted. "I'll help you. Here is the release handle. Count to three—one—two—three—then pull this orange handle. Keep your hand on the release when you go out, but don't pull it until you reach three. Three! The chute will open fast. There are red guidelines on each side to turn you. Don't worry about them, you won't have time to learn how to use them. Keep your feet together when you go out the door, and make sure they are together before you hit the ground."

We didn't have safety helmets, or even hats, to protect us from pine branches if we landed in the trees, or did a crashing roll in the brush. The slipstream was tossing Liz's hair, and I had to admit she looked romantic when she faced the open door.

I didn't have time to explain that if she did a forward or backward somersault out the door with her legs spread the chute could deploy between her legs. That's not a good way to start a jump.

"I get it! Count to three!"

Mac turned and watched us, his hands on the yoke. The plane was losing altitude but he pushed the nose down, raising the tail, to prevent the chutes from tangling there, to give us a better chance.

"Go!" he yelled.

"Put your hands on the sides of the door," I shouted in Liz's ear. "We don't know what this plane is going to do!" I took her right hand off the door frame and placed it over the orange handle. "I'll give you a little push."

Liz turned for a second, smiled at me, and gave me a look that said—if this doesn't turn out well, Casey, I'm going to have your ass!

I glanced below at the tall trees and small meadows. We had no choice. "You're ready!" I shouted in the wind. She was looking down. "Look up and out!"

"C'est la vie," she said, and nodded.

I gave her a light push and she didn't move. Then I lifted her and shoved at the same time, and into the open sky she went. One, two, three—pull the orange handle. And she did. An orange and white canopy blossomed below, like it was supposed to. Then I threw the survival pack, placed both hands on the sides of the door, and dove into the sky, above the mountains, into another world, and unknown terrain. I tried to keep an eye on Liz at the same time. We were less than nine hundred feet. Too damn low and dangerous.

The pilot chute popped and the main chute deployed with a ragged snap. I turned with the guideline to look for Liz, and she was swinging back and forth under the canopy and dropping rapidly into the edge of some trees. She hit a tall ponderosa pine in a puff of yellow pine pollen and the orange and white parachute snagged and wrapped itself over the top of the tree.

Now it was my turn. I looked for an opening in the meadow, had to miss a tree or there would be big trouble with both of us hung up. In the last seconds before the ground came up, I pulled down and planed with the front risers to get some forward momentum for the roll. It was a controlled crash, resembling something of a jumper landing, and I was on my left side on the ground. Several boulders were hidden in the tall brown grass. Just missed them. The smokejumpers, if they had been there on the ground watching, would have given me a five out of ten on that landing. Nothing was broken or bleeding and I stood up and unsnapped the chute and the harness, then turned to the sky when I heard the distant sputter of the Otter breaking the stillness. Mac was nursing the plane north to the Middle Fork. Good luck, I said silently. Standing there in the meadow, I again made the Sign of the Cross. This business was making me religious. Mac needed all the help he could get.

"Casey, for God's sake, get me out of here!" Liz hung thirty feet up in the branches of a tall ponderosa at the edge of the meadow. It could have been worse.

I ran across the grass, stopped below her, and looked up.

"Well, Mr. McConnell, what do we do now?" she said.

"Are you okay? Any scratches, twisted ankles, shoulders out of line? Or is it just your dignity?"

Liz was hanging from the risers of the chute. The orange and white parachute was securely draped over the top of the pine. I judged the chute safe enough to hold and not slide off if she bounced or moved around, or if a wind came up.

"No, I'm fine. Please figure out how to get me out of here."

The smokejumpers have equipment to extricate themselves from tree landings: hundred foot let-down ropes, climbing spurs for a partner to climb the tree, and chain saws to remove branches or snags. We had none of this equipment, only a climbing rope if I could find it.

"I threw out my survival pack. It has a sixty-foot rope." A plan was formulating on how to get her out of the tree. "I'll look for the pack—it fell somewhere between where you landed and where I came down."

"I haven't landed yet. In case you haven't noticed. I'm still up in this fucking tree." Liz's feet were thirty feet above me. I could throw her a pocket knife to cut the risers or shroud lines, but the drop could break her leg or ankle.

"I'll find it," I said, and started back across the clearing.

"Casey! I see the pack from here. Over there, into the trees. Red, isn't it? Looks like a flotation device?"

"That's it, the only flotation device this side of the mountain." I ran into the trees and brought the pack back to the meadow and spread the equipment on the ground below Liz. "There is a long climbing rope here but I can't get this heavy rope through the branches next to you. I'll make a light rope out of my parachute lines and throw it up."

Three of the shroud lines made a good lead line after cutting and tying them together. I wrapped one end around a small rock, the other end to the climbing rope.

"I'm going to throw this line and rock over your head. Hold your hands in front of your face, if my baseball throw isn't so good."

On the third throw the rock made it between the branches. Liz grabbed the shroud line and let it thread through her hands, then hauled up the climbing rope. I pulled it around the trunk of the tree and belayed it there.

"Now here's the tricky part. I've tied a bowline loop at one end of the climbing rope. I'll haul it up by pulling on the rope over the branch above you and around the tree trunk. When the loop is at your feet, step into it with both feet, and I'll take up the slack around the tree. When you can stand upright, the slack should be out of the D-rings. Then unsnap the two metal D-rings on the parachute. Whatever you do, don't turn loose of the yellow climbing rope. Then I'll lower you down."

"I get the picture. And if you drop me, I'll kill you."

"I won't. The rope is over a large branch. You may drop a foot when the slack goes out."

Liz stepped into the loop, and I pulled on it to lift her, which did not go easy. She unhooked the riser snaps, and held onto the heavier rope. This was the tricky part. I slowly lowered her to the ground.

When her feet hit the grass, she straightened up, stepped out of the loop, blew on both of her hands, said "Wow," and then came toward me. It took me but a second to drop the climbing rope, which was wrapped around me for the second belay, and then take her in my arms. She gave me a long hard kiss on the lips.

"You are my hero again. Twice in three weeks."

"Anytime," I said, and smiled. "I love this. You smell like a Christmas tree." I took a handkerchief from my pocket and wiped the dust and pine pollen from her face. "God, you're beautiful when you've been parachuting."

"You've been out in the mountains too long." She laughed.

The sun dropped behind the ridges and the gray clouds were piling up as we watched. A chill hung in the late October afternoon.

"I hope Mac made it to the river. Landing in the water is not much better than landing on rocks."

It was time to plan the next move. "Mac called in a May Day before we jumped but he didn't have time to tell us if it was acknowledged." I kept searching the mountains to the north in the direction of the Middle Fork, praying I would not see a black smoke cloud. There was none, but the canyon of the Middle Fork was out of view. Mac was a good pilot and if anyone could land an airplane back in there he could.

The tops of the pines and firs swayed in the wind. Small swirls of dust rose and fell between the shrubs in the meadow. The sun had disappeared. The mountains were changing and a cold and isolated feeling hit me. I looked at Liz.

"We need to move down off this high country before this weather sets in. There could be snow in these clouds. We are above Rush Creek, which flows into Big Creek, which joins the Middle Fork downstream, not far from your lodge."

"And how far might that be?" Liz asked.

I hesitated. "Twenty miles as the crow—"

"—flies," she interrupted. "We're not crows."

"We can walk downhill and be at Rush Creek tonight. There's an old Indian trail there we can follow to Big Creek. This weather looks bad, and I suggest we move out. The chute in the tree will be a marker for anyone looking for us, like a helicopter, tonight or tomorrow. We can mark our direction with rocks at the bottom of your let-down rope."

We spread the contents of the survival pack out on the ground. Like a couple of kids with an Easter basket, we looked over the contents: dried macaroni and cheese, powdered scrambled eggs, dice-sized potatoes with dried carrots and dried onions, and a can of rabbit pate. Rabbit pate? In the backpack was one down mountain sleeping bag, a lightweight nylon tarp with tabs, waterproof matches, a compass, Swiss army knife, tungsten cook pot, small metal cup, twenty-five feet of lightweight nylon cord, and a leather-covered flask.

"And what's in that flask?" Liz asked.

"That flask holds a pint of Bombay Sapphire gin."

"I might have known." She laughed.

"There are no olives or vermouth, but once we drop lower and set up a shelter, we can have a party."

"I remember your parties. At least we won't be disturbed by anyone. Who in the world would find us out here in the mountains?"

"Who indeed. We're on our own tonight."

"If you get me drunk, can I trust you?"

"Not at all." I smiled.

The daylight was fading and if Mac got through on the radio for a rescue there was not a logical reason to stay at the meadow. At one time we heard a plane in the distance but the sound faded; it could have been traveling through. In the morning a plane or helicopter, if there was going to be one, would spot the parachute in the tree.

The weather could change rapidly in the backcountry. Both of us were wearing light gray sweatshirts, not enough protection from an early snow this high in the mountains. I shouldered the backpack, walked across the meadow, then stopped and took one last look at the orange and white chute hanging in the tree. I made some marks in the dirt, saying ALL OK, then a rock arrow pointing north in the direction we would take. Snow tonight in the high country would cover the marks and probably the rocks.

We stepped out and quickly entered a dense pocket of fir and spruce. The timber grew thicker as we descended. Small glades in the forest made walking easier and we took advantage of the openings. From these meadows we could better observe our route off the peaks.

"The parachute I stuffed in my pack will make a nice comforter tonight," I said. "I've spent many nights sleeping in a parachute in these mountains. With some luck we can be down on the slopes above Rush Creek before dark, then tomorrow Big Creek and the Middle Fork. The temperature is dropping fast with this weather coming in."

Liz and I walked between the tall trees, sidestepping back and forth in copses of cottonwoods, circling impenetrable alder thickets at soggy seeps, and picking up our pace when we crossed the meadows. Game trails wandering from the ridge to the creek provided short-lived avenues of travel. Tracks of elk, deer, and wolves came and went on the forest floor, soft indentations pushed into the bare dirt under the tree limbs.

We knew we were not alone.

The winds aloft pushed the clouds down, bringing a feeling of isolation. Darkness was coming. We both sensed an urgency to move out of the high country. The alpine meadows were above us now and we entered the dark timber. The rain picked up with a rustling noise in the trees, finding its way through the branches, spotting our sweatshirts. Liz moved easily through the forest. She was in excellent shape, right behind me moving through the thickets and the timber.

"We should make camp soon, before dark, before the storm really hits us," I said, turning to Liz. "Keep your eyes open for a nice flat spot in the woods, below some solid looking trees, near a brook, or if not that, then better yet, look for a Motel Six."

She stepped closer behind me in the walk through the wet forest. Her long legs moved smoothly around the boulders and the clumps of bear grass in the clearings, and she easily stepped over or the fallen gray logs.

The clouds were lower, and in a short time, we would be walking in them, or the fog, as the weather people call it when clouds surrounds you. I was trying to stay away from the brushy bottom and keeping my eyes open for the old Indian trail down Rush Creek.

"How is this for a camp?" Liz pointed to a level place with grass under the tall firs, with rocks for a fire, only a stride or two from a small brook. "This is perfect, and not a bear or wolf in sight."

The spot would provide protection from the wind, and even snow if the weather got colder. I erected the nylon tarp, tying the parachute cord to the tree limbs, fashioning a shelter in the shape of a sloping tent, then stacked more branches on the ground for a mattress. The wind was increasing and I sealed the edges with more branches and rocks. Liz laid the sleeping bag and the parachute side by side inside the shelter: an elegant camp bed, good enough to display in a sporting goods store. Inside the survival pack was a candle lantern. I hung that from a tab in the center of the roof.

For the campfire, I set flat rocks on edge to reflect heat and light into the opening of the shelter. A Boy Scout leader would have been proud. We collected firewood, built a fire, and then sat side by side below the trees in front of the flames.

"This is a nice camp," I said.

"It is very cozy," Liz said. "God, I hope Mac made it."

"He might have had enough power to fly to Big Creek. When we jumped from the plane he had no altitude to spare."

"Mac has flown us into the ranch before. If anybody can land that Otter, Mac can."

"In the meantime, we can break out early and push on to the Middle Fork and your lodge. There may be snow on the mountains in the morning. A plane or helicopter will be looking for us at daybreak." I didn't tell Liz the clouds looked permanent and would likely be here in the morning. The visibility in the forest was only twenty feet. The steady rain and the fog and the darkness made the night complete. The woods were silent and for a moment we were hypnotized by the flames.

Liz organized the meager food supplies in the survival pack. "Tonight I'll cook up the macaroni and cheese, then tomorrow the scrambled eggs and instant coffee. If we're out here any longer you will have to chase down an elk."

"It is time to break out the gin." I poured the Bombay from the flask into our only cup and handed it to Liz. "The Scouts always said 'Be Prepared.' This is a high-class martini cup. We can take turns."

The rain continued to fall. Liz and I sat next to each other under sheltering branches next to the fire.

"This weather isn't bad. In fact, it's romantic. If time had stopped in our lives, we could consider this our honeymoon," I said.

Liz turned from the firelight and gave me a long look, which I couldn't decipher. She took off the camouflaged hunting cap I had given her for the hike. In the firelight her cheeks were rosy from the walk down the side of the mountain. She looked prettier than ever. She removed her sweatshirt and threw it onto her sleeping bag in the shelter. "It's warm in front of the fire."

I leaned forward and threw a dry branch on the fire.

It was my turn on the cup of Bombay. No ice, no olives, just straight gin. "How did you like your first jump?" I asked.

"It was a rapid exit from the plane, but we were so low. There was no time for the fear factor to kick in. And no time to enjoy the ride."

"We were dangerously low—eight or nine hundred feet when we stepped out. The parachutes worked perfectly or we would have been toast. You did great. Now that you are a parachutist, you can add another notch on your belt."

"That's doing it the hard way. Thanks for getting me out of that tree."

"That was easy. You came down that rope like a pro. The hike off the mountain was almost like old times. We rode horses into the hills. Remember?"

"Of course I remember. Are you getting nostalgic? The difference is that we had more romance and less excitement."

"That we did."

"Have there been many women in your life?" Liz looked at me seriously then, firelight on her face.

None like you, I thought, but didn't say it. "Some."

"Anyone serious?"

"One."

"Married?"

"No. We lived together for three years."

"And?"

"I guess we didn't love each other enough to get married. I went back to the Middle East again. She married an actor from California. Doing well, I'm sure. That was a long time ago."

"Did you think of me often?"

"Yes."

The campfire suddenly got higher and brighter as the dry branches caught the flames.

Neither of us said anything after that.

The fog stirred from a light breeze through the trees and the damp smell of the pines came up from below. A wolf howled down in the creek bottom. Another wolf answered, in the distance.

"They won't bother us," I said.

"I know. I love it here in the mountains, wolves or not." Liz threw a stick on the fire. "What do you think caused the plane engine to misfire and conk out?"

"I think the guy I saw in the trees was a terrorist, left over from the fight, and he sabotaged the plane during the night. Mac said he probably unscrewed some spark plugs, which could vibrate loose in flight. Or maybe he put something in the fuel tanks, screwing up the mixture. If it had been water in the aviation gas it would have shown on the drain in the pre-flight procedure. Mac was very good on the pre-flight. I watched him."

"Do you think there are still terrorists around?"

"Yes," I said, "I called Link about that earlier today." *Today? That seemed like ages ago.* I told Liz about the green Cessna, the flight over her lodge, my exact questions to Link on that plane, and why it was always around when we were near the hostiles or the Middle Eastern people.

"If the rescue aircraft haven't spotted us tomorrow, or picked us up by helicopter before we reach your ranch, I think we should approach with caution. Link will probably have a SWAT team there, but if he doesn't, we will need to make other plans."

"Like what?"

"Like me going in alone, you staying hidden in the woods."

"That's too dangerous. Our cell phones and your weapons are in the De Havilland."

"I know. I feel insecure out here without a weapon."

"Who in the world can find us?" she asked. "Even the terrorists don't know about the headwaters of Rush Creek."

"Probably not. The plan is that if we see any of them, we'll drop our gear and take off fast, move deeper into the timber. I know you're in great shape—saw that in our hike today."

Liz looked pleased by that. "I run, do some yoga, and occasionally compete in a triathlon."

"Thought so," I said.

"So you remembered."

"How could I forget?"

"You must have had a memory lapse in the desert. There were weeks when I didn't hear from you."

"That was the Second Gulf War. We went in on the border, virtually alone. I was trying to keep my team alive." I handed her back the cup of gin, now almost empty. "We really didn't need olives, did we?"

"Of course not." She handed the cup back.

I took the cup and filled it with the diminishing Bombay.

The rain continued to drip through the trees, and we kept the flames dancing with dead branches and small logs that were within easy reach. The flask of gin was empty. Liz prepared the freeze-dried package of macaroni and cheese in boiling water in the tungsten pan. We talked far into the night, about the summers we spent together, about Mike, and Link, and Jammer, and Baker, and the great times we had together. We knew we could do anything then, and the world was waiting.

The gin, the campfire, the night, and the solitude had all done their job, especially the gin. A bear could have walked into camp, sat beside us at the campfire, and we wouldn't have noticed.

"It's time," Liz said. Her brown eyes were wide and glowing in the firelight. She had removed the camouflaged hat.

"For what?"

"For bed."

The fire was burning itself out. The fog moved in to take over the camp. Rain continued to hiss when the water hit the last of the embers. I crawled into the nylon of the parachute, and folded my sweatshirt for a pillow. Except for my mountain boots the rest of my clothes stayed on.

Liz opened the zipper of the mountain bag all the way to the bottom, turned her back to me, unbuttoned and took off her blouse. She unfastened and removed her bra, and I was feeling out of the picture. I was supposed to do the unfastening. She reached over and picked up her sweatshirt, exposing her breasts for a moment. She dropped the sweatshirt over her head and pulled it down. I was sitting on my parachute bed, my arms around my knees, when she made a circle with her hand that I should turn my head. Being of upstanding character, I did.

Before climbing into her sleeping bag, she slipped off her jeans. I rolled over in the parachute, losing myself in the slick material, but there was an open steering slot in one of the panels. A great technical feature, the side openings in these controllable parachutes. She was wearing black bikini panties.

Damn, she has terrific legs!

"Goodnight," Liz said, her voice muffled by the down bag. "Thank you."

The rain coming through the trees and the fog made little splash noises on the roof of the shelter.

"Goodnight," I said, rolling the other way in the orange and white nylon. I arranged my sweatshirt for a pillow, and lined up with the slot in the parachute to keep an eye on Liz. I tossed around several times to get the kinks out of the parachute bed, and when I looked at her again she was asleep and breathing softly.

Dry Martinis

The rain had stopped during the night. A fog rolled up from Rush Creek and a morning chill hung in the air. The tall firs twenty feet away stood dark and ghostly, barely visible. With the daylight the forest creatures came alive. A pine siskin ran down the face of the tree next to our shelter. The tiny bird picked at the bark, gave us a quick look, chirped twice, more of a trill, then turned and hopped its way back up the tree, just as fast. I was at the same time struggling to untangle the parachute from my arms and legs.

Liz hadn't moved but when I turned to see if she was awake, she was looking back at me with wide eyes through the top opening of the sleeping bag, and she was smiling.

"Morning. How did you sleep?" I asked.

"Like a baby." Liz laughed. "Made it through another night without being eaten or shot." She moved to unzip the sleeping bag. "How did you sleep in the parachute quilt?"

"Did some tossing and turning." I put my hand on her foot which she had smoothly slipped out of the bottom of the sleeping bag and was moving along the seam of my jeans. "I had a dream we were sitting by the fire, drinking gin, and made wild love in the forest."

"In the wet pine needles?"

"In the soft dry sleeping bag."

"You're making that up."

"Part of it."

"Remember, I've only been single for a month. God bless Alec. He tried, but our life together was unraveling. Everything we did was about him. He was obsessed with making money. But that wasn't even working these last several years. He was taking risks. Maybe it had never been that wonderful. That's all behind me now. Let's talk about us. You and I have miles of hiking today, so I best get dressed."

"And miles to go before we sleep," I said, quoting an old poem. "Don't move. We can't get up this early." I slid off my jeans. Liz waited a moment, then her toes began tracing an imaginary line up my leg past my knee. Her finger touched the scar on my cheek. "Almost gone," she said.

I rolled over, pulled some of the panels of the parachute over us, and kissed her.

"We're together again," I said, and slipped her black panties down her thighs, past her knees, over her toes, then flipped them into the trees.

"I'll never find them again," she said, laughing.

"It doesn't matter up here in the mountains."

"So you say. I think you planned this, making me jump out of an airplane, and now taking advantage of me." She didn't laugh or say anything for the next twenty minutes, because my lips were on her lips, my arms around her.

The little bird ran down the tree again, trilling twice. I pulled on the nylon panels and closed the shelter opening.

"It's dark in here," she said.

"It's perfect."

"For what," she said.

The sleeping bag was open and she moved one leg. Then she moved the other.

The moment, and there were many, could have lasted forever.

Liz trembled and gave me a long hug, her arms tight around me. "I can't believe us," she said. "Never could. Here we are, making love in the Idaho wilderness, with nothing but the clothes on our backs, one sleeping bag, a parachute, and a package of freeze-dried eggs."

"We have each other," I said, reaching for my shirt.

"Maybe we always have," she said.

I threw back the folds of the parachute, walked into the trees, picked up her panties, and handed them to her. "I found them. You're gorgeous. Can I sit here and watch you get dressed?"

"You're a lech!" Liz laughed. "But a nice one. Yes, if you'd like." She began fastening her bra. "Next a breakfast of scrambled eggs and coffee."

Liz slid her panties on, then her jeans. "If you'll build the fire, I'll make us a gourmet breakfast of freeze-dried scrambled eggs, French style."

"Whatever the hell that is."

"You'll see."

The fire warmed us, and the eggs and instant coffee tasted like a classy breakfast, there in the fog. I didn't ask her what the French thing was: she might have thought I wanted to lure her back into our shelter. The pine siskin came down the tree again, pecked at a bug on the bark, then ran out on a branch above us. It circled around the limb, and flew to the top of the tree.

"The little bird knows what is going on," Liz said.

"He peeked. Now he is telling us to get moving."

We broke camp, pushed our belongings into the pack and I hefted it onto my shoulders. I brought out the compass, set a heading of 180 degrees to Big Creek and the Middle Fork, and put it into my shirt pocket. "In the fog, it's easy to get turned around, even going downhill. The last thing we want to do is to get stuck in the bottom of a brushy draw."

A section of blue sky opened in the fog at the top of the mountain. We glanced up, and the clouds closed up again. "The pilots call that mountain obscuration."

"Well named," she said.

Then we heard the plane, the sound muffled in the fog. The plane flew over us, came back again, and then the throaty hum faded into the distance.

"They're looking for us. There is no reason to stay here in the clouds," I said.

"Where's that old Indian trail?' Liz asked. "Did the old Indians move it?"

"Maybe. Those old Indians were crafty."

We started walking again, energized by the sound of the plane, the daylight, and the sleep and romance under the trees. After an hour moving through the timber and the meadows, we came to the Rush Creek trail, an easy hike down switchbacks to Big Creek. We were in the bottom of the canyon when the clouds lifted. A cabin was there, no one around, and the door was locked. We left the cabin as is, and faced the cold and fast flowing waters of Big Creek. I hefted the pack again and we waded the creek, holding hands on the slippery rocks and getting ourselves wet in the process. We climbed the bank, broke out of the willows, and came to the trail leading to the Middle Fork.

I turned on the trail and looked back at Liz. She had a sad and forlorn look on her face. "We're almost home again," she said, "and I was thinking of Mac. He made us jump and saved our lives."

"Mac's a great pilot—he can land anywhere. The plane was lighter without us. With luck he gained some altitude."

Except for the uncertainty of Mac, walking the creek trail was almost a joy. The fog had burned off and the sun was overhead. The sky was cloudless and a deep blue. Two sandpipers flew down the creek, several feet over the water, their raspy cries the only sound in the forest. Three elk appeared above us, walking slow below some rock outcroppings.

I watched the trail, an old habit, looking for boot marks or anything else. Deer and elk moved on and off the path into the forest, as some animal notion told them to do. Distinct horse tracks, heavy with riders or gear, marked the dust and dirt and took the opposite direction, upstream. Outfitters and hunters.

We were five miles down the trail when a helicopter flew over us just above the tree tops. We waved and a minute later a note fluttered down on a red streamer. The message read:

> WILL PICK YOU UP AT THE PACK BRIDGE DOWNSTREAM WHERE BIG CREEK JOINS THE MIDDLE FORK. SIGNED, CAL EVERETT, DEPUTY SHERIFF.

"And just when I was enjoying this little outing with you," I said.

"Yes, it's been fun, but we've run out of food—except for the can of rabbit pate. Where did you get *those* field rations?"

"They were French army rations, picked up in Europe, been in the hangar for years. The French include rabbit pate in their field food. The troops in the French Foreign Legion love pate and wine. I knew them well."

"The first two meals were very good," Liz added. "And when we get to the lodge, I'll toss the pate and grill us a steak."

A white helicopter, its rotors slowly turning, sat hunkered between two big pines on the east side of the pack bridge. Two men stood next to the skids when we walked up. Deputy Sheriff Everett introduced himself. We shook hands with him and Ed the pilot.

"We'll take you back to the lodge," Everett said. "Get some food and rest."

"But first, tell us about Mac," Liz said.

"Mac Alistyn is fine. Takes more than a glider ride in an airplane to kill him. He had enough altitude, crossed Bear Trap Saddle at fifty feet and set the Otter down at Cabin Creek. Landed short and tore up the nose gear. Two mechanics are flying in to fix it."

"Thank God," Liz said.

"Link Barrett is waiting for you back at your lodge, with two shooters. We think the terrorists are still out here. We have deputies at the roads leading from the backcountry."

The helicopter lifted off and in fifteen minutes we were back at the ranch. Link came out to meet us when the chopper landed next to the rail fence. The two SWAT agents were nowhere in sight. Cal the deputy sheriff went inside, and the pilot did an after-flight inspection around the helicopter. Link said the sheriff's people weren't needed now and they planned on leaving before dark. He would go out with them.

"You think there are terrorists still out here?" Link asked me.

"Yes, I saw something at dusk, looked like a man, then the Otter was sabotaged."

"No proof of that yet. Maybe something in the fuel. We circled the lodge and the airfield on the way in; didn't find anything unusual."

"Don't forget that feeling in the back of my neck. It's still there."

"Bittner and Carter are out in the woods, camouflaged, and you can't see them. They will come in at five for supper, and they will stay the night with you and Liz."

"That's good. My firepower and our duffel are in the plane at Cabin

Creek. Your shooters can sleep in the second guest room, but I hope they'll alternate surveillance shifts during the night. I'll suggest that to Liz."

"They will. Who's staying in the first guest room?"

"Me."

"You and Liz must have spent a cozy night in the woods," Link said.

"You ever spend the night in a rolled up parachute? Don't answer, I know you have."

"You're dodging my questions."

"One step at a time. Let's get rid of these hostiles first."

"We're working on it." Link keyed his field radio and ordered Bittner and Carter back to the lodge. Fifteen minutes later they both suddenly emerged, stepping out of the forest, carrying their Remingtons.

"Seen some man's tracks up there on the mountain, Boss," Bittner said. "Might have been a hunter. Didn't find any near the house. Lots of tracks in the field, though, where you park the planes and helicopters. Could have been anybody's."

Link gave the two SWAT agents tactical instructions for the night. They would provide security for the lodge until the territory around the grounds was secured. Link would fly in another six agents in the morning in the Blackhawk to canvass the woods and fields out to a two-mile radius. In the late afternoon, he, along with the deputy, boarded the helicopter and returned to civilization.

The lodge was cold from being closed up. I built a fire in the great room, making a mental note that more firewood needed to be cut and split for the lodge before winter set in.

Liz and I stood on the deck watching the helicopter disappear over the top of the breaks. The line of sunshine moved up the side of the canyon. Three mallards flew up river, looking for a place to settle for the night.

"It is beautiful out here, isn't it," Liz said. "Except for the unknowns."

"That too will pass."

"The perennial optimist. Nothing bothers you, does it?"

"Not much. I was never smart enough to let things bother me."

"I don't believe that."

"It's true." I put my arm around her waist. She didn't move.
"Did it ever bother you we never married?" Liz asked.
"Yes," I said.

She was almost as tall as I was, with the western boots. Her large brown eyes were making me giddy. Then she took my hand and moved it from her waist. She smiled at me, and walked into the lodge.

I watched her for a moment, then picked up the binoculars and glassed the edges of the airstrip.

Kentucky Long Rifle

At five o'clock Bittner was walking from the horse barn to the lodge when I heard a thud, saw Bittner fall, then heard the rolling report of a high-powered rifle. Son-of-a-bitch. Carter was nowhere in sight. I looked for Liz, ran to her in the kitchen, took her arm and pushed her into the great room. "I heard the shot," she said.

"Stay away from the windows."

Bittner was down, but trying to crawl. His rifle was knocked out of his hands.

"Don't move!" I shouted to him, remembering the tactics used by the Taliban snipers in the Afghan mountains. If you moved you'd get another round. If your partner ran over to help, he became the second casualty. Happened time and time again in the infantry until the line platoons learned.

Where was Carter? I had to get Bittner's rifle.

The sound of a high-power rifle shot rumbled high up on the side hill. Carter or someone else was shooting. Carter?

"Don't move," I shouted again at Josh Bittner. He looked at me with blood pooling around his waist.

"Can you hold out? It'll be dark soon," I said in a low voice from behind the door frame, which wasn't the safest place to be. Liz crouched near the stone fireplace.

Another rifle shot boomed above us, echoing through the canyon. Darkness came fast in the trees below the breaks. I had to take the chance and bring Bittner in.

"Josh, I'm coming for you. I'm going to grab your feet and pull you into the lodge. It's gonna hurt."

"I'm okay. Do it."

I sprinted the thirty yards to Bittner, grabbed his ankles, pulled him roughly across the grass and through the door, a method not first-aid sanctioned. I prayed the sniper wasn't smart enough to register his rifle where Bittner lay, only to touch the trigger again when darkness came. A sniper's trap.

Liz came into the kitchen and in the dark we pulled off Bittner's flak vest and shirt. The bullet had hit the edge of the vest, then went through his side.

"Fuck, I'm fine," he said. We kept him down, cleaned the wound as fast as we could and put a compress on the bullet hole. The slug missed the vitals.

"I've got to get your rifle. Where's Carter?"

I took the radio off his suspenders and called Carter. No answer. "If he's close to the hostiles he'll turn off his radio," Bittner said, sounding fuzzy and going into shock. Liz covered him with two blankets.

"I've got to get that rifle." I sprinted to where Bittner had lain, blood splotches on the grass. The rifle was gone. Damn, should have asked the sheriff for a weapon. After making two fast circles in the dry grass, I knew I was pushing my luck, and ran to the lodge. Who picked it up? Another hostile? Somebody had been shooting up on the side hill in the trees. Where was Carter?

"Somebody took the rifle," I whispered to Liz. "My rifle is in the airplane at Cabin Creek. If these guys charge us, you go out the opposite door and head up into the breaks. I'll stay with Bittner and try to work something out."

"No. I'll stay with you. I have a .22 automatic pistol in my bedroom. I'll get it and load it. Haven't used it for years."

"Get it and bring it out here. Can you do that in the dark?"

"I can do a lot of things in the dark."

"Of course."

"Keep your mind on business. Turnabout is fair play," she said.

"I'll try to contact Link on the radio. Using the satellite phone on the runway is too dangerous."

Liz went into her bedroom to get the pistol. I was on the radio in the great room trying to get somebody, the sheriff, the FBI, the Forest

Service, anybody. The only contact was Cal, the midnight operator of a ham set in Alabama. The same guy.

"This is Cal. Y'all still fighting them terrorists up there in the mountains?" *He must sleep during the day.*

Yes, and could he call the FBI in Boise and tell them we were under attack, and to bring in a team to the Phantom Ranch immediately. I gave him the number.

"Phantom ranch, you say. That sounds dangerous. I'd sure like to be up there to help you with them terrorists. Was in the Navy once. I was a cook. I can shoot real good. Okay, I'll get on it."

"Thanks Mister Cal. Call back when you have made contact. Got to go."

Liz screamed from the bedroom. A pop, pop, popping sound came through the room, loud and clear. The automatic pistol. *Christ! They're in the house.*

I ran for the bedroom, stopped with my back to the wall next to the open door, and looked in. The double doors to the deck were open, and blood was on the floor. There was no Liz, no one.

I had no weapon, nothing. Bittner was in the kitchen not making a sound. Maybe he was in shock.

I'm going after that bastard. I did have a weapon—the long rifle above the fireplace. I grabbed a chair, dragged it to the fireplace in front of the fire, stepped up and reached for the Kentucky.

Someone behind me yanked the chair away. I jumped to the floor and a bloody arm came around my waist. I dropped the long rifle, grabbed the arm and rolled. The other arm came up, holding a combat knife. I dropped the first arm, grabbed the second arm and lunged into the attacker.

The terrorist stepped back. Blood everywhere. The assailant was young, early twenties, Caucasian, a lone wolf, and he wanted to kill me. Blood ran down his arm and the side of his shirt. His eyes were sunken and red, a killer, crazed, wounded, and for a moment I could smell him. He blinked. He was scared. *You can't match your ass-hole buddies in Afghanistan, you miserable turn-coat. They didn't smell as bad as you.*

This assailant was bleeding everywhere but he wasn't going to stop or run out of blood soon enough. He lunged at me again.

The long rifle with the spiked bayonet was on the floor. I grabbed it and jabbed the bayonet at him twice. He parried each time, the knife out in front. *Trip the trigger!* The rifle was a percussion ignition. I pulled the hammer lock back, trying to scare him to run, knowing it was futile. He circled around, tried to jump over the leather sofa and fell back. He gasped, was weakening. I jabbed at him again with the spiked bayonet, then pulled the trigger. A cloud of smoke and an ear-splitting boom filled the room.

The Kentucky long rifle was loaded and primed!

The sound was deafening. At a distance of five feet the smoke covered the terrorist's face and he jerked backward and fell. The .50 caliber rifle ball took out his lower jaw and the back of his head.

I dropped the rifle and ran out to the deck looking for Liz. Carter came around the side of the lodge, his rifle at the ready. "God damn," he said. "These bastards don't give up!"

Liz came running into the great room from the hall, slamming another magazine into the pistol she held in her hand. "Oh my God! He's finally dead."

The man's brains and blood were all over the red and yellow carpet behind the sofa. The pine logs in the fireplace burned brighter. The fire was saying, "Keep going, nothing changes here."

"I'm okay," Liz said. "The man came through the French doors just as I loaded the pistol. Blood was running down his arm. He had a rifle and dropped it."

"And you unloaded the pistol on him. You hit him several times. You and Carter and Alec, bless his soul, saved my life. The badass was weakened or I couldn't have fought him. Alec had loaded the long rifle, which shocked me when I pulled the trigger, and sure as hell shocked that terrorist."

We ran back to Bittner in the kitchen. He was groggy, but he was looking at us. We told him there was one less hostile, probably the one who shot him in the yard. Bittner managed a grin; "Glad you got him." He wanted us to give him a weapon should anybody else rush the house.

Carter handed him his nine millimeter and Bittner put it under his blanket.

"I'm slipping," Bittner mumbled, "exposing myself like that."

Carter said he was up on the side hill watching the lodge when he saw Bittner walking to the back of the lodge, heard a rifle shot and saw Josh fall. "Another guy came out of the edge of the woods, and I tripped the trigger on him. I finally located the second asshole, the guy who shot Josh. He was moving to finish Josh, when I shot and winged him, but lost him in the trees. He must have run down to the lodge."

"He ran into the bedroom and I emptied the Walther on him," Liz said.

"You hit him three or four times, after Carter shot him," I said. "He was bleeding everywhere. He was wounded bad. Both of you saved me."

"There's not much left of him," Carter said. "He's a white guy. It took three of us to take him down."

"And I never fought anybody that smelled that bad," I said.

"You shot him because he smelled bad?" Carter smiled.

"That was a good enough reason."

Carter looked around, surveying the mess. "We will let Mr. Barrett's team do the forensics and clean up this place."

"How did you know they were terrorists?" I asked Carter.

"They weren't hunters. Both of them had taken up sniper positions facing the lodge. I watched one of them with binoculars, couldn't see the one who shot Josh. The boss also told me about the De Havilland being sabotaged. When one of them shot Bittner, it was open warfare."

"Think there are any more out there?"

"The dead man up in the trees is Middle East," Carter said. "The guy in the next room looks like an American, a nutcase. How in the hell do they recruit these freaks to kill their own people?"

"Ours not to reason why," I said.

"Ours but to do or die," Bittner added, lifting his shoulder and grimacing.

"Into the valley of death rode the six hundred."

"Tennyson," Bittner said, flat again on the bed.

Liz looked from one to the other and back. "We're in a gun battle here and you guys are reciting poetry!"

"Why not?" I said. "I think the hostiles are gone for now, or they would have come in for the fight."

The radio crackled. Baker was on the air. "What's going on, Casey? Calvin from Alabama radioed me again and said you found more terrorists back there in the mountains."

I told her about the latest action. Link had come in and left us with two FBI shooters. There was a firefight. One FBI agent, Bittner, was shot and wounded. I asked Baker to relay to Link to bring in a helicopter to land in the dark. Bittner needed to be evacuated right away. "He has a stomach wound. Tell Link to bring a doctor."

Baker called back in fifteen minutes. She said Link had ordered a Blackhawk and would arrive at Phantom at first light.

"Can't they land at night?"

"No. First light. Link said the aircraft they have is not night equipped. Link said to stay under cover; don't expose yourselves. There could be more hostiles." Baker's voice was rising. "Casey, did you copy?"

"Yes, I copied. Did you find any more information on the green Cessna? I know the tail number was a fake, and the man we saw at the bar, Fauod Saeed, I think is their leader."

"Was he one of the guys you took out?"

"We're working on it."

"Just like old times," Baker said. "You and Link and Jammer. And now you and Liz. I'm jealous you know. Let me talk to Liz."

And she did.

The helicopter touched down at dawn. The doors opened and Link and six camouflaged SWAT agents disembarked. The shooters disappeared into the edges of the forest. In moments they had surrounded the lodge, the barn and field.

Liz was in the lodge sleeping. Carter and I were tending to Bittner. After the agents had reported by radio to Link that the perimeter of the lodge was secure, the doctor and the two EMTs ran inside to administer to Josh.

"What a mess in the big room," Link said. "Bodies follow in your wake."

"They must like me, the freakin' zealots."

He didn't smile this time. "There have been too many of these people coming into our country, Casey. They join up with local thugs. I hope we have all of this bunch."

Carter's rifle was slung on his shoulder. He took the nine millimeter from Bittner, ejected the clip, pulled the slide back, reversed the procedure, putting a cartridge into the firing chamber, then slid the Beretta into his shoulder holster. "I didn't want him to get a fever and shoot himself." Carter was in his element, not tired from the night's adventures. Carter was a Navy SEAL and thrived on this action.

"Bittner wanted to keep the pistol," he said. "I told him we were secure now. The doctor has him stabilized and the helicopter will take him to Boise."

"It was every man for himself last night, and every woman too, when Liz shot the bad guy." I told Link the details of the previous night.

Thompson, the deputy agent, camouflaged and carrying an M4, told Link they had come across the dead terrorist at the edge of the trees. "Must have been quite a shot, Carter, what was the distance?"

"Two hundred yards."

"Got him good."

Combat soldiers had no feelings for terrorists who kill unarmed innocents. Unlike enemy soldiers, terrorists do not follow the rules of war, if there are rules.

"The hostile was sitting there, watching the back of the lodge, like a cat over a mouse hole. I was watching him. There was another guy stalking Bittner. I evened the score. Then I saw the other guy but just winged him. Liz and Casey finished him off."

"He was on a suicide mission," I said.

We stood on the deck when the Blackhawk lifted off with Bittner, the doctor and the EMTs. Dawn was breaking in the backcountry. The sunshine touched the trees at the top of the breaks.

"The helicopter will bring forensic people back with them, and they will write a report on what they find. We'll need you at headquarters again," Link said.

"I'm getting to be a paperwork junkie."

"You don't prevaricate on the answers to their questions, do you?" Link asked, knowing that I might stretch the truth to the government.

"Of course not," I said, and winked at Carter.

"Will somebody move the bodies out of here?" I asked. "Or do we have to bury them? The bears will be coming around." Carter and the deputies had carried the dead terrorist to the edge of the woods.

"Yes," Link said. "The deputies will take care of them."

Link continued, "On another issue, we're still trying to determine who killed the bikers in Wyoming, and what part Saeed played, if any."

"They're are getting a lot of cash from somewhere. I suspect Middle East black market oil money."

Link shrugged and walked outside.

The SWAT shooters took turns coming into the lodge kitchen for breakfast. Liz slept late, showered, and changed into clean clothes. She had applied make-up, brushed her hair, and wore faded jeans and a red checked ranch shirt when she walked into the kitchen. I thought she looked terrific.

"Good morning," we said in unison.

"And a good morning to everybody. God, the living room. Where is the terrorist?" I told her Carter and the deputies had taken him out of the lodge.

"What a deadeye," I said, and put my arm around her waist, handing her a cup of coffee. "Where did you learn to shoot a pistol?"

"You gave me lessons once upon a time in the desert, on a picnic. Remember?"

"A picnic in the desert. Of course, a picnic."

Link looked at me and smiled.

At mid-morning, the sunlight reached the bottom of the canyon and the grass of the airfield sparkled with dew. We sat in the kitchen, eyelids drooping from the warmth of the wood stove and the loss of a night's sleep. A hawk shrieked on the edge of the pines, making Link and me jerk. Carter nodded off on a side chair next to the wood box, his rifle across his lap. His head fell forward every few minutes. The screech registered. He moved, but didn't open his eyes. He looked contented. Carter could sleep on a rock pile in a mortar barrage.

The woods were silent around the lodge. Cottonwoods along the river rustled from the noon winds, yellow leaves falling and floating in the river. A woodpecker hammered on a hollow tree, hesitated a moment, then picked up the drumming. I visualized the black and white head pounding at larvae in a gray snag, at a speed the human eye could not follow. The woodpecker stopped, then started again, a distant lonely staccato sound. When the bird had finished that old tree, all was quiet in the forest. The world was serene again.

Ours not to reason why, I thought, and drifted off.

Three Fires

"**Twin Falls tower calling Phantom Ranch,**" an unfamiliar male voice said.

I came back on the radio, wondering what this was all about. "Go ahead, Twin Falls."

"This is Wellington at FAA Twin Falls. I need to speak to Captain McConnell."

I didn't bother to tell the caller that I hadn't been a captain for many years. When I identified myself, Wellington told me that Lorraine Brindell was flying into the backcountry.

Baker! Flying in here, into the path of the terrorists? "Coming into *here?* The Middle Fork? That's crazy!" *What was Baker up to?* I glanced at Carter and raised my eyebrows. He was checking out his .308, the barrel pointed up. Carter pulled the bolt back, inspected the open receiver, then turned to my radio conversation.

Wellington continued, "She told me to tell you she is flying into McCall, picking up a Forest Service official, some smokejumpers, and will land at the river airfield in an hour."

"They can't come in here—it's too dangerous. We may still have hostiles out here."

"I'm just the messenger, Captain," Wellington said. "Lorraine and a guy named Deming are flying in to the river country."

I'll be damned—Baker and Jammer! Why was Baker using my military rank with her peers? She wants to sound more official with the FAA.

"Wellington, try to contact them in the air. They're probably flying with a Forest Service pilot in the Twin Otter. They need to return to their base. The FBI is here, and we think hostiles are still in these woods. Ask Loraine—we know her as Baker—and Jammer Deming to contact us here at the ranch as soon as they can make radio contact."

"I'll pass the word, sir," Wellington said, and keyed off.

Link walked into the lodge after I cradled the radio mike. "You won't believe this, Link. Those two adrenaline junkies are flying in here today."

Link cracked a grin. "Which two junkies? You know a lot of them."

"Baker and Jammer."

"I believe that. We need to stop them."

"Twin Falls tower says they're already in the air. They're on their way."

"The Forest Service does what it wants to do. I hope Jammer brings a sharp Pulaski." Link made a face when he took a swallow of coffee.

"Coffee a little strong for you, Boss?" Carter said.

"Might have guessed you made it."

"Hot and black," Carter came back. "The way I like my women."

Link laughed. "You sailors are all alike."

"That's what Mr. McConnell said. The two of you should have been in the Navy," Carter said, as he wiped an oily rag down his rifle barrel.

Twenty minutes later the Twin Otter flew over the field at three hundred feet, the pilot looking over the runway for deer, elk, or horses, then turning and landing smoothly on the grass, close to the lodge where he could turn quickly, if the situation required. Jammer must have advised the pilot to stay away from the trees.

Link, Carter and I went out to the rail fence to meet them. The side door of the De Havilland was open, removed for the firefighters, the stairs dropped and Baker appeared in the doorway, first off. Her blonde hair caught the wind from the idling propeller, and she reminded me of royalty, greeting the waiting paparazzi. She was flushed, as pretty as ever, and I knew this was what she loved to do.

Jammer came off the plane next, followed by six smokejumpers who stiff-legged the steps, their parachutes unhooked from the D-rings and left somewhere inside the plane. They stopped, holding their helmets, looked around, smiled and laughed with each other, which is what jumpers usually did.

Link and I greeted Baker, kissing her on the cheek, then pulled Jammer aside, near the rail fence, away from the pilots and jumpers.

"Jammer, we need to talk," Link said. Link stood an inch taller than Jammer. Link moved closer, looking serious, and told Jammer that he,

Link, was in charge here, and why didn't the Forest Service call him before flying a plane load of jumpers in here? "Furthermore, what in the hell is Baker doing out here?"

"Thought you and Casey might need some help," Jammer said, not intimidated by Link's questions. "Baker said the only contact you had here on the river was through her and some ham radio guy in Alabama."

"And why did you fly in six jumpers?"

"There are three fires just north of here," Jammer came back.

"I didn't know that. And did you know we suspect there are still hostiles out here in the mountains?"

"I did suspect that," Jammer said, "and I'll tell you why. The fire season is almost over but two of our late season lookouts reported three fires all within five miles of each other. There hasn't been any lightning in the clouds that came through these mountains in the last week. Furthermore, the fires started in the canyons."

"In other words, not on the ridges, where the lightning strikes," Link said.

"That's right, near Forest Service trails. There aren't many trails north of here. We plotted them—after we flew over the smokes this morning. We checked the terrain from the air."

"What does that tell us?" Link said. "The fires may have been started by the hostiles."

"Possibly. That's why we didn't use the jumpers. We flew over the smokes at two thousand feet above the highest ridge. I've learned my lesson. What is the range of an AK47?"

"Too close for the De Havilland," I said.

"Not to worry about the fires. It's late in the season for them to do much damage to the woods anyway," Jammer, the fire boss, added.

"Those fires could have been arson, deliberately set," Link said.

"When plotted on a map, they were more or less in a straight line, back in the wilderness area."

"In other words, somebody walked or flew that country and started them," I said.

"The three fires could have been ignited by a man walking, dropped at a remote air field and picked up at another position, twenty-five miles away. Would be easy," Link continued. "We can check the location of the fires to determine what backcountry airfields are close by."

"There must be a band of radicalized terrorists out here," I said. "They want to do more damage than burn some trees." Link nodded in agreement.

"We've taken out eight of them. There are more out here," I said.

"The three forest fires are a diversion. The real target is something else, a hell of a lot more strategic than trees. A target that will create fatalities," Link said.

"The mastermind is Saeed, flying the green 206," I said.

Jammer walked over to his jump crew, who had found some deck chairs and spread out on the grass next to the lodge. They had opened their Forest Service lunches and two of the jumpers were finishing their sandwiches. Baker and Liz were inside the lodge, talking with the FBI agents and waiting for the sheriff's deputies to move the bodies and finish the inspection.

Link and I stood next to the rail fence. Two of the firefighters got up and walked over to us. They had taken off their heavy jackets and wanted to talk.

"Are you going to supply us with guns? We know how to use them," the tall jumper said. He was fifteen years younger than Link and me. "I hear this is a combat zone along the river." His partner was watching him and concealing a smile.

"Hell," Link said, "you guys don't need guns. You got shovels and Pulaskis."

"Thought we'd ask. Our boss had all the fun."

"We wouldn't call it fun," Link said, with a serious look. "Casey and I were jumpers once. We know how you guys think. You don't want to pass up a good fight."

"You got that right," the second firefighter said.

"Smokejumpers don't change." I smiled at Link.

"Stand by, we might need you," Link said, and walked into the lodge.

I made small talk for several minutes, then the tall firefighter and his partner walked back to talk with Baker.

The afternoon slipped away; the FBI shooters alternated their positions, coming into the lodge for breaks. The Twin Otter was dispatched to the Salmon airport, leaving Jammer and the jumpers at the lodge.

The leaves on the cottonwoods along the river rattled on the afternoon breezes. I paused in the quiet to listen to the bugle of a bull elk up high in the timber. All was too serene—the silence before the storm. Link came out to join me, and said he felt the same way. "Casey, let's have a talk with Baker."

I knew what he meant. Baker was in the kitchen. I nodded to her that Link and I wanted a word in private. We walked to the big room.

"Baker, we love you, but why did you come back in here with Jammer?" I asked. I remembered the days when she and Jammer were a pair. Was something in the wind again? She didn't mention any kind of a tryst when we were dancing at the Rustlers Noose, when her dog was shot, or the wild romance in the morning.

"I came in to help you and Link track the Cessna on radar. I have contact from here with the FAA. We're assisting you guys. The FAA is with us on this, Casey. The pilot is probably your Middle East friend you met in Sun Valley and saw again at the Rustlers Noose."

"If it's the same guy, Baker. We're not sure."

"She's right, Casey. Baker has been in contact with headquarters and FAA most of the afternoon," Link said.

"We are intercepting words like 'explosives' and 'hospitals,'" Baker said. "Salt Lake radio reported they lost him on radar—must be flying low in the canyons." She excused herself to go back to the radio.

"These people don't care who they kill—men, women, and children," I said. "The terrorists—call them what you will—go into a building and shoot. Why. Because they can. The victims are innocents, unarmed, rich or poor, young or old, Gentiles, Jews, and Muslims. Can't shoot back. Doesn't make a difference."

"You're getting that feeling at the back of your neck, right?" Link added. "I have the plan for night security."

"Good. Do you have an extra rifle? Mine is at Cabin Creek."

"Take Bittner's. Don't shoot yourself, eh?"

"I'm glad I had that Kentucky rifle. That was a nasty bastard."

"Yes, it was," he said. Link glanced toward the lodge window. "Liz will have memories of that room and the stone fireplace. They won't be good memories."

"Liz is resilient. She's tough," I said. "Both of these women are—Liz and Baker—super tough."

"And fearless," Link added.

"And fearless," I said.

Link looked in all directions around the house. "We'll bring the shooters in closer as it gets dark, keep them around the lodge and this end of the airfield, around the Blackhawk and the barn. The men can alternate in the lodge for chow and rest. They can take turns sleeping with the jumpers in the bunkhouse. Carter and Thorgard will take shifts staying awake in the lodge."

I retrieved the bottle of Maker's, took two glasses out to the deck, and poured. The drinks were waiting when Link returned. Two glasses clinked. "Cheers. Like other times. The Hindu Kush. Mike should be here," I said.

Link lifted his glass. "To Mike, wherever you are."

"To Mike."

"He was a hell of a combat soldier."

"Yes, he was."

"Things happen." Link wasn't going to the maudlin side. "Why do they happen when you and I are together?"

"You love it. That's why you were a Green Beret, and why you're in the FBI. It's in your DNA. You can't stay away from danger. Maybe you should join a monastery somewhere back in the mountains. Find a cloudy peak. You could pray, read books, drink wine, plant flowers, chase the nuns, that sort of thing."

"It wouldn't be long before you'd bring a band of guerrillas to the door."

"Then we'd have a hell of a party. I'm going to reload that Kentucky long rifle."

"This is good bourbon," Link continued, setting his glass on the deck rail, and keeping his eyes on the trees near the river. "Just one."

"Maker's 46."

"Alec had a lot of class."

"Yes, he did."

"Women and whiskey." Link gave me that smile again.

"One woman," I said. "Don't ask."

"I won't." We settled in our chairs, eyes searching the far canyon walls and the timbered slopes.

Two ducks flew up the river, a foot above the surface of the water. Silver ripples in the water followed them. The last rays of the sun stretched out at the top of the breaks, the sky a deep blue, cloudless, a great evening for flying.

Somebody else thought so too.

The sound of an airplane came around a rocky promontory, the rumble and direction of its engine telling us it was lower than the occasional high-altitude fly over. We both turned, instantly alert. Planes along the river were rare, but not unknown. Occasionally an aircraft flew up or down the Middle Fork, especially during the hunting season when air charters took hunters in and out of camps. But the sound of the engine of this plane was penetrating, echoing in the canyon walls. This plane was flying low and fast, just above the treetops.

"Move back, closer to the wall so he can't see us," I ordered, like the combat days in the mountains.

Link contacted the SWAT agents by radio and asked their locations. One came out of the woods behind the lodge, camouflaged head to toe, his face darkened, body impossible to locate in the waning light. He waved his rifle in the air, showing us his position, then disappeared. The other shooter ran out from the trees halfway down the field, waved to Link, then he too vanished. The others called in from the edge of the field.

In less than a minute the green plane came around the nose of the ridge upstream, lost altitude and flew down the grass runway under full power, fifty feet above the ground. "Back against the wall," Link said.

I looked around for a weapon.

The pilot didn't land, but flew above the runway at a high rate of speed, and over the rail fence, brought the nose up and roared over the lodge, flying downstream. "For Christ's sake, Link, it's the Cessna! What is he planning to do, strafe us?"

"He's taunting us," Link snapped. "Casey, go in the lodge, alert the others. I'll tell the shooters to take up positions outside the buildings."

The plane flew a mile down the canyon, then, under full power, did a one-eighty turn and came back up the gorge, straight for us.

"Out of the lodge now!" I shouted. The pilot could be on a suicide mission. Liz, Baker, and the agents needed no coaxing. They moved with hair-trigger speed out the back door and were into the trees when the green plane roared over the lodge going back upriver.

"I saw one person in the cockpit." Link came around the corner of the lodge holding an M4. I was hoping he had another one.

I took Liz's arm, leading her farther into the trees.

The green plane came over the big pines and the pilot cut the engine power. He was going to land! Another suicide freak, wanting to meet his God. Six rifles, including Link's, were trained and centered on the prop and swinging with the plane as it came closer. The plane bumped down on the dry grass at the far end of the field. "Hold your fire!" Link commanded. This must be FBI rules of warfare. We hadn't been fired upon. The green Cessna hadn't been classified as a hostile. *Not yet, Link!*

What is the pilot going to do? I was kneeling next to Liz. She squeezed my hand. The shooters were waiting for the word to fire. Suddenly the pilot gunned the plane, picked up speed on the field, and began a take-off. He must have seen someone, got a warning, or decided this wasn't the right time to die. The brown grass waved and shimmered behind the plane, the propeller revolutions at a max, the sound so violent it echoed in the trees. The nose wheel lifted, and the plane came off the ground, skimming the pines next to the lodge with only feet to spare. This time the pilot kept going. In a moment the canyon was quiet.

"Hold your positions until I advise you," Link radioed the agents. He turned to me. "I'm calling regional and alert them that a green airplane is on the loose."

Liz sat in the woods at the base of a big ponderosa, her arms around her knees. I sat down beside her and took her hand.

"I'm fine, Casey. First it was Clint, then Alec, and now this. If that terrorist comes back and crashes into my lodge, I'll kill him."

"If he doesn't do it to himself, there are eight guys here who will help you."

Carter walked over, holding the sniper's rifle. "These guys are crazies. Link, any idea who the pilot is? Can Baker and the FAA give us some help? I think I could have popped him with .308."

Link came right back. "The tail number, the paint job on the plane, and the name of Fauod Saeed are all fake. Aliases. They started something big at the old mine, are really pissed, and I suspect are planning something new."

"Saeed is their leader. He manages to stay out of the line of fire. He brings in radicalized terrorists to create havoc. And recruits lone-wolf crazies," I said.

"Hey, that's an insult to Idaho wolves," Carter said.

"Point taken," I said.

We gathered in front of the lodge, watching the canyon and the river. Link said, "A helicopter will be in tomorrow with forensic agents and will take you and Liz back to Owyhee Crossing. We're tracking the Cessna, and are getting radio intercepts of his position and messages."

"I was certain he was going to suicide into the lodge on his last approach," I said.

"Thought the same." Link was looking downriver.

The night had turned black, deep in the canyon before the moon came up. The SWAT shooters had moved closer to the lodge, taking turns sleeping on the deck. Baker had found an extra bed near Liz in the master bedroom. The smokejumpers were sleeping in the bunkhouse, but far from turning in, they were having a merry time: their laughter echoed in the canyon.

"I'm going to the bunkhouse to visit the jumpers," Baker said. "I know most of them from the summers."

"Okay. Don't get my crew drunk," Jammer said.

After Baker was in the bunkhouse we could hear the laughs increasing. Link and I looked at each other. "She's probably telling some jump stories we've never heard." At eleven o'clock Link contacted the shooters again, telling them to move closer to the lodge and barn. A night bird whistled once back in the trees.

Liz looked at me over the kitchen table. "I think they've all turned in over there in the bunkhouse. It's finally quiet. I'm going to bed,

Casey. Best go over and escort Baker back here, before the night gets too short."

I walked around the barn and opened the bunkhouse door. All was quiet. The red-haired jumper was dimming the Coleman when I walked in. The other firefighters were in their sleeping bags, some looking up at me from their bunkhouse cots.

"Where's Baker?" I asked.

"Baker? She left here an hour ago."

A hollow feeling hit my stomach.

I walked back, thinking we might have passed in the night, checked out the lodge deck, whistled once, moved around the perimeter of the helicopter parked by the rail fence, whistled to one of the sentry shooters, heard him say he hadn't seen anyone. I returned to the lodge. Link was crawling into a sleeping bag on a cot in the hall. Carter sat at the kitchen table. The lanterns were turned down. Liz stood in the doorway to the big room.

"I can't find Baker!"

Link and Carter were spring loaded. Link went to the deck, radioed the sentries. Carter pulled his nine from its holster and ran to the bunkhouse. Nothing!

They both returned looking serious. Liz went down the hall to check the bedrooms. Nothing.

"Baker Brindell wouldn't get lost in the dark walking from the bunkhouse to the lodge," I said. "You couldn't lose her in the middle of the Amazon jungle."

The moon had come up over the rim of the breaks. An eerie light was filtering through the high branches of the pines. A wolf howled once, far away.

I picked up Bittner's rifle and quietly walked into the forest behind the lodge, stopped and listened. Fifty feet away was the tree line where I had put an arrow through that hostile three weeks before. If someone moved in the moonlight now I would see them. The woods were silent. The night was telling me that Baker wasn't there, that she never existed. If those bastards had snatched her, they had to be very good.

The lights in the lodge and bunkhouse went off. Baker was gone.

Hostage

Jammer was a man possessed. He ran from the lodge to the bunkhouse, circled the barn, ran back to the kitchen, and slammed the kitchen door. "Jesus H. Christ, they have her."

"Stop!" Link snapped at Jammer. "Quiet. They're out there."

"Let's make a plan," I said. "Keeps the lights off."

"Give me a gun. Somebody give me a fucking gun!" Jammer was looking straight at Link in the dark.

Link put his hand in front of Jammer. "Not yet. No noise. Not a sound. Doesn't seem like they could grab Baker so easy. They could have shot her. Could have shot some of us."

"Maybe she had one too many with her jumper friends and wandered off into the forest," Carter said, coming into the group. Jammer gave Carter a hard look. Jammer and Baker weren't a pair now, but Jammer defended her at every chance.

I stepped between Carter and Jammer. Carter and Jammer Deming were two guys you didn't want to get riled up. It was possible Jammer was still in love with Baker.

"Baker could drink any two of those smokejumpers under the table, and run a marathon afterwards," I said.

"I think they want a hostage," Link said. "We've wiped out most of the hostiles here, along with the explosives they stored. They have another plan. Another Twin Towers."

"Let's get Baker back first," Jammer said.

Link was in command. This is what he was good at, what he was paid to do. This was his game. "We have six agents here," he said. "Two of them will secure the Blackhawk, two will disperse around the bunkhouse and barn, and two will be stationed outside the lodge, one in front and one in back. That leaves four of us: Carter, Casey, Jammer and me.

Carter, give Jammer your pistol and extra magazines. You and Jammer stay inside the lodge, near Liz, and the radio. Casey and I will try to pick up Baker's tracks, or anything else we can find behind the bunkhouse."

He stopped to let his plan sink in.

"It's dark and dangerous to move around in these woods. Ambushing will be easy for them. Casey and I have done this before."

"Let me go with you, Link!" Jammer was getting himself worked up. "Baker and I go way back. You know that. I can't stand the thought of someone hurting her."

"I know you can't. Our shooters have night vision goggles. You don't."

"I can follow in Casey's footsteps. I won't shoot him."

"Okay, Jammer, but follow my orders. Explicitly. And take off that damn red hat."

The three of us moved out slowly, studying the ground for sign, the trees for dark shadows, and any other clue we might find.

The tall pines were quiet.

We had moved less than a hundred yards into the trees uphill from the landing field when Link raised his left hand. His right hand held his pistol, and his finger was on the trigger. I saw his fingers move, I froze. Jammer saw me and did the same. We waited. Five minutes passed. Link motioned us forward, his fingertips giving us directions. Link and I had been in combat a long time together, it seemed like years, and we could read each other's minds.

Link froze again, and nodded toward the ground. Below the tree branches were two distinct tracks, scuff marks made in the needles and dirt, like something—a body—had been dragged, with the person's heels a foot apart, showing the direction of travel.

Link pointed to a pine branch on the ground, several feet from the scuff marks. The piece of wood was three inches in diameter, broken to a length of three feet, and one end black with blood. It looked like a crude baseball bat.

Jammer saw the scuff marks and the branch at the same time and looked at me. In the darkness I could see the panic in his eyes.

The moonlight was fading. The night became black. A light breeze came down the canyon carrying the smell of pines. I turned slowly and looked back in the direction of the lodge and bunkhouse. All was in darkness. I slid my thumb forward and took the .308 off safe.

We followed the scuff marks through the trees for fifty yards, then another fifty, when Link motioned us to halt. He made a signal for me to come forward, but put a hold on Jammer, directing him to stop. The double motion gave me a feeling of dread.

I stopped twenty feet behind Link. Then he made a "look forward" sign with his fingers.

Laying out there between the big trees was a body. Link made another motion that he would go up first; I would stay back, out of the range of a booby trap. From what I could see the person was lying face down, arms forward and askew.

I came up beside Link. The person was a man, and in the dark not anyone I recognized from the bar at Rustlers Noose.

Link pointed to the victim's head. His skull was crushed, black hair soaked with blood. From what we could see of his face, it too was battered, his nose shattered. Blood streaked down his cheeks and chin.

"Baker did this," Link turned to me and mouthed.

She had been busy. Baker would not go easy.

Jammer came up and we showed him the body, the battered skull, and the broken tree limb. He shook his head.

There must be two or three hostiles out here; how else could they drag one of their own. Then they got tired and dropped him, and continued with Baker.

Link made a motion to return. We did, and were just as wary of being ambushed on the way back to the lodge as we were on the way out. We radioed the team we were returning. When we knocked on the kitchen door, the others were on edge and waiting.

They had seen nothing.

"Baker is alive," Jammer said, trying to convince himself. "Who else could have killed that bastard?"

"They didn't know they grabbed a wildcat," I said.

"When she saw the chance, she grabbed that club in the woods, and broke the hostile's head open," Jammer said.

"Baker could have been shot. They want a prisoner," Link added. "To tell them what we have here, and what we know."

"She won't tell them squat," Jammer said. "She'll die first."

I wasn't so sure of that. "She is alive for one reason. As a hostage. These guys are planning something big."

"I think you're right," Link said. "Something really big." The sky above the eastern ridge turned morning gray. Liz was in the kitchen. She had refused to go out with the first helicopter. Now I was going to insist. Carter sat close by, drifting in and out of sleep again, but I knew his reflexes were razor sharp, and like a cat, he was hearing everything.

"We'll get Baker back," I said to Liz. "Pity those bastards, once Jammer catches them, and he will, I guarantee."

Everyone was tired, a little punchy. The coffee and frying bacon smelled good. "What is the plan, Link, to rescue Baker?" I asked.

"Sheriff Bronski is flying in four more deputies to the ranch. Four more have been dispatched to the trailheads on the river."

"What is *our* plan?" I asked.

Link paused. "Wait," he said, and held up one finger. Then we heard the plane.

A single engine white plane came silently up the river, its prop barely turning above stall. It drifted over the lodge, almost without power, then set down two-thirds of the way up the grass field, a thousand yards from the lodge fence and the parked Blackhawk. The pilot has balls, I thought, and he made a perfect landing in the cold morning air, taxied another hundred yards to the edge of the trees, and stopped. The plane's running lights were off.

Four sets of binoculars at the lodge were positioned on the white plane. Six telescopes mounted on rifles were also focused on this new arrival. Hell, I thought, this isn't the green Cessna. It could be anyone, even a friendly. The prop kept turning. The side door opened. No one came out of the plane.

"Hold," Link said, and radioed the command to the shooters.

Two men came out of the trees. They were close together, struggling with something, and that something was Baker. I could easily see her, wearing the black turtleneck sweater, a white bag over her head and her hands tied behind her back. The two men pushed, grappled and shoved Baker up the steps and into the plane. They climbed aboard and the door was closed.

"Hold," Link commanded again. "They have a hostage. Too far for a shot."

We could hear the engine of the white plane rev up, a dust cloud blowing back through the grass into the trees. The pilot put the engine to maximum power and the plane lifted off the runway halfway down the field. The white plane flew over our heads and the lodge. There was no tail number. Somebody had painted it over.

"Okay," Link said, dropping his binoculars inside his open shirt, and turning to the team standing there. "We have a lot of work to do. Let's get busy."

South to The Desert

Link's radio crackled. He picked up the head set. "The FAA is tracking the white plane—the 185—on radar. It left the Middle Fork two zero minutes ago—twenty minutes that is—to an unknown destination." I heard him say the tail number had been painted over, and a female hostage was on the plane.

Link listened for a minute, then gestured for attention. "They have picked up radio intercepts. The aircraft is flying south on a west-southwest heading of two-three-five. That heading will take him into the Owyhee Mountains and over the Owyhee Reservoir if he continues on that course."

"The pilot is talking to someone, somewhere, an accomplice," Link continued, going back to the UHF radio.

Carter and Thorgard patrolled around the lodge, alternating trips to the pines in the back. They were communicating with the agents in the trees and on the side hill above the river.

"The FBI has been talking to the regional office and the authorities are watching the events unfolding," Link explained. "Region is in contact with the Idaho State Police and the county sheriffs. All decision-making offices are monitoring the direction of a white 185 flying from the backcountry. The Feds want to know if it's loaded with explosives. I can't tell them. They're the ones who have intercepted the words 'explosives' and 'target.' The plane is on a course away from populated areas and into the desert hills."

"That heading will take them over the Snake and our timber plant at Owyhee Crossing," I said. "I have those compass directions memorized from the Middle Fork."

"You would," Link said.

"It's revenge. Saeed knows me, and he wants to get back at me because I took out his people in the mountains."

"Does he know that's your timber plant?" Link asked. "If that plane is full of explosives I'd think Saeed would have bigger fish to target than your timber plant."

"Hey, I happen to like our plant and people. With that lumber there, the place would make a nice torch. We need to contact them, and tell them to evacuate—return for tomorrow's shift."

Link could see some sense in that. "Do it quietly. We don't want to panic anybody."

"If the plane continues on that heading, he will be over the Owyhee reservoir in about thirty minutes, and then onto the Alvord Desert," I said. "He can't get away. If he lands in the Alvord we can drop a team in and surround the plane."

"We are working on that," Link said.

I got on the satellite phone to Ellen at the plant and told her not to ask too many questions but contact Tony and vacate the premises. "Send the crew home for the rest of the day. Make it a short work shift. Do it right away and do it quietly. I'll explain later. Include yourself and the office staff."

"You sound serious," Ellen said.

"I am. You need to have everybody out within thirty minutes. Can you do that? Did you copy all that?"

She said she could, then disconnected.

Link gathered the shooters around him. "We're going south. Check your ammunition and water." Jammer moved up and stood beside Link. I knew what Jammer was thinking. Link looked at him and without a word, shook his head.

A chartered Islander flew in from Cascade with four more armed deputies. Their mission was to patrol up and down the river for five miles, then provide additional security and act as a listening post at the lodge and the airstrip. They also brought in more rations.

Link advised regional HQ that all was clear on the river. The FAA and the military were tracking the white plane. They had lost the green Cessna on radar. "He has nowhere to hide," Link said. "I suspect he is flying into the MOA—the military operations area—in the Owyhee desert. He probably doesn't know that."

"We have his general direction," Link continued. "We'll take that course in the helicopter. The sheriff at Owyhee County has been notified. The smokejumpers will return to McCall when the Twin Otter comes back. The sheriff's deputies will provide security."

"I'm going with you, Link," Jammer said.

"You can't, Jammer, it's unofficial."

"I followed your orders in the woods last night," Jammer said. "I owe them. When I get my hands on them, I'll rip their arms off. They have Baker." Jammer's face was getting red.

And I thought a Pulaski was messy.

If the smokejumper leader had been anybody other than Jammer, Link would have cold-cocked him right there. "You're too involved. There's too much at stake—that's why you can't come with us." Link adjusted the pistol in his shoulder holster—again—then moved closer to Jammer, looking him in the eye.

"These people have no respect for combatants, noncombatants, women, or children. We think the white plane is carrying explosives. We don't know the location of the green Cessna, but we'll find him. It also may be filled with explosives. I assure you, our priority will be to protect Baker, but I cannot say what will happen if we determine the planes are on a deadly mission, and Baker Brindell is on one of the planes."

"Son-of-a-bitch."

The old military rule: sacrifice one to save many.

"I won't carry a weapon," Jammer said. "I'll stay behind Casey."

Link wasn't as tough a guy as he looked. "Will you follow my orders explicitly, regardless of what happens?" Link asked.

"Yes."

"Uh-uh." Link was going to bend. "Explicitly?"

"Fuckin' aye. Explicitly." Jammer's fingers were crossed behind him.

Link gathered the six SWAT members around him, plus Carter, Thorgard, and myself. "Here is the update on the terrorist activity. The FAA and FBI are tracking the white plane, which as you know has two known hostiles on board, plus the pilot and a hostage, Baker Brindell.

The plane is on a heading south to the Owyhee Desert. We have been getting radio and phone intercepts about targets, hospitals, military facilities, and city malls. We think some of these targets are ruses, set up to divert us. We also suspect they are on a suicide mission. Nine of them have been taken out; eight by us and one, probably by Baker. Many more remain. We do not know the location of the green Cessna. We think a man calling himself Fauod Saeed is the mastermind and is piloting the Cessna. He'll let the sheep kill themselves, and being the leader, will fly off and hide somewhere."

Link continued, "We will follow the white plane, out of sight, and make plans as we go. An F15 will also be circling above us. The Air Guard is bringing in some A10s and Apaches from Boise. I can assure you that their official position is that we will not allow either plane to fly toward a populated area. If they land, get on the ground and take orders from me. There is a hostage with them."

I knew what Jammer was thinking. He wasn't in the military *or* the FBI. He was going to save Baker. Hell, we all loved Baker as much as Jammer. I walked over to the table and opened an aviation chart, drawing a line from the Middle Fork to the Owyhee Desert. My fingers traced the heading the white 185 was flying. The hostiles were not taking a direction leading into the cities, not yet. If either plane turned north, the authorities wouldn't hesitate to take them down. The Air Guard A10s could easily do that. I didn't want to think about that.

"Link," Jammer said, "the three forest fires were diversions. The green Cessna is also a fake lead, a feint, a diversion."

"They know we will shoot them down, hostage on the plane or not, if they fly toward a populated area," Link said.

"They're targeting the power grid," I said. The others looked at me.

"The high-line electric transmission line runs from Oregon and crosses the Owyhee Mountains with power service to Idaho and states to the east. The utility companies and federal authorities have drafted alternate power plans if hostiles disrupt the major power grids by cyber sabotage. But physical destruction of remote transmission towers is another matter." I continued to lecture, my hands in front, like a professor. "How many states to the east would be affected if the major line was taken out?"

Link, Jammer, and the shooters looked at me. The authorities must have thought of that. Perhaps they hadn't. "How long would it take to put contingency power plans in place? Would they be effective?" I asked.

"It's possible," Link said. "Let's saddle up."

Liz walked into the big room and handed me a cup of coffee. She was going back to Boise on the Twin Otter. "Let's come back later, Casey, after all this is settled."

"Stay at my place in the hills, and you can take a commercial flight to Nevada in a day or two. I'll call Tony and ask him to meet you at the airport."

"You're on. The camp at Rush Creek was nice, but I'm sure your home in the country will be perfect." Liz winked, and walked out to the plane.

Link was on the radio, looking serious, talking to some high brass. He wore his tailored sun-bleached camos we wore in the infantry, to look as gung ho as possible. His sleeves were rolled up above his elbows, like the Marines. All he needed were the Ray-Bans.

"The pilot has altered his direction west and is tracking on a heading of two-hundred and seventy degrees," he said. "That will put him near the town of Wagontire, Oregon in fifty minutes. We are getting intercepts of 'hospital,' and 'INL.' He also must be running low on fuel."

"The Idaho National Laboratory?" I said. "Both facilities contain radioactive material. If the terrorists get hold of that, they could poison a hell of a lot of people."

Link was back on the radio. "The white plane did another course correction to the east."

"And that heading will take him where?" Thorgard asked.

"To the middle of the Owyhee Mountains," I said, interrupting Thorgard and answering for Link, who was looking at a chart. "I have every compass heading memorized down there."

"He's circling back," Thorgard said. I glanced at him. I gave Thorgard a serious look. He was a muscular and mean-looking son-of-a-bitch, carried an M4, with extra magazines around his waist. A combat knife was strapped to his thigh. Thorgard was ex-Army, sported a full red beard, and had dark tattoos on one side of his neck. He had applied streaks of black camouflage above his beard. He was a throwback to the Vikings—well trained and disciplined. He was good with answers to tactical questions.

A minute later Link returned to the deck. "We are going to take him out," he said. "A decision that was made above me."

"Best thing I've heard all day," I said. "But first we have to rescue Baker."

"Once a Green Beret, always a Green Beret." Link nodded, punched Thorgard on the arm, and walked back to the commo table in the big room.

Jammer was looking at me. "If anything happens to Baker," he said, "there won't be enough of those bastards left for the crows to pick at."

"We can't go in shooting: we'll make a plan."

Neither Jammer nor I worked for the FBI, and we didn't take orders from them, or from Sheriff Quentin Bronski and his posse. We'll make our own plan. *I've got a rifle—just need a pistol.*

"Let's move out to the chopper," Link ordered. And we did.

Destroy the Power Grid

"I have the distance and direction to the white plane," Warrant Officer Dyke Dawson, the Blackhawk pilot, said to Link. Dawson was a pro. CWO Follette, the co-pilot, also had the look of an experienced pilot. Follette sported a thin dark mustache, and spoke with an accent. "He sounds French," I said to Link. We were stuffing equipment bags under the bucket seats.

"He is French," Link said. "Follette was a pilot with the French Air Force. Has a combat record from their skirmishes in Africa. He is now an American citizen."

I knew we had the right guys when I saw them flying the chopper in the river canyon.

Six SWAT agents sat in the helicopter, three on each side, their rifles held muzzles up. The shooters applied camouflage paint to their faces. Two of them ran their fingers over their cartridge magazines. Jammer and I sat in jump seats behind Link and Sergeant Crockett, the crew chief and machine gunner. Crockett wore a pair of OD cargo pants and a military-issue brown tee-shirt. He moved like a cat inside the Blackhawk. We were told he had some experience with the machine gun. We'd need him when the battle started.

In a moment the lodge, river, and pines were far below and behind us. It was a somber group because we knew Baker was a hostage out there in the terrorists' plane. "How close should I be, when we catch him?" Dawson asked Link. The speed of the Blackhawk was equal to the Cessna's. We had headsets and were communicating easily in the chopper.

"Stay close enough to keep him in sight," Link answered.

The white plane had crossed the Snake River, heading south, when we spotted him.

The pilot maintained the same heading as he flew over the towers of the electrical transmission power line. This line was the major part of the power grid running from Oregon and California in the West through desolate Idaho desert country to transmission stations in the East. The steel towers loomed high and ominous, although they appeared diminutive and out of place next to the massive rocky cliffs and canyons.

If the hostiles were going to dive-bomb their plane into a building in one of the Idaho cities, they could have done that by now, but they were flying south, into the mountainous desert. We scanned the sky for the green Cessna. Nothing. The hostiles could be planning a coordinated attack.

"Their objective must be the power grid, Link," I said. "The transmission towers."

"Maybe," he said.

The helicopter pilot and Link were talking on their headsets. Link came back into the cabin and motioned for attention. "The hostiles' plane landed in an unmarked field in the next valley. A dirt road runs next to the field, leading to Route 95, thirty miles to the east. I will notify the sheriff to block that road and proceed to this location. We will land on the opposite ridge top, in defilade—stay behind the line of the ridge and observe what these people are doing. Split up in pairs. You know how to do this. Do not skyline yourselves. Move to within five hundred yards, then proceed on my command. They have Baker as hostage—hold any shooting until I give orders."

Dawson brought the Blackhawk down through a cloud of dust in the only opening in the field of sagebrush and juniper. We ran under the rotors and stopped behind some boulders. I crossed my fingers the hostiles hadn't put scouts on the ridgetops.

The pilots, Crockett and the shooters stayed with the bird. When we exited, Sergeant Crockett was checking out the M240 mounted machine gun, still oiled from Afghanistan.

Link, Carter, Jammer and I spread out and walked a half mile through the sagebrush, then climbed to a low saddle overlooking the field. I carried Bittner's sniper rifle. Jammer was unarmed, without even a Pulaski. I knew he was biding his time until he could get his hands on a weapon.

The afternoon was clear, cool, and deathly quiet in the desert hills. Piles of white cumulus broke up the sky to the north. Two hawks circled above and behind us, screeching. The smell of the sage and the dried clumps of grass were a welcome change from the exhaust of the helicopter. Two mule deer jumped up from their beds and ran to the ridge. I hoped they wouldn't spook the people at the plane.

We approached the low place between the two hills. Link crawled forward first, his binoculars in one hand. He appeared as a camouflaged bush on the skyline, then he motioned me forward. Parked in the grass was the white tail-wheel plane, the 185. Next to the white plane was the green Cessna. We counted four men and one woman—Baker. A beat-up faded black pick-up truck was pulled up next to the planes, and the men tied Baker to the front bumper. Her hands were also roped behind her back. Baker could run like the wind, and the hostiles were taking no chances. Two automatic rifles leaned against the side of the truck, far from her reach.

Four of the men unloaded gray bags of what looked like explosives from one plane, then the other, piling them in the bed of the old truck.

"They're not using the planes as missiles," Link said.

"They could be taking the truck to the transmission towers."

"My thoughts exactly."

Jammer crawled up behind us. "We have to get Baker out of there."

I could tell he was working himself up.

"Wait," Link said.

"For God's sake, we can't wait too long. They could—"

"I know," Link said sharply. He was in command. I looked at Jammer, gave him another flat "be cool" movement with my hand.

A second pick-up truck, bouncing at a high rate of speed over the dirt ruts, drove up and parked next to the planes. Two men stepped out with rifles. Both looked rugged, dirty, swarthy, North African. One of the men untied Baker from the bumper, then two of them pushed her into the back seat of the second truck. She must have said something to one of them, because the man slapped her across the face. Baker didn't flinch.

"I'll kill that bastard," Jammer snarled. "Tear his fucking arms off. I'm marking the guy—the one with the long black hair and gray ball cap." Jammer was using my binoculars.

One black pickup was loaded with backpacks and explosives. From where we were, we could hear the slamming of the tailgate. The hawks circling the ridge to our left answered the noise with screeches. *Hope those birds won't tell.*

Baker was in one of the trucks. Two men jumped in each truck. Two other men—the pilots—stayed with the planes.

"We'll follow those trucks from the air. Keep the other four agents here to watch these other two," Link commanded. He radioed the two shooters on the right and the two on the left, who had crawled to within five hundred yards of the airplanes. Link instructed them to stay, but not to move on the men and the two planes until he gave the order from the bird. They still had the hostage in one of the trucks.

The time was two o'clock when I checked my watch in the Blackhawk. We were observing the two trucks from miles in the air. They took a dirt road that circled the tops of the canyons, dropping into a large reservoir in the desert. Their dust clouds were easy to follow from the air. There was nothing secret about their moves.

"This is no diversion," I said to Link.

"The transmission towers," he said, and radioed his headquarters.

Headquarters told Link to advise them if the trucks stopped at the transmission towers.

The electrical lines came from the west over the top of a low ridge. One steel tower rose close to the top of the hill, the next several hundred yards closer to us on the downslope. We couldn't land the helicopter anywhere near the trucks or the towers. Dawson set the bird down over a mile from the far side of the hills. The crew chief produced a spotting scope and we grabbed it and jogged back as close to the towers as we could and still stay unobserved.

Two hostiles pulled Baker from the truck and tied her back to the front bumper. She was bucking and twisting, took a kick at one of them, as the terrorists moved the explosives. Baker must have thought she was dead anyway. Jammer and I were getting our hackles up, glassing Baker, then glancing at Link. Link continued to look through his binoculars, ignoring us. The insurgents moved boxes of explosives from the pick-up beds and placed them around two of the steel I-beams of one tower. They were in a hurry—not good if one is working with C4 and detonators.

Two of the terrorists then threw some boxes into the second truck and bounced their way across the rutted terrain, where they packed explosives around the support structures of the second tower, farther up on the hill. The truck then came back to the first tower, and a conversation took place between the men.

"We have to get closer," Link said. "I don't like this. We need to take our chances and get within rifle range."

We crawled at best we could down a dusty creek bed, and came out three hundred yards from the trucks. Hunkered down in the small arroyo we could see the men—two were Mideast types and two Anglos—wiring up the detonators to both towers. At one point they all faced the second tower two hundred and fifty yards away. An explosion boomed and raked the valley. Pretty dumb, I thought, if the lines came down they were under them.

Nothing changed for a few seconds. Then as the smoke cleared the tower began to heel over, gained momentum and toppled. Sparks and fire flew as the wires contacted the sage and brush. Then the tower stopped before grounding, suspended by the heavy transmission lines. But the terrorists had done their job.

"Those dirty bastards," Jammer said. He had acquired binoculars from the crew chief.

We watched as the four men stood, looking at the destruction of the second tower. Not a complete failure, but enough to interrupt power for a long time. The men moved rapidly, placing more explosives around the steel beams of the first tower. One of the men untied Baker. She rolled to one side and two of the men grabbed her and tied her to a vertical steel column, one of the four structural members making up the tower, only feet away from the packed explosives.

"Let's move," Link said. "Carter, take out the one with the black hoodie working on the detonator. Casey, the other one. I'll take out the third guy next to Baker."

We were ready. "Now!" Link said, his cheek pressed to the stock of the sniper's rifle.

Three rifles cracked. Three hostiles dropped. Carter, the trained sniper, was cranking the bolt of the Remington for the fourth insurgent. He was too late. The fourth man jumped out of the truck, ran to Baker, cut the ropes, grabbed Baker and jerked her toward the truck. She kicked him and he punched her hard. Baker staggered and he grabbed her shirt, lifted and pushed her into the backseat of the truck. She appeared to be hurt, maybe unconscious. We could see him pull a pistol, and point it at her. Then he dropped the pistol, and jumped on her to retie her wrists and feet, fumbling around, looking for more rope in the backseat of the truck.

"Should I take the shot through the windshield, Boss?" Carter asked. He was ready.

"No, hold," Link said. "Too risky."

"That guy is going to pay," I said.

Jammer was silent. He had a terrible look in his brown eyes.

The terrorist started the engine, gunned the truck, went flying over the ruts near the tower, bounced and fishtailed, doing over sixty, when the black truck came to the first curve going up a hill. A cloud of dust twice the size of the vehicle followed them up the grade.

Link radioed for Dawson to pick us up in the Blackhawk, and told Carter to check the bodies of the hostiles.

The dirty black pickup was easy to follow. How were we going to get Baker back alive? The Blackhawk pilot flew the bird above the sagebrush, following the terrain, the track taking us up, then down, one dry canyon after another, heading back to the two airplanes.

I knew Jammer was about to explode. He turned to Link. "Drop Casey and me on the other side of the hill from the road, out there about five miles, and we will ambush that son-of-a-bitch on the downslope." He gave Link the hard look, the kind only a former wildcatter could give. I knew why Jammer was the boss of the firefighting unit. He had the binoculars from Crockett, the crew chief, and had conned CWO Dawson out of his .45 Long Colt revolver and a box of cartridges. Dawson and Follette had turned and were watching us for directions.

"Okay." Link nodded, and said something to the pilot.

Dawson added power, went up high and took a circuitous route miles ahead of the truck, dropping Jammer and me below boulders halfway down the slope from the top of the hill, not far from the road. We moved like wolves through the brush and the rocks back to the road, taking advantage of any fold in the ground or rock outcrop.

"He is going to be coming fast," I said to Jammer. The truck came across the top of the hill, the dust cloud betraying his position. Then the vehicle started down. The driver slowed for the first curve, then the second. I looked into Jammer's eyes, seeing something there I had never seen before. They were almost glowing with energy, a savage hate, a revenge. I loved Baker as much as he did, and we needed to be smart, and steady. I didn't have a plan how we were going to stop the truck without hurting Baker.

Jammer had a plan and made the decision for both of us. He jumped up, ran through the sagebrush at right angles to the road, the long revolver out in front. We were above a short cutbank on our side, and when he got to the edge Jammer leaped, landing on the road fifty yards in front of the pick-up. He stood up in the road, his feet spread, the long-barreled revolver out in front, pointed at the windshield of the truck, the terrorist braking with surprise, back tires bouncing on the corrugated dirt, the truck straightening and headed straight for Jammer. I was thirty feet behind Jammer, and caught a glimpse of the driver, black beard, black hair, a deadly look, accelerating straight at the smokejumper leader. Was Jammer out of his mind?

Jammer pulled the trigger. The revolver bucked and a small hole appeared in the windshield where the driver's nose would be. The truck swung to the bank, started up the slope, then rolled back, tilting on its side in a spray of pebbles and dust. I ran up and smelled gasoline. We didn't have much time. Jammer jumped to the right, his legs like springs, the revolver pointed at the terrorist through the shattered windshield. He didn't need the pistol—the front of the cab was a bloody mess. I kept my eye on the driver, but my attention was getting to Baker.

She was upside down, kicking to get into the front seat. The doors of the truck were jammed and with a rock from the road I smashed the side window. "Get me the fuck out of here," Baker yelled. I dove through the smashed window into the truck, pulled my knife, cut the ropes around Baker's wrists and ankles, then pushed her up and out through the window, stepping on the body of the terrorist.

Baker had lines of tears streaking down her face, smearing the dirt and the sweat. She moved quickly, cutting one hand on the broken side window. She didn't notice the blood.

Baker grabbed Jammer and threw her arms around his neck. "God, I knew you guys would get here," she said and planted a very wet kiss on his lips. She turned to me. "Casey," she said, and started to tremble.

"We were watching you," I said. "All the time." I put my arms around her and held her, and she stopped shaking.

Jammer took another look at the bloodied terrorist, his pistol a foot from the mess which was his head. He came walking around the front of the toppled truck, glancing left and right, like the battle wasn't over.

"He's the guy that saved you," I said, nodding toward Jammer.

"You never forgot me, did you?" Baker put her arms around Jammer again.

"Not for a moment." Jammer's arms were around Baker's waist, the gun still in his hand. "Never. For that, I'd rescue you every day."

We left the truck and the dead terrorist right where they were. "Give the buzzards something to eat," Jammer said.

I radioed Link, told him Baker was safe, and gave him the details on the situation on the road. "You can pick us up here in the bird. Do you have contact with the agents near the planes?"

"Yes, this isn't over yet. They have no hostage now. We will move in on them. Unless they received reinforcements, we count two hostiles at the planes."

The sound of the rattle of automatic weapons came to us on the afternoon winds.

"It's not over until it's over," I said, turning to Jammer and Baker, still hugging each other.

"Here comes the bird," I said, breaking up the new romance. The rotors continued to spin while we climbed aboard.

Link nodded to Baker, who was flushed from her adventure, pointed to a jump seat, and said, "I'll see if Crocket has any coffee." Her streaked blonde hair was askew, and she brushed it back and put on a headset.

"How many in the planes?" Link asked Baker.

"Three in the white plane; I was the fourth person. The green Cessna came in with the pilot, Saeed, and another person. The other person looked like a businessman. I wasn't close to them. I think Saeed is the leader. Saw him in the bar at Twin. There are still two of them with the planes."

Link's face was stony. "Our SWAT team says they are taking automatic fire from two hostiles somewhere west of the planes. They have one agent badly wounded, don't think he'll make it," Link said.

Sergeant Crockett went from helping Baker to the M240 mounted on the starboard side of the Blackhawk. He had already pulled a can of ammo out, loaded the breech, and was looking over the firing mechanism. Six cans of ammo were stowed next to it on the bulkhead.

"Sergeant Crockett," Link shouted to the crew chief. "Crank up that 30 and fire on those hostiles and their planes at my command."

"Yes sir. Will love to, sir!" Crockett said. "At your command!" he bellowed, pulling back the bolt of the machine gun, and giving Baker a wink.

We could hear the occasional single shots of the .308s, answered by the fast fire of the hostiles' automatic weapons.

"We are going to use the machine gun from the Blackhawk. What is your position from their planes?" Link asked the team leader.

"Three hundred yards to the south," the SWAT shooter said.

"We will come in over your heads, on a north heading." Link circled his fingers, the pilot nodded, and Link beckoned to the crew chief. "At my command. Keep the rounds on and around the planes. Our agents are three hundred yards to the south. South is that way," Link barked and pointed. From five hundred yards out, coming in over the heads of the SWAT agents, at an altitude of four hundred feet, the M240 fired. Casings flew in the cabin, the bullets with tracers hitting the ground around the planes.

Tracers again. Hoo-rah! More fires.

The helicopter circled to the south for another run. "Concentrate on the planes this time," Link said to the gunner.

"Can't tell if the hostiles are down," the ground shooter said. "Try again!" The bird came in from a different direction—south-southwest—on the next pass. Two hostiles were running for the planes. "There is your target, Sergeant," Link commanded.

We could see the rounds going through the white tail-dragger and kicking up dust on the other side across the field. The propeller was not turning, and the pilot was probably dead. But the green Cessna was taxiing through the bumpy field. The tail was up, and it lifted off, banked above the sagebrush and flew down a stream bed.

Link barked to Dawson to drop the Blackhawk where the agents were located, and pick up the wounded agent.

The team leader gave us the clear on the landing zone, and in we came. "Agent Westmoreland, sir," the team leader said, appearing out of nowhere and addressing Link. "One hostile dead, and one of our guys in bad shape."

Baker and Sergeant Crockett had already moved out of the Blackhawk with the stretcher. One of the agents was pumping on the chest of the wounded shooter. Baker removed his vest and tore off his shirt.

In a moment Crockett was back. "He didn't make it, sir," he said.

"Son-of-a-bitch, let's go," Link said to the pilot. "Get me Colonel Brant at the air base at Mountain Home."

We climbed aboard the Blackhawk, a somber group.

I Owe Them One

"**The direction of flight of the hostiles**' plane is north. We do not know his intended target," Link said. "Authorities above me have deployed two Air Guard A10s and two Apaches out of Boise. They have the armament to take out the small plane. It will be only minutes before they make visual. We're all together on communications. The Feds call it 'cowboy control.'"

CWO Dawson, flipping switches in the cockpit, glanced behind him, making certain all was secure. His gaze stopped for a moment at the bloody covering over the SWAT sniper, and he nodded to Sergeant Crockett, making a military gesture to him that we were lifting off and to stay alert, as if Crockett needed that. The machine gunner was already estimating the range to the canyon walls. Crockett glanced at Baker, who had her head bowed, her hands in front of her face. Then Baker straightened and looked at the machine-gunner.

Jammer was seated next to Baker's shoulder. "We'll find him and finish off that son-of-a-bitch—once and for all."

Link stood behind the pilot on the lift-off, communicating with the FAA and an authority from central command out of the Idaho Air Guard.

Link turned to me. "He is flying at a heading of zero-four-zero which will take him to Boise or the airport south of Boise. He can reach the commercial air terminal or the Idaho Air Guard facilities at that heading. If his target *is* the INL—one hundred and seventy miles to the east—he'd never make it."

"If it is Saeed, he is on a suicide mission," I said. "Most of his team are dead."

"Let's hope so, but I wouldn't count on it," Jammer shouted over the noise of the rotors.

Link was communicating with the officer in charge of the Air Force fighters. "They have word from the top to take him down. That means the Pentagon. We'll follow their command."

A heated conversation followed between Link and the military authorities. I turned, looked at Baker, and raised my eyebrows. The red welt on her cheek was turning purple and swelling.

"I want to kill that bastard myself," Baker shouted over the engine noise. "For him," she said, nodding at the covered body of the federal agent.

The Blackhawk had gained a thousand feet of altitude as it flew northeast of the reservoir and entered a deep canyon. The width at the top—the rocky edges—was less than a half a mile. The depth of the massive geological cut was twice that distance. I had flown Whiskey Bravo over this desolate land many times and I knew the canyon was oriented south to north with a small stream hidden in the rocks and willows at the bottom. Small intermittent blue pools of water indicated a stream bubbling north. The gray canyon walls next to the Blackhawk were jagged, rocky, nearly vertical. Clumps of juniper rimmed the low arroyos.

We flew low into the canyon, over a herd of wild horses feeding near the broken rocks at the top of the breaks. Some of them lifted their heads at the noise of the helicopter. I pointed the mustangs out to Baker, but her mind was somewhere else.

"Two A10s and two Apaches have lifted off from Boise," Dawson barked back at us. "The Cessna's direction of flight is north."

"Not good," I said. "What are the F15s doing?"

"At altitude and circling far above us," Link came back.

The Blackhawk was moving north, flying lower into the canyon. The wind from the open door had pushed back the gray canvas tarpaulin covering the fallen SWAT officer. It wasn't a pretty sight. Baker was seated near the starboard door. She stood up and tied off the bloody cover.

I saw Link raise his shoulders and shout at Sergeant Crockett. "We've lost him on radar!"

"What the fuck—" Crockett said.

"He must be down on the deck and turning back to the south," Dawson shouted, his concentration immediately in front of him.

Crockett jumped from his bucket seat and took a position behind the machine gun.

"Move to the doors!" Link shouted to the SWAT officers. "Cover all terrain—stay vigilant! Control thinks he turned a one-eighty and is moving south. The A10s and Apaches have split up."

I looked over Link's shoulder, scanning the terrain and cliffs to the north. Williams slowed the Blackhawk to a hundred and fifty knots. "He might be coming down this canyon," Link said, turning to Sergeant Scott. "Give me an ammo count."

"None, sir," Crockett said, rattled. "Thought we had six cans. Used up four in the desert. The other two were empties! Sorry, sir."

Link didn't miss a beat. He directed two shooters to the open starboard door—agent Ramos to shoot and agent McKirk to spot.

"Aircraft at twelve o'clock, sir," Dawson reported on the intercom. "Dead ahead, five miles out."

"Keep the aircraft to starboard," Link directed the pilot. "Let him pass to our right."

"The plane is not changing course," Dawson said. "He might have us as a suicide target."

"Hard to port and down, when the aircraft is at a thousand meters."

And the pilot did just that. If the Cessna was planning to collide he didn't have enough space or time. The aircraft flew past the Blackhawk with a combined speed of over three hundred mph. He was four hundred meters to the right.

"It's him!" Jammer said. Link nodded. We had all seen the green Cessna.

"Follow him, Dawson!" Link commanded. "Stay on his port side. Shooter ready!" Link barked to Ramos, who was sitting, rifle pointed out, elbows on his knees supporting the stock and barrel. Ramos cranked a cartridge into the chamber.

After Dawson turned the one-eighty, the green Cessna was a mile ahead of us.

"You can catch him!" Link said.

"We're at one hundred and eighty knots. We can do it."

"Stay seventy-five meters to his port. He might blow himself."

The Cessna was now at three hundred feet above the bottom of the canyon. We were so low a herd of mule deer, heads down, feeding in the grass, stunned by the noise, bolted and ran around a rock outcrop.

The Blackhawk was gaining. The Cessna had to slow when the ground suddenly jumped in front of him.

The hostile's plane banked and veered right. Dawson flew the Blackhawk in tandem, behind him and to his left. The terrorist pilot then swung back to the left. Was he trying to crash into the helicopter? Dawson was thinking ahead of him, coming back on air speed and banking left. The gray basalt walls were too close; Dawson slowed and gained altitude.

Link radioed control. He received approval to fire and turned to Ramos. "Commence firing at one hundred and fifty meters. Use tracers. Aim for the pilot."

The shooter was over his scope, steadying the rifle. McKirk was above him, next to the open door. The wind rippled his shirt; he had taken off his cap and was using binoculars.

The Cessna suddenly picked up speed: its nose went up, the plane banked to the right, and still dangerously low, flew up a side canyon.

"He's not going to get away," Dawson said on the intercom.

"He's moving in the direction of the reservoir," I shouted to Link.

"That's good. We do water."

The Blackhawk was within two hundred meters of the hostile. "Target, sir!"

"Go—aim for the pilot." Link was giving orders like a Green Beret.

The SWAT sniper was good. Crack, crack, crack, three shots, almost like automatic fire, the bolt on the rifle moving fast. The last round was a tracer, brighter than usual in the darkening clouds over the reservoir. Ramos pushed new rounds into the magazine.

In the side canyon the Cessna banked left, putting the plane at an angle in front of the Blackhawk. A rifle barrel showed in the window of the Cessna behind the pilot and automatic rifle fire erupted. Bullets thudded into the Blackhawk.

Ramos said "Ooof" and fell backwards onto agent McKirk, who was concentrating on calling the shots.

"Son-of-a-bitch!" Link shouted. "They have a shooter."

Link and McKirk pulled Ramos away from the door. McKirk was tearing off his vest.

"I'm okay," Ramos said to Link. "Push me back."

"Back off!" Link shouted to the pilot. "They have a rifle." Dawson jinked to the right, above and directly behind the Cessna, making a tougher target for the hostile rifleman.

Baker grabbed Ramos's Remington. In an instant she was sitting on the deck, her elbows planted solidly inside her knees. She slammed cartridges into the magazine. Dyke Dawson slowed the bird, putting another hundred meters between the helicopter and the Cessna.

"Let me have the rifle," I shouted at Baker.

"No! I'll do it! I was shooting before I could walk."

"Baker, for Christ's sake!"

If she could shoot like she did everything else, she'd knock him out of the sky. McKirk had moved to help Ramos. I swung around to get more cartridges for Baker.

"You bastards!" she said, pulling the trigger, cranking the bolt, firing two rounds. A small piece of fabric flew off the fuselage. The Cessna seemed to wobble. The pilot jinked again and increased the distance between the two aircraft.

"I'm okay, Link," Ramos said. McKirk cut his fatigues. Blood spotted the dressings he was pressing to the side of Ramos's stomach.

I slid a box of tracers to Baker. The tips of the rounds were painted red. She glanced at me, then pushed the red-tips into the rifle.

Baker fired two more rounds, the last one hitting the metal tailwheel assembly of the Cessna, showering sparks. Dawson pulled the Blackhawk up to avoid the cliffs. I handed Baker three more cartridges.

"Windage and elevation, Mrs. Baker!" Ramos yelled. "Windage and elevation!" He was up on his elbows. McKirk grabbed his shoulders, trying to keep him down.

"He thinks he's John Wayne," McKirk shouted. "Rio Bravo this ain't."

"Take the rifle, Sergeant Crockett," Link ordered. Link didn't want her exposed in the doorway.

"No!" Baker shouted, without taking her eyes off the Cessna. "I owe them one."

Baker fired another round. Crockett moved toward her, reluctant to carry out the order. He put his hand on her right arm, but like lightning she worked the bolt and squeezed the trigger. The Remington bucked.

"Stop! Leave me alone!" Baker snapped at the sergeant. I handed her two more red-tipped cartridges. Baker slammed a cartridge into the breech, and glanced down at the rifle. In that instant the green Cessna exploded.

Flames, smoke, pieces of wings, empennage and Plexiglas flew past us. Dawson swung the Blackhawk to the left to avoid the fireball.

Saeed was carrying one hell of a cargo of explosives.

Ramos and McKirk raised their right arms with fists. Baker turned to us with a smile that covered her whole face, obscuring the bruises. "I told you I'd get those assholes!"

"Where did you learn to shoot like that?" I asked, my arm around her, squeezing her shoulders.

"In the desert hunting antelope." She opened the receiver of the Remington and handed it to McKirk. "Antelope are harder to hit than an airplane."

Dawson banked the helicopter and we watched the pieces of the terrorists' plane fall and scatter over the top of a rocky hill. Everyone began shaking hands. Baker moved forward and gave Sergeant Crockett a kiss on the cheek, then she hugged Ramos, who suddenly looked better.

"Windage and elevation indeed!" Ramos said, touching Baker's cheek. I was slapping everyone's back. CWO Follette recorded the location on the GPS. Link radioed for a forensic team to get to the crash site as soon as possible to provide security.

Dawson landed the Blackhawk on an open knoll, two hundred yards from the wreckage. Baker and I walked to the site; debris was scattered everywhere. A crumpled black corpse was draped over granite rocks. We thought we identified Saeed, but Baker didn't linger. "The bastards," she said. "I hope this is the last of them."

"I doubt it," I said. "These freaks are on a mission of death. They want to kill Americans and themselves."

"Over here, Casey." Carter gestured to me. "Here's the shooter."

A body was lodged between two large clumps of sagebrush. The body was not charred like the first one.

"God, I can't look at any more bodies," Baker said. I stopped her, and she walked back to the helicopter.

Carter pointed to a partially blackened AK47 lying on the ground, then nodded to come his way.

We stopped next to the second body. Enough unburned skin and patches of clothing remained to identify Hanson Porter the Third.

"I know him," I said to Carter.

"You know all the dead people." Carter shouldered his rifle. "Let's get out of here."

Link waved us back to the Blackhawk. Was one of those charred bodies on the granite rocks Saeed? I wouldn't bet on it. Link said I should give a description of Saeed to his people, from meeting him in Sun Valley and later the bar. Height, weight, hair color, and clothes. Said I would. Somehow, I wasn't sure the body was Saeed. He was a man who would make somebody else do the dirty work. Neither Baker nor I wanted to linger at the crash. We'd had enough.

Baker strapped herself onto one of the bucket seats, turned and gave me a V for victory sign. I smiled, gave her a thumbs up, took one last look at the charred wreckage as the helicopter gained altitude. Somehow I expected I'd have more encounters with hostiles.

Sheriff's deputies were en route to secure the crash site. They could sort it out. We had some urgency to get Ramos to the hospital, although he told Baker it was only a scratch. He and McKirk were talking about her shooting, shaking their heads, praising her marksmanship. Baker had found some tissues to wipe the blood and dirt from her face. I looked at Baker again. She was looking at me. Her look was serious—and lingered. Then we both smiled. We had secrets.

High in the cloudless sky, three turkey vultures, black dots, circled in the afternoon thermals off the reservoir. The wild creatures know these things.

In The Spring

There's a breed of men that can't sit still,
The kind that don't fit in,
They break the hearts of kith and kin,
And roam the world at will.
~ Robert Service

AFTER THE FIGHT IN THE DESERT we separated. The Blackhawk landed in the field next to my house in the hills. CWO Dawson gave me ten seconds to disembark. From there he flew to the heli-pad at the hospital to admit Ramos. McKirk and Carter stayed at the hospital with Ramos. Link went to his office to answer questions and write reports. Jammer asked the sheriff's deputies to drop him off at the jump base to finish the fire season, and Baker, after the examination of her bruises by the ER doctors, went back to directing air traffic.

Liz was at my ranch house, delivered by Tony the day before; he had met her at the airstrip along the Snake. We sat at the breakfast table next to the large windows. While Liz admired the view of the valley farms, I admired Liz. "Your pajamas are very pretty," I said, "but next time, could you bring the black panties and bra you wore at our Rush Creek camp?"

She looked at me, smiled, and ignored that. I had told her of the fight in the desert the day before. Now, I was getting into the details.

"Are you still a soldier, Casey?" she asked.

"Of course not." We finished sausages and hot cakes, the coffee hot and black. I poured again and smiled to myself, thinking of Carter.

"What are you smiling about?"

"Carter."

"Are you, Carter, and Link in some secret military unit?" Liz asked.

"No, but lately, I seem to have my own private army."

"You do. When you call they come from everywhere. Please don't go off to any more wars, or for God's sake, bring them here."

"Not planning on it." I shook my head, and smiled with a modest grin.

"Fauod Saeed is dead, isn't he?"

"His name was an alias. Carter and I looked at a crumpled corpse on the rocks. Yes, we think that was him. Not sure."

"From Sun Valley to the mountains to the river to the desert. We couldn't get rid of him," Liz said.

"He's gone."

"Are you certain?"

"I hope so," I said, and took a sip of coffee. Actually, I wasn't sure. Link and the authorities would sort that one out.

"Then we are together again. Alone," Liz said, and smiled.

"I wish you could stay here forever," I said.

"Yes, but—"

"I know. Your flight to Reno leaves in three hours. We can take the red airplane to the main terminal. I'll fly down to your ranch in four or five weeks, if that's a good time for you, after you settle everything in Nevada. I need to spend some time with our operations here. Then you and I can sit down and discuss what in the hell we did out there along the river in the backcountry."

An hour later Whiskey Bravo bumped and the tires squealed when the plane touched down on the runway at the Boise Air Terminal. We taxied to the private tie-down. Liz had a reservation on Southwest Airlines, leaving us an hour to spare. The propeller on the plane flashed and stopped, and I opened the side door panels. Taking off her headset, Liz did the usual pull-up on the overhead struts in the cabin and swung her legs to the outside step. I placed my hands under her legs and helped her down. She smiled and gave me a mischievous look.

"This is getting to be fun," she said.

"We'll go for more plane rides—back to the Middle Fork, or maybe the Bahamas."

"Promises, promises." Liz laughed. She straightened up and smoothed her hair.

"I'll remember our wilderness camp on Rush Creek and have dreams about you."

"You mean the bottle of gin and the wet pine needles?"

"Better than that. Your hair. The firelight on your face," I said.

"The camp was wonderful, in the forest, by the fire, in the rain, under the parachute."

"We could do it again, whenever you want to."

"Life with you is too damn exciting. Do you think we should wait another fifteen years to talk about this?"

"This time I'm not waiting," I said.

The conversation was over when the manager of the private terminal, driving the courtesy car, dropped us off at the outside check-in.

Two cars stopped behind us, doors opening, college boys jumping out, laughing, some holding carry-ons, others computer tablets.

Liz received the required baggage chits from the counter agent, paid for some extra weight, and pocketed two claim checks. She turned to me and I put my hand on her waist.

"I love you," I said.

Liz knew I was going to kiss her, and she put her arms around me. I took her hand and led her three steps from the door, away from the college crowd.

"Go for it!" the college boys yelled. I smiled back at them.

A long kiss goodbye.

"Casey?" It was a quiet question. The wind down the terminal drive was ruffling her hair. "Let's go back to the river. And this time stay awhile."

"You'll have some memories, and not good ones," I said.

"No—I won't. If you're with me. Those years are behind me."

"In the spring," I said.

The electronic doors opened again. "In the spring," she said, turned, waved, and entered the terminal.

I waved back.

The noon wind was gusting and the American flag snapped outside the terminal. The smell of sagebrush from the desert to the south came with the wind. I walked back to the private hangers, thinking of Liz.

Whiskey Bravo was waiting. Small threads of brown grass blew across the runway. The red rudder on the vertical stabilizer was swinging from the gusts. The next time I'd tie down the control stick to stop the flutter. I bent over to check the bullet holes on the bottom of the fuselage. Steve had done a good job. I opened the cowling, went through the pre-flight again, climbed into the cockpit, and turned on the engine.

The Lycoming sounded great, and I swung the plane around and taxied to runway one-zero-right for departure to the east. On the radio the control tower gave Whiskey Bravo clearance for take-off. The noon wind blew strong from east-southeast. *Hold the stick a little tighter. Take some right rudder.* A quick look to the left and right, then a roll-out to the white line in the center of one-zero-right.

Then I heard a voice. The words were clear over the vibrations of the engine. The voice could have been the wind.

"Let's go back to the mountains," the voice said.

The tail wheel was down on the tarmac, eager to come up. I stretched against the shoulder harness to look over the cowling at the white center-line of the runway in front.

"In the spring," I answered.

The voice was silent.

From the cockpit I glanced at the far mountains on the left. To the north, past the tree lines of the pines on the distant ridges, the sky was a deep blue.

All was quiet. The air controllers in the tower were silent. I knew they were watching me, using their binoculars. The world was waiting. The propeller turned, idling. Take one last glance at the instrument panel.

"All right, Whiskey Bravo, we'll fly tomorrow."

I pushed the throttle forward. With the head wind, the prop a blur from the full throttle, and a promise, the red airplane leaped off the runway and into the sky.

The End

With Thanks To . . .

To Rod Snider, pilot and former smokejumper, who remembered a short backcountry airfield—long ago abandoned by the Forest Service—in a high meadow at the headwaters of Phantom Creek, south and up from the main Salmon River. A gutsy pilot could have landed there in the long grass.

To John Paine and Liz Kracht for their work in reviewing the original manuscript.

For discussing, reading, and listening to the stories: Ted Filler, Bill Rother, Bo Campbell, Austin "Bear" Young, Earl Dodds, Suzanne Rainville, Loree Nugent, Melinda Langston, Shelley Seewald, Michele Bancroft, Rochelle Cunningham, Neal Davis, Nick Richy, Larry Satterwhite, Megan Richy, and Andy Filler, for his computer skills.

And last, and certainly not least, to Dennis Held, for his usual great job in editing.